# The Kingpin's Call Girl

# content notes

Please be advised that this book contains content that may be upsetting for some readers. Should you prefer detailed information in order to have the best reading experience, use this link or the QR code above.

https://annikamartinbooks.com/content-notes/

# The Kingpin's Call Girl

ANNIKA MARTIN

# Chapter One

## EDIE

New York breeds plenty of predators in designer suits, but the men in this hotel bar are something else entirely. They're sleek. Hard. Dangerous.

Steel and diamonds instead of flesh and bone.

And worlds away from the college boys I'm used to being around.

Even their hands seem bigger and rougher. *More.* When guys come up to the bar, I try not to focus too hard on their hands or think about them touching me.

Bender promised me it wouldn't go that far, but I'm not stupid. I'm not in the safe, regular world anymore. This is a luxury hotel run by the Albanian mob, heavy with old money, dripping with chandeliers, a place that is so far beyond the orbit of my life, I might as well be on Mars.

It's 10:07 p.m. on a Saturday night...10:08 p.m. on a Saturday night.

I need to stop looking down at my phone; I really, really do.

I'm trying desperately not to drink all of my gin and tonic in one gulp, but it's hard because I'm hyper-conscious of my dress, which is fire-engine red. The back goes down to my butt crack, and don't get me started on the plunging front.

I feel exposed to every eye in the room. I guess that's the point.

Is this how my sister felt?

*Feels* I correct myself. How my sister *feels*.

Because I know she's not dead—she can't be. She can't get to a phone, that's all. Or maybe she's on some kind of whirlwind trip where she's partying so hard she lost track of what day it is. What week it is.

I close my eyes and say a little prayer that that's what happened.

There's a thin plastic rain poncho rolled up in my purse. This will be over in three hours and twelve minutes, and then I'll put the poncho over my dress and walk out of here and give my report to Bender. I'll go home and scrub off my makeup and wear pajama pants for the next ten years.

A notification flashes across my phone, a faint beacon from my other life—my *real* life. My roomie, Odetta, likes a post of mine.

It feels like a world ago.

I take a breath. I've stood here too long.

*It's okay to stay mysterious,* Bender said, *but as soon as you get centered, take a fucking breath, turn around, and smile at him.*

The *him* in this case is "Iron Jaw" Dardan, a low-level mobster and member of the Ghost Hound Clan. Bender told me that Albanians call themselves clans instead of mobs or gangs or mafia families.

In addition to having a thing for women in sexy red dresses, Iron Jaw Dardan has cold eyes and a belly like a beachball, and he's old enough to be my father.

*You don't have to fuck him; you just have to sit with his group and listen to their conversation.*

I'm supposed to remember names, places, and dates. Easy enough for a history major.

I take another sip, letting the alcohol burn. Bender gave me thirty dollars to spend, and it barely covered this drink, plus a tip. It seems like an outrageous waste, considering I had to sell my dining hall punch card just to buy books.

*Just get the invitation to sit,* I remind myself. Sit and listen. Bender has promised to drop the charges against me and help me find my sister if I complete this one simple assignment.

He gave me a picture of a woman who has a major 1970s hairdo the stylist called a "Farrah Fawcett" to bring to the beauty salon. Apparently, Bender has been studying the tastes of this guy named Dardan, the one most likely to bring me to the table.

I rip a tiny corner off the napkin and then another and another. I can name all eighty-three Roman emperors and every pope from Saint Peter to the Reformation, but fooling a bunch of hardened criminals? I don't see how I can pull that one off.

I take another sip and try to channel my anger instead of my fear. Criminals are just stupid brutes who can't get ahead the right way, so they take the wrong path, that's all.

For a second I imagine my sister, Mary, laughing at me for that kind of explanation. Mary is obsessed with criminals. It's how she got sucked into the life she's leading now. Growing up, Mary was always the one who cared for me and protected me, especially after Dad left. I didn't realize until way too late that she needed me to protect her.

Well, I'm protecting her now. But I need to find her first.

I force myself to turn around. I glance at the corner booth, and sure enough, Dardan is staring at me. I know it's him from the pictures Bender showed me.

I hold the stare suggestively long, but inside, I'm trembling. There's a reason cops don't send civilians into undercover work. Like maybe they're terrible at it!

*Charges dropped, sister located,* I remind myself as Dardan licks his lips. I just have to get invited to the table.

I turn back to my drink, giving the bartender a nervous smile like he's my last lifeline to civilization. In truth, I left civilization the minute

I walked into this place. They could shoot somebody in the face here, and the busboys would clear the body away with the empty glasses.

The bartender slides a small bowl of nuts my way.

"Thanks," I whisper.

He picks up a glass and wipes the rim.

Growing up, my sister and I were the only ones who ever remembered each other's birthdays. At some point, we made a vow to always sing Happy Birthday to each other. No matter where we might be, the call would be placed, and the song would be sung. If one of us is dead, the other goes to the grave and sings it.

But when I tried to call Mary on her birthday two weeks ago, her number was out of service. I tried again and again. I tried her friends.

Nobody had seen her.

I went to her last apartment in a shabby high-rise "with a view of Rikers Island!" Mary once joked. Her angry, drug-addled Irish roommate said she owed rent. He couldn't remember when exactly he'd last seen her. Three weeks ago, maybe.

I filed a missing person's report, but the person taking down the info couldn't have been more disinterested.

I finally headed to Emerald Avenue down in Southeast Bronx. Mary would work the street there when she needed cash; my plan was to show Mary's picture around.

That's when Bender and his partner arrested me.

I pleaded with them and swore I wasn't a hooker. I explained how desperate I was to find my sister and that a solicitation charge on my record would destroy my dreams of being a high school history teacher.

Right before I was booked, Bender took me aside and said he'd found a way to get me out of the jam I was in... if I did this thing for him.

It sounded easy enough at the time.

I check my phone to make sure it's got reception and that the sound is turned up. Bender is going to call me at 1:20 a.m. to get me out of here. He promised that he'd personally come into the place if he had to. Three hours.

"What if this guy wants to exchange money for sexual favors before 1:20 a.m.?" I'd asked.

Bender said it wouldn't happen because "the chatter" said they'd be hanging out until dawn working out plans. But I could always make an excuse and leave.

I catch Dardan's eye in the mirror and look away.

*Don't seem too eager,* Bender told me. *A little bit of resistance is part of the package you're selling.*

Just as I'm gathering my nerve to walk over, Dardan appears beside me. "She'll have another." He puts money on the bar. "What's your name, honey?" His breath smells of mint and onions.

"Honey," I say.

He leans in closer. "Well, isn't that convenient."

I go for a Mona Lisa smile. *Don't be eager.*

"You looking for a date?" he asks.

"You a cop?" Bender told me to ask that.

"I look like a cop?" he asks.

"You're not answering the question, soooo." I shrug.

"I'm not a cop," he says.

"Two an hour. Grand for the night."

He reaches around and grabs my ass. "You gonna make it worth my while?"

I force myself to smile like it's a joke. Is it a joke? I don't know. I just have to get invited to the table and memorize names, dates, and locations.

"Send it to our table," he tells the bartender. "Come on."

I shove off the bar, balancing on my heels.

He takes a chair outside of a circular corner booth and makes me sit on his lap.

I settle in, trying to center myself more on his legs and less on his crotch. *Hate criminals*, I think.

A waiter sets down a fresh gin and tonic.

There are five men and two women, but no one gives introductions.

"New around here?" a jowly man across the table asks. He has a heavy brow and a baby-blue sports jacket. The woman next to him is watching me with hooded eyes. She has glossy brown hair like a model, and I get the feeling she's the one who wants to know.

"Just passing through," I say. "On my way to Vegas. I have a modeling job set up." More stuff Bender told me to say. If I'm just passing through, I won't be as threatening to the women whose territory this bar is.

"Modeling for who?" the woman asks.

"Lingerie line," I say.

Dardan roams his eyes down my front for about the tenth time.

I force a smile. My B-cups are playing C for the night, thanks to a lot of padding.

"I think you got what it takes to make it big in that business," he says.

I force another smile, fantasizing about making a citizen's arrest—Dardan and the other men. These are the kinds of men who lured my sister into their stupid life of easy money, danger, and drugs.

They all have opinions about Vegas—some hate it, some love it, and for one strange moment, they're like normal people. Everybody I know has an opinion on Vegas. I tell them I've never been there.

"Be careful," the woman with glossy hair says. "Most of those photogs are pervs. Get your pay up front. Nothing on spec."

I nod and thank her. It's sweet that she's giving me advice.

The talk turns to cars, and I get the feeling that was the topic before I sat down. I start taking notes in my head.

At one point, Dardan gives my thigh a squeeze, like he's testing out an avocado. I try not to stiffen.

Mary told me that a lot of prostitutes take designer pharma to stay relaxed and mildly floaty. Maybe it would've been smart, but I'm not used to drugs, and I need to stay sharp to hold up my end of the deal for Bender. I'll over-deliver, and he'll have to come through.

Mary and I were just kids when Dad took off for parts unknown; she was twelve, and I was nine. Our little family was already struggling, but Mom went off the deep end, swinging wildly back and forth between being deep in drink and being deep in prayer, a grim cycle that involved lots of tears and unpredictable punishments.

We quickly learned it was best to stay small and out of sight. Mary tried to keep my spirits up. We'd do dance moves in the scrubby field out back or try things on at the H&M in town, making plans on what to buy if we ever had money. Sometimes, she'd smuggle candy into our shabby little bedroom. It's a favorite memory, the two of us sitting on a bed strewn with candy, music playing softly from her phone.

It never occurred to me until later that she stole that candy. Or that she gave up her time with her friends to care for me and protect me from Mom's increasingly creepy boyfriends. She even stayed around home a few extra years so as not to leave me alone there.

While Mary was focusing on me, I was focusing on getting into college. I studied as hard as I could and earned a big scholarship. Anything to escape that life of poverty, demons, and despair.

And now it's my turn. I'm going to find Mary and give everything I have to pull her up and out of wherever she is, too.

So I sip my drink slowly and pretend Dardan's legs are just a shitty, lumpy chair. I try not to notice when he leers at me.

That's what I'm doing when he jolts as if electrocuted. He practically throws me off his lap in his haste to stand. I clutch the chair back, trying to keep from toppling over in my stilettos.

All eyes lock onto a figure gliding toward us through the dim light. He moves with predatory grace, like a dark raptor stalking its prey. Two grim-faced men flank him.

A collective intake of breath ripples across the table, followed by a hoarse whisper from somewhere on my right: *Luka.*

Even the pronunciation of the name is fierce, the vowels long and strong.

His rich, dark hair seems to have grown out from a severe military cut—the hair of a soldier too long in the field—and his chocolatey eyebrows point to the sides like swords.

His perfectly tailored charcoal suit accentuates his athletic build; a crisp white triangle peeks elegantly from the breast pocket. His dress shirt is classic white; his tie is black, broken only by a strange gothic tie clip inset with a gleaming red stone.

Everybody's standing now. Those trapped behind the booth are doing their best to stand or to at least straighten to give the appearance of standing, as if this Luka might smite them down if they don't show the proper deference. They're also falling all over themselves to greet him. *"Didn't expect you!" "So nice to see you!" "To what do we owe this honor?"*

Luka rumbles his acknowledgment with a severe gaze that seems to assess the past, present, and future of each speaker.

His presence is intense, like weather or electricity. He changes the atmosphere in a new and dangerous way.

I stiffen, telling myself I'm not impressed.

This guy is just a criminal, no different from the criminals who preyed on my mom during her long stretches of drunken gullibility and no different from the criminals who lured my sister away from me, away from the dreams we had.

*Loser, loser, loser.*

Right then, Luka's brown eyes snap to mine.

I can't breathe.

I can't think.

His gaze pins me where I stand, mesmerizing. Merciless.

A shiver licks up my spine.

His masculine beauty cuts hard as diamonds. His lips are cruel. But his deep brown eyes... are the eyes of an angel. And I have this strange sense that he can read me with those eyes, even my inner thoughts.

But then I pull my mind back together and straighten.

He can't read thoughts, and he's not special. And if he thinks I'm impressed now that his gaze is on me, he's wrong. If anything, I hate him even more, though I keep my expression perfectly pleasant because I'm here for my sister. And also? Not an idiot.

As if in a dream, he comes closer. Now he's close enough that I could slap his face. Not that I would. Or even could. The nearer he gets, the more immobilized I feel.

And those eyes.

The way he's looking at me, I feel translucent, like one of those tiny, see-through fish where you can see its big heart pounding inside its skin.

Even Dardan's arm on me seems less corporeal—more fog than flesh—like Luka is the only solid thing in the room, and if he wanted Dardan's arm off, he could make it vanish with one harsh thought.

I swallow, knowing I should say something. *It's nice to see you* seems odd when we don't know each other.

"Greetings." I force a smile.

Did that sound weird? Sarcastic? Something you'd say to an alien?

Thoughts seem to flit behind his dark, angelic eyes.

Somebody says something about a plan, and he finally turns away from me, leaving me almost gasping for breath, a fish out of water.

I fight to get my fear under control, or maybe it's awe. Because really? Who is he to assess me and silently mesmerize me or what-ever the hell he did?

I remind myself I'm helping to take him and his crew down, so that's a plus. Not enthusiastically helping but helping.

Luka takes one of the chairs like it's his throne, and his bald-headed right-hand man takes the one next to him, which forces everybody to squish into the booth. I end up sandwiched between Dardan and another guy.

The other man who had flanked Luka coming in, a big scary blond who looks like a villain from a military thriller set in the Arctic Circle, stands next to Luka's chair because, apparently, Luka is the king, and he is the king's soldier.

A waiter swoops in and sets a drink in front of Luka.

Another waiter sets down plates of food, narrating all the while. "Fried cheese with honey and walnuts, Albanian American bruschetta topped with a spread made from roasted red peppers, feta, and olive oil, finished with a slice of prosciutto and a balsamic glaze. Crispy eggplant stuffed with *gee-zuh* and Italian mascarpone. Fergese stuffed mushrooms. Warm rosemary bread. Can we bring anything else, Mr. Zogaj?"

Mr. Luka Zogaj lifts a hand in a kingly wave. "That'll be all."

My mouth waters. It all just looks so delicious. I focus on stir-ring my drink with the little red straw while Dardan settles a possessive hand on my thigh.

Luka instructs people to eat, but they remain frozen until he samples an olive with imperial indifference; only then do they cautiously reach for the food. The men, anyway. The women abstain, so I follow their cue, even though I could inhale the entire basket of rosemary bread if they let me.

I manage to create mnemonic devices for each man I get a name for. Ghost with his pale skin, Cyrus like a cyclops, Rick with slick-Rick hair who worked with Gianni. I don't need a memory device for the grand poo-bah, Luka Zogaj, the center of the universe, smooth as polished stone with his sooty lashes and his perfectly disheveled battlefield hair.

I grab my napkin and fold it into a tiny square, and then a triangle, and then a smaller triangle, and then I sneak another glance at him.

He swishes his drink as he talks. When he catches me looking, I quickly look away because criminals like him don't deserve attention.

If karma were real, he'd be burning in utter agony. That is what I wish for him—to suffer tenfold for every bad thing he's done.

My hatred for him feels like heat under my skin.

I fold my napkin into increasingly tiny shapes.

# Chapter Two

## LUKA

Is that scorn I detect? This is something new.

Who looks at me like that?

It gets my blood racing.

This girl—it's like somebody snatched her from a quaint farmhouse, poured her into a garishly tight red dress, plastered makeup all over her fresh-scrubbed cheeks, and styled her light brown hair like a doll. The look is perverse in a way I can't tear my attention away from. I want to peel everything away from her and get to the heart of her and the heat of that scorn.

And then there's her glittering gaze. That gaze is the key thing about her. Incandescent. Silently raging at us. At me.

She thinks people won't notice.

But I see everything. I always have.

Also, *'greetings?'*

But what am I doing? This outraged little whore in this completely wrong outfit is not where I need my attention. A king doesn't lower himself to notice every trembling peasant in his kingdom.

I settle back into my chair and put my attention on the situation at hand.

The men are nervous. They have questions. Why did the new boss—the *kyre*—come down the mountain with his attack dogs to sit with the low-level guys? And most importantly, who will I kill next?

I like nervous people. Nervous people are stupid people, and stupid people show me things they shouldn't. I like to see those things.

I swirl my drink, getting a sense of the men as they bluster on.

I took over a month ago, and I'm still no closer to finding out who carried out the killings all those years ago down in South America. But I will. There's nowhere in this world they can hide from me.

Dardan says something, and Orton and I exchange glances, having both come to the same conclusion: Dardan doesn't have the information we need. He's the kind of man you send for a threat, not the kind my brother would've trusted with secrets. A sledgehammer, not a lockpick.

I turn to Gianni and ask him about the coke delivery. He gives me just enough information to be useful and not waste my time, so he could be somebody to pull out and question.

And then there's the girl.

The harder she rages, the hotter her gaze grows. Is it possible this is her act? A lot of the whores adopt a persona for the job, and she could be going for the angry ingénue. Then again, it really does seem like she's trying to keep her face blank and simply failing.

Which makes her all the more fascinating.

Compelling.

I want to unwrap her. Provoke her. Mark her as mine.

She's all wrong. And she's fucking riveting.

She could be up to something, of course. People who seem wrong usually are. She could be a plant from a rival clan, a snitch, a girl desperate for money, or a newbie drug addict.

But it doesn't matter what she is. Nobody touches this organization, and nobody touches me—not anymore.

I focus back on the chat about the uptown crew—not easy with her blazing so hard with... what? Judgment? Anger? What is it about this girl on her high horse, so fucking above it all? Well, that'll change at the hands of a guy like Dardan.

Something unpleasant churns in my gut.

And really—the outfit. Good god.

So wrong. So fucked up.

Though sometimes a man wants fucked-up things. And I always take what I want.

# Chapter Three

## EDIE

Luka toys with his glass, fingers moving with the sort of graceful precision that could turn to lethal strength at any moment. Faded scars crisscross the knuckles of his rough, weathered hands, and veins run along the backs like raw power.

He is another species from the college boys I'm used to with their pampered hands and recycled hot takes on Marvel movies and craft beer.

He wears a bracelet of wooden beads on his left wrist, and a tattoo peeks out from beneath the shirt cuff on his right; I can see a bird's wing, some roses, and part of a sword.

It's most likely a two-headed eagle. I know from my medieval studies that the Albanians love the two-headed eagle. It's on their flag, their products, and a lot of their clothes.

The chat moves on. I take my mental notes, trying not to look too hard at Luka or his hands.

Sometime later he takes off his jacket and turns up his shirt-sleeves, revealing a few extra inches of his muscular forearms, and that's when I see it—the full tattoo.

It's not the two-headed eagle I expected from an Albanian mob guy. No, Luka has a one-headed eagle with an extra talon.

I blink, stunned. I know that symbol from my medieval symbology class. It's Prince Arianiti's eagle.

Arianiti was a 15th-century badass who led uprisings against overwhelming odds. He was underappreciated and never given his due but kept fighting anyway.

He was all about resilience and resistance, which resonated with me during one of my hardest semesters. I was constantly choosing between books and food and dealing with my mom's drinking and criticism about "wasting money on school." That defiant eagle carried me through.

I look away, unfolding my napkin and folding it up again.

Arianiti's eagle. So weird.

But what of it? So the asshole has a cool tattoo. He probably doesn't even know what it means.

I force myself to tune back into the conversation. Dardan is arguing with the man named Cyrus about what date Wednesday was, and suddenly, everybody's arguing. I want to blurt out the right answer or tell them to look at their phones, for fuck's sake, but I'm not supposed to draw attention to myself.

Luka observes, though, silent as a sphinx. Does he know the date? Of course, he knows the date, but he doesn't say it for whatever reason.

Never mind. Just over two more hours to go, and then I'm gone.

Luka and the guys start talking about the Knicks while the women stay quiet. I'm staring down at the table, listening, willing myself to be invisible and trying to ignore Dardan's leg, which is suddenly pressing more against mine.

I check the time. Is the clock even moving?

Luka shows a slight interest in the problems of somebody named Zedd, and now everybody is falling all over themselves to tell him what they know about Zedd's corner guy getting robbed, desperate for Luka's approval. The theory seems to be that a rival gang was behind the robbery.

Criminals stealing from criminals.

I amuse myself by imagining the great Luka in an orange jumpsuit. That's what he should be wearing. Not whatever cashmere Italian suit he has on, sitting there all larger than life like a runway model fresh from a designer's evil fashion show.

With a tattoo that he doesn't even understand the coolness of.

Sometimes, I think I feel the intensity of his gaze turned back on me, but then I think I imagine it. Either way, I try not to look at him. I'm barely even here—that's how intensely I'm willing myself to be invisible.

And so what if he does see through me a little bit? So what if he's somehow figured out that I'm not actually an experienced hooker? I doubt I'm the first impoverished woman to try her hand at sex work.

They're still on the thing with Zedd. Luka has questions. He wants the corner guy brought to him, and no, he doesn't care that the corner guy turns out to be fourteen and it's the middle of the night.

Luka takes one of the guys' phones and puts something in, and then he takes Dardan's phone and does the same. I don't look at the numbers he's punching in. Some protective instinct is telling me I don't want to know.

My own phone is at the ready, and in two hours and fifteen minutes, Bender will call with a supposed family emergency to get me out.

And I'll never have to be near these hateful criminals again.

# Chapter Four

## LUKA

Are they actually fighting about today's date? Look at the fucking phone, I think. But again, the nervousness. Except for her, the nubile prostitute and her holier-than-thou scorn, so above it all, like she alone doesn't have a dark side.

Say what you will about the other people at this table; at least they know they have dark sides. They know they're capable of doing monstrous things when monstrous things need doing. You have to respect that.

There's a dusting of freckles over her nose that she tried to conceal with makeup. So many little secrets waiting to be uncovered.

Her lips are formed into a rosebud of judgment, a configuration that makes her top lip plump out. It comes to me that her top lip is too large to fit exactly with her bottom lip; it has more volume, I suppose you could say, an imperfection that is fucking hot.

I imagine those lips around my cock as I fist her hair. This girl on her high horse transformed into a beautiful little beggar, tears of need bleeding down her cheeks as she begs me to use her in whatever way I see fit, greedy for my cock, pleading for my touch, desperate for my next command.

I force my mind back to the situation at the table. Orton's drawing people out with careful questions.

My being here is the culmination of months, if not years, of hell, and I'm analyzing her lips?

No.

Everything is riding on obtaining the information I need. There are more people who need killing. It's everything.

She takes a sip of her drink through her straw and licks her lips —just the inseam.

The guys reply to Orton, still wary of what my presence here means for them.

I can hardly blame them for feeling that way. I showed up out of nowhere, sliced up their leader in the grizzliest way possible, and declared myself king. I'd be wary, too. But that's the Albanian clan life for you.

I feel her gaze burning. She's studying my tattoo—again. A lot of people look at the tattoo, but it's different with her.

"Got something to say?"

She sits up ramrod straight. "Excuse me?"

"My tattoo." I hold out my arm. "Did you have a good look?"

Her eyes widen. "No—I mean yes. I guess."

"And? Conclusions?"

"Uh... it's an interesting design."

Dardan feels the need to insert an opinion here. "It's an eagle," he explains to her. "The symbol of Albania. It's on the flag."

"Oh! The flag? Cool!" She gives Dardan a big, bright, fake smile.

Dardan puffs up. The best way to manage a man like Dardan is to puff him up, and she seems to know that.

She definitely knows more than she's saying. At a table full of people trying to shine the spotlight on themselves—how smart or badass or attractive they are or how much info they have. But this one? She's hiding her light under a barrel with the ferocity of a badger.

"No," I break in. "You have something to say. You're going to say it."

She turns to me in shock. I note with some satisfaction that those freckles are more pronounced now.

"I didn't have anything to say. I just didn't think that's what your tattoo was, that's all."

"What did you *think* it was?"

"An interesting design."

"You really are one of the worst liars I've ever met. Don't do it again."

"W-what?"

"You said, 'I didn't think that's what it was,' which implies you thought it was something other than the eagle from our flag. And now you're going to tell me what that something would be."

Her gaze flares hot.

Dark enjoyment pulses through my veins.

I raise my brows. "Well?"

People have fallen silent. Everybody watches her. Maybe they think I'm going to kill her. Dardan frowns. He doesn't like his whore talking to me.

"Well, I thought it might be Arianiti's eagle. Just... whatever—"

"Excuse me?"

"Arianiti's eagle. He's a prince from... some old history book."

I narrow my eyes. It's a very obscure thing to know. "What else?"

She furrows her brow. "What do you mean, 'What else?'"

"When a person uses the phrase 'what else' in the way that I just did, it's a request for elaboration."

She raises her chin, taking offense now, and, God, there's that scorn. Something dark and wicked swells inside me.

"*And* I like old books. I like to read them."

"Old books." There's more where that came from, and apparently, I just can't stop myself. I raise my brows, waiting.

"I have a memory for random old things," she adds.

"Random old things," I say.

"Yes."

I'm about to go at her harder when I feel Orton's gaze on me.

We're here for a reason, and it's not antagonizing some little hooker.

"I still remember the score in the third inning of the final game of the World Series when I was ten," one of the other hookers offers.

"I remember my address from when I was four," Gianni says.

Dardan's hooker has fixed her gaze on the breadbasket.

She hates us with the fury of a thousand suns—she really does. I hated criminals once. I can barely remember what that was like.

"Any questions about the upcoming operations?" Orton asks, getting us back on track. "Ask now, or you all have my number."

People nod. There's logistical chat, but Ghost has something to say—it's obvious from the way he cranes his neck forward.

I raise my brows at him.

"Mr. Zogaj—" Ghost begins.

"Luka," I say.

"Luka," Ghost whispers like he's summoning the dark lord instead of just saying my fucking name.

I sit back and steeple my hands. *Here it is,* I think. *What everyone wants to ask. What did my brother do to deserve what I did to him?* It's the million-dollar question.

"Speak up," Orton says.

Ghost straightens. "The men are just curious about the beef with your brother."

"And you're curious, too," I say.

Ghost gives a half-shrug. "It's just that... nobody knows what he did..." *To deserve such a terrible death,* he means.

Ghost asking the hard questions. I make a mental note: This guy is leadership material.

"You want the story," I say. "You want to avoid the same fate."

Ghost nods.

Expectant gazes fix on me.

When there's some gruesome violence seemingly out of nowhere, people want to know why. It's a hardwired human instinct and the reason people turn their heads when they pass an accident.

*What did they do to make it happen?*

"Do you know what loyalty is?" I ask Ghost.

He punches his fist to his heart, a distinctly Albanian gesture.

"That's right," I say. "Be loyal, be straight with me, be forthcoming, and I'll make you a fucking prince. Cross me, hide information from me, and you'll see just how dark a man can go."

Ghost nods.

It's too late for the men I'm hunting—I'll kill them no matter what they do—but for everyone else in the clan, it's true. Don't give me a reason to kill you, and I won't kill you. Simple.

The two men I'm hunting aren't here at the table. Orton and I are pretty sure of that. A couple of them are just too young, and the rest we've ruled out, but they may know something that leads me to them.

Not that I can ask them outright; nobody needs to know why Orton, Storm, and I have come to town. Nobody needs to know our intention.

Never show your hand. Ever.

The little hooker sits there, secretly raging on in her personal little maelstrom. What is it now? Has she realized she's shown too much of herself?

That scorn, though. And the tattoo thing. And how much she clearly hates us. But it's more than that. There's a primness to her like she's truly innocent.

Innocence.

*Please.*

Everybody has their price, and everybody has their breaking point. Every innocent person is capable of taking a hacksaw and cutting out the soft parts of themselves.

You cut and cut until there's nothing left but cold, hard bone, merciless as the moon.

# Chapter Five

### EDIE

I think about the pint of chocolate chip cookie dough ice cream in the tiny fridge back at the dorm. It's my prize for the end of the night, and if Odetta eats it, I will go ballistic.

*Don't make a scene,* Bender warned. *Don't draw attention.*

I've resisted looking at Luka—his tattoo and his arms and hands and angel-devil eyes—for at least thirty minutes, a record I'm feeling proud of, considering he's a darkly glittering black hole that sucks you in.

Why did I say all that stuff? I'm supposed to blend in, but I couldn't be chill. Anyway, there's no law against prostitutes reading old books.

And then I can't help it again. I look up at him, and both Luka and Dardan catch it.

Dardan's hand is still on my thigh, and his hand is not happy. He's squeezing—hard.

*Don't make a scene.*

I grit my teeth and try to push his hand off without making said scene, but then he squeezes harder. It starts to really hurt, so I turn to him and find him scowling at me. I push at his hand under the table, but it only squeezes harder.

Like somebody actually put a metal vise on my thigh.

"Stop," I whisper.

He doesn't stop.

Suddenly, Luka stands up.

Everybody scrambles to follow suit, just like before, and Dardan is forced to lay off and clamber out of the booth with the rest of them.

I follow along, standing next to Dardan but not too near. What's happening? Are people leaving? I smooth down my skirt, unsure how to handle this. Will Dardan expect me to go somewhere with him now? Bender said they'd be in the bar all night!

The waiter comes, and Luka asks him to see if some suite is open.

Are they going to meet in private to talk about super-secret things? Bender won't be happy, but that's not my problem. I'm holding up my end of the agreement; that's what counts.

The waiter returns. The suite is available.

The men exchange discreet glances. Like me, they're waiting to see what the new king does next.

Luka's dark gaze pins me in place with an almost supernatural power.

And then he's coming around to me, the group parting with ease.

It seems surreal that he's coming to me.

My blood runs cold and then hot and then icy hot when he stops in front of me and sets a finger under my chin. "She any good?"

"Don't know yet," Dardan growls beside me.

Luka shifts his molten brown gaze to Dardan. He says nothing. Just a look.

Dardan stiffens. "With all due respect—"

"With all due respect, *what*?"

Dardan goes pale. "W-with all due respect," he bites out, "I want to pay for her. For your time with her. As a gift."

Luka keeps his finger on my chin, but his dark angel eyes are fixed on Dardan.

The finger is gone, and Luka Zogaj moves to stand in front of Dardan.

One of the women catches my gaze. She points to her eyes and then points at the floor. She's telling me not to watch. What does she think is going to happen, exactly?

I avert my eyes all the same. I'm buzzing with so much fear I can barely feel my face.

"Please," Dardan begs. "Let me pay for the whole night for you. For your time with her. As a tribute." He reaches into his pocket and peels off two five-hundred-dollar bills. He shoves them at me, and I fumble to take them.

"B-but I actually can't stay," I say, handing the money back to Dardan. "I have to go."

Dardan does not take the money.

"Really have to go." I may as well be talking to the wind.

Luka throws a few bills on the table. "Have another round, guys. Don't wait up."

Luka sets a hand on the small of my back. "Come on."

"What?"

"Now." He urges me forward through the open doorway toward the hotel lobby.

"I really do have to go," I say, knees shaking as I walk, money clasped in my fist.

We head through the lobby to a dark elevator alcove. He hits the up button on the elevator.

"I have to go," I whisper.

"You gonna turn into a pumpkin?"

"N-no."

"Are you working or not?" he asks.

My mouth goes dry.

"I was working, but now I'm not..."

He touches my cheek, leaving a trail of electric shivers. "Is this your game?"

I'm a rabbit, frozen in the spotlight of his dangerous beauty.

My breath comes too fast.

My sex fills with a dark ache.

No, no, no, no. This man can't be turning me on. He is not turning me on. He's just a dirty criminal. A bad person.

"Well?"

"It's not a game," I manage. "I might have a family emergency..."

"Might?"

"I—I..."

He grabs my hair. Heat blasts through my core.

No man has ever grabbed my hair like this. Possessive. Hard.

It's wrong. So wrong.

But, God, the feeling of it. Some wicked part of me wants it tighter. And I want to keep the money, too.

He turns my head so I have to look up into his eyes.

Here in the empty, elegant little alcove next to the elevators, I'm getting lost in a bad man's beauty.

He'd probably stop if I told him, but my skin buzzes all over like my blood has transformed into pure lightning.

I've never felt like this before. And I want more.

"Yes or no?" he asks.

"Y-yes," I hear myself say.

He tightens his hold on my hair, twisting it like he knows what I need, and brings his warm lips close to the tender shell of my ear. "The reluctant nubile. Innocent. Scornful. It's good."

My core goes melty.

My back flattens against the wall as he presses his thigh between my legs. Everything in me flares to life. He's hitting a place nobody has ever hit before.

"It's good. Got it?"

I blink. Was that a question? An order? I always know the

answer. My study skills are impeccable. My color-coded organizational skills are second to none.

But now I can't even think.

"Got it?" he asks again.

"Got it," I whisper.

His hard thigh against my sex feels better than all the vibrators in the world because a vibrator can't twist my hair and fill me with aliveness. A vibrator can't be so dark and wrong as to take my breath away.

A vibrator can't pierce me with pure, delicious, sparkling lust.

He presses in harder, watching my face as he does it like he's learning me, analyzing me.

If he does it again, I swear, I'll come.

"Keep it up."

"Okay," I breathe.

He twists my hair a touch tighter. He kisses my neck and presses higher and harder between my legs.

"Right. There," he whispers warmly in my ear.

*Right there.*

And the horrible thing is that he's right. Right there. He found my spot.

I don't know if I hate it or love it.

He's a criminal, a killer.

I'm near to coming now. Thirty seconds with this guy, and he's able to do something that a good-hearted college boy couldn't achieve with an hour of toil between my legs.

Even a vibrator and my roomie gone for thirty minutes is no guarantee I'll get off.

He pulls back, watching me with an evil glint. He's compelling me like a vampire or something.

He's the kind of man I despise. The kind of man who corrupted my sister.

I try to get back to the place where I hate men like this. He's a killer, of that I have no doubt, and you have to be deranged to kill another human.

"The scorn written all over your face is delicious," he says, owning my clit with his hard-cut thigh. "I'm going to take you up there and fuck it right out of you."

I want to tell him that he's wrong. He'll never change my opinion of him, and the badness of his character is an objective fact, but I don't want him to stop what he's doing.

What's wrong with me?

A rumble sounds behind me. He yanks me away as the elevator door opens, and then he walks me in backward, eyes hard on mine.

His hands are between my legs, stroking me.

I gasp, flooded with heat.

"Jesus... fuck... so fucking wet..."

I want to deny it, but my body's responding to him like he flipped some forbidden switch.

"I need you wet for how hard I'm going to use you up there."

So... arrogant... I think as I melt against the elevator wall.

He watches my eyes with that insufferable smirk, like he already knew this would happen. Like my reaction is just another victory for him to claim.

"You think I can't own you with one finger, baby? You're gonna spread those legs and take everything I give you."

"Whatever," I spit out, even as my hips betray me by pressing against his hand. "You don't own anything."

"I own you right now," he whispers against my ear, breath hot on my skin.

Well, *that* shouldn't be hot. Why is it hot? It's outrageous—the sheer arrogance of this man thinking he can claim ownership over me. But it's like some primal part of me craves his raw, brutal dominance.

He kicks my legs wider, and I let him. Good god, it's maddeningly hot.

He jerks me higher against the wall, positioning me like I'm his personal plaything to arrange however he wants. His finger is strong and precise between my legs, creating spirals of sensation that radiate through my core and make my knees weak.

"Everything," he says, his voice a dark promise that sends shivers down my spine.

"We'll see about that," I say with all the contempt I can muster, but my voice trembles.

"Yeah," he says, eyes dark with triumph. His fingers work relentlessly, each stroke leaving a wake of unwanted pleasure. "There we go."

I realize here that he thinks I'm coming.

Where could he have gotten such an idea? Does he think he knows me better than...

Something swells inside my belly—airy and bright. My vision is pinpoints of light, and a hurricane of feeling builds inside me.

I clench my muscles, fighting it. He doesn't get to do this. He doesn't get to be the one.

I cry out, and an explosion of sensation quakes through me.

"That's it," he says as I shiver to pieces.

If he wasn't holding me up with his body, I'd fall.

*He made me come.*

*A horrible criminal.*

*In an elevator.*

A bell. Doors.

I'm gasping as he picks me up and puts me over his shoulder, firefighter-style.

My mind reels. I'm jelly. Another door. A lavish room.

He plops me down onto the bed. He's the lion, and I'm the dead antelope that he's going to feast on.

I stare up at him, stunned. A wild tremor goes through me because how dare he treat me like that?

He gazes down at me like he feels my angry thoughts and maybe even likes them. He's perverse.

But I feel so weirdly alive.

He turns away and pours himself a drink. "If you have to pee, you better go now."

"I don't have to pee," I say.

His voice is a low rumble. "You sure?"

Deep down, I know this is my opening, my chance to tell him I'm not really down for this.

He's the kind of person I hate. But I'm desperate for more of him. In school, we'd call this a paradox.

"I should know."

He shoots back his drink. Downstairs, he was sipping like he didn't care for alcohol, but everything's different up here—for both of us, maybe.

# Chapter Six

## LUKA

I can hear her soft, sharp breaths behind me. Those lips parted just so.

Even if I couldn't hear her, she's practically vibrating with emotion. Where the fuck did Dardan find her? God knows what he planned for her. Not that it matters.

I tell myself that this was in no way a rescue. I'm the last person to be in the rescue business.

I took her because I could. Because I like to take what's not mine. Nothing more. Nothing less.

I pour another drink.

My voice, when it comes, sounds eighty percent normal. "Then strip. Now. Unless you don't care about the dress. Keep the heels on."

No sound, not even the rustle of fabric. She's probably still where I put her, glaring at me with her full wattage. I pull off my tie. Maybe I'll use it. Maybe I won't.

She's fucking delicious, and I have this sense that I might not ever get enough of her, which is probably a good reason to send her away. But I won't be doing that.

I turn to her. "What the fuck are your clothes still doing on? You don't like the dress? Is that it?"

"I hate the dress," she whispers, eyes sparkling.

She's different. I should ask her about Arianiti's eagle, but that's not the point. It's the spark that's the point.

I approach her slowly, my eyes never leaving hers. When I reach her, I grasp the edges of her plunge-neck bodice between my fingers, feeling the delicate fabric and sensing her breath quicken in anticipation. With deliberate slowness, I pull the sides apart. The fabric surrenders with a soft, satisfying tear, parting down the middle to reveal the swell of her breasts in a push-up bra, her skin flushed and warm.

"You like it better now?" I ask, my voice dropping to a whisper as I take in the sight of her. "I know I do."

She watches me from under her eyelashes, this indignant little girl who's thrown herself to the wolves for whatever reason. A little lamb to the slaughter. I don't have a taste for lamb, but I do enjoy a few things that would make her quake in her ten-dollar hooker heels.

"Take off the bra and touch them," I growl.

She frowns. Doesn't move. She's thinking about it a little bit. Struggling with herself. She'd do it if it were her alone or with anybody else, but she doesn't like that I told her to because she doesn't want to take orders from the Antichrist or whatever I am to her.

She's just too fucking delectable, and she has no idea.

I take her hands and put them on her breasts. "Not a request. And don't just phone it in."

She takes off the bra to expose pretty breasts and nipples, pink and swollen.

I narrow my eyes as she moves her trembling fingers around on her nipples with a disdainful glare.

"Jesus, yes. Whatever you do, you can't stop looking at me like that."

"Looking at you like what?"

"You know what. The heat. The hate."

She purses her lips, doing that judgmental thing where her top lip swells slightly over her bottom one, creating that perfect pout of contempt.

"What are you thinking when you look at me like that?"

She shakes her head.

I fist her hair and force her to sit up. "Tell me the truth—or else. And I'll know if you're lying."

"I—I'm thinking... you're a bad person."

"You got that right. There's not a good bone in my body. What else?"

"You're a horrible criminal. You take what doesn't belong to you, and you deserve none of it."

"Meaning you? I took you, but I don't deserve you?" I ask, all the better to provoke her.

"Yes. You don't deserve me."

"No, I don't deserve you. But look at me about to take you. I'm the twisted-up criminal who's gonna use you like a little whore and make you love it."

"You won't make me love it. You think might makes right, but you're wrong. It doesn't."

"Did you actually just say that? But might does make right, doesn't it? If it didn't, you'd be in charge. But you're not, are you? Tell me who's in charge."

"Have you always been this horrible?" she asks.

God, people so rarely show me their edge like this.

"Oh, no, I used to be a good little boy, but that turned out to be a farce."

"Being good is never a farce."

Fuck, I cannot get enough of her and her prim act and her cherry-smelling lip gloss.

I let her go and cross the floor to the desk where I left my drink. Like a signal to myself that I'm in control. I'm running this show.

I take a nice big swig. There are a lot of things I should be doing right now. Acting on some of the information I learned tonight, for one.

But here I am.

Sometimes, you just have to get a thing or a person out of your system: hunger, thirst, a man who needs killing, a woman who needs fucking.

I turn. "Change of plans. Scoot back and pull up what's left of the skirt."

I can practically hear the thoughts racing in her mind.

"Now. Fast, or you won't like it. Panties off. Leave the stockings."

She shimmies off her panties, down her long legs and past her thigh-high stockings, and scrambles all the way back so she's sitting against the headboard.

"Legs open," I say. "Keep touching your tits and looking at me like that. I am so enjoying the angry vibe. That's what I'm gonna fuck out of you. You'll be smiling when I'm done."

"I won't," she whispers.

"What was that?"

She keeps gripping her tits and showing me her pussy, but it's the scorn I crave. "I won't smile."

I take another sip.

"My smile is mine," she adds, glaring at me.

"Well, this is getting better by the second." I put my glass down and pull off my belt.

Her pulse beats rapidly in her neck.

The fact that she came before and still wants more is part of the reason she hates me right now.

We both like wrong things—that's what I know right now. And we both need to get each other out of our systems.

She glances toward the window now, defying me.

"Look away from me one more time, and I'll bring this belt into the mix. The tie. The belt. Or maybe you'd like that."

That gets me the look back.

"My tie binding your wrists. A hard leather belt against the tender flesh of your ass. Nothing you can do about it. Nothing whatsoever…"

Her breath speeds. She's picturing it—me tying her up and hitting her with the belt.

"Or is that what you want?"

"Doesn't matter to me either way," she tries. "It's all the same."

"Little liar."

Her gaze flares, nourishing something inside me.

I unbutton my shirt slowly, letting her watch as each button slips free. I peel it away, then strip off my undershirt in one fluid motion, my St. Michael medallion catching the light as it settles back against my bare chest. My pants follow, and my cock springs free, hard and ready.

Her chest rises with a sudden intake of breath. I let her look her fill, and she does, cheeks pink.

Most whores are on drugs, but I can tell this one's not. She's raw to everything—I see it in her eyes. The muffled sounds from Middleton Road coming up through the triple-pane windows. The cool feel of fine linens under her ass, the soft kiss of the air between her legs.

I give her a wicked smile. "The tie sounds a little good, though, doesn't it?"

She raises her chin. Wordless defiance.

I unwrap a condom, still holding her gaze.

She looks younger with her makeup smudged, her honey-colored hair messed up, and all that fire in her green eyes. The freckles. This—this is the real girl, I think.

Not that it matters. This is a one-time transaction.

I toss aside the wrapper and roll the condom on with ruthless efficiency.

Her eyes shine with a look I know well. She's on the edge of something, but everything's too real.

She's new at this, no question. If I was a good person, I would make her leave right now.

Too bad I'm not a good person.

I sit at the foot of the bed and set a finger on her ankle.

She hisses out a breath as I trace a line over the top of her foot, slow and steady toward her toes.

"I'm too old for you." I pause at the tip of her middle toe. "Too rough. Too wrong. And it's working for you, isn't it? All the dagger stares in the world won't change that."

She snorts in contradiction.

I continue over the ball of her foot and watch her face as I hit the tender underside. She's determined not to show me anything, but she's already shown me everything. Except how she knows the tattoo, but the night is young.

*I—I'm thinking... you're a bad person.*

I get up from the bed and loom over her.

*You're a criminal.*

I wrap my hands around her ankles.

Her gaze burns.

I yank her down in one swift motion, bedding tangling around us as I pull her beneath me. With deliberate movements, I part her legs and position myself above her. Still holding her gaze, I nudge her entrance with the thick head of my cock, the silent tension between us electric.

And wait.

She arches up just a little, needing it, even as she tries to keep a blank expression.

Yeah, we both like wrong things, but I'm the only one here willing to revel in it.

I pulse in, little by little.

She gasps, breathy now with excitement.

I push on, enjoying every inch of her magnificently tight, wet cunt.

She grips my biceps, nails digging into my flesh like she's trying to hold me there, keep me inside her.

Good with me.

I thrust all the way in finally, seating myself deeply inside her. Right then, something in me stills, like some essential calm has settled over me.

But then I'm back to business, focused on what we're here for, namely fucking her and consuming her. But instead, I'm losing myself inside her.

Her angry gaze fades as pleasure takes its place. Something swells in my chest at this, as if her pleasure is everything.

"Stop that. Don't start acting like you like it. Got it?"

"Oh, don't worry. I don't like it," she snaps.

"Good, because that's not what you're here for. This is a transaction."

"Wasn't... liking it."

I bury myself so deep in her. "Ungh. So tight."

She makes a little sound of pleasure, followed by a haughty snort. "Whatever. You're horrible!"

"I *am* horrible. That's why I'm in charge."

She's clutching my shoulders, sweaty palms against hot flesh. "A dirty, twisted criminal," she gusts.

Her words are gasoline on my blaze.

I change my angle, my speed. I can tell from her body when I've found the place that will make her unravel, and I'm merciless, rubbing deeper and deeper, obliterating her walls.

It's good. Too good.

I grab her wrists and pin them to the bed. The harsh way I'm holding her kicks up the heat in her eyes.

She's in over her head, wanting more of what I'm giving her, even if she doesn't know what it is.

I lean in and bite that sexy top lip, holding it loosely in my teeth.

"Mmm," she breathes. "Guh." She makes a few other sounds before she stops herself, like she's determined not to show enjoyment.

I could eat that lip. I force myself to let it go.

"Fuck," I say, burying myself inside her. "Fuck."

I feel the clutching swell in her that tells me she's coming, though you wouldn't know it from her face, which is scrunched in harsh concentration because she is really committed to not appearing to enjoy it.

But she's bad at hiding things. Bad at hiding her scorn, at hiding her pleasure. Her building orgasm.

"You can't hide from me, baby. I'm inside your house. I know everything."

"Buzz off," she manages through the waves of an orgasm that I happen to know is raging through her, judging from the way her hot, wet cunt is milking my cock.

A whore who tries to hide that she's coming and says buzz off. She's fucking priceless—she really is.

I grab her hair while she's still coming. "Look at me."

She doesn't have the wherewithal to disobey—that's how hard she's still coming, lips parted, cheeks pink except for those pale freckles.

The attitude is gone. I fucked it out of her—for a moment, at least.

Eventually, she comes to her senses and snaps back to scorn-girl mode, full-on glaring at me.

Who looks at me like that? All that harsh, aggressive energy. My cock feels dangerously hard.

This whole thing she's got going gets me off in a way I didn't think was possible anymore, and I'm fucking her savagely now, coming like a motherfucker. "Jesus."

She clutches my arms as I explode into her. It's a full-soul, time-space-continuum-in-flames orgasm.

"Fuck," I pant.

I hover over her, and for one bizarre moment, I have a sense that we're sharing the same strange frequency. There's a feedback loop of the big bad getting off on the prim, scornful miss and the prim, scornful miss getting off on the big bad.

It's too much... something.

I pull out and roll over, but it takes a while for me to get myself back.

"Fuck," I say again.

Some time passes—I have no idea how much.

I rouse myself enough to sit on the edge of the bed. My brain feels like a tossed room, all the clothing and papers pulled out of the drawers.

I always know what I'm doing, always in control. One disorganized fuck isn't going to change that.

I focus on the view out the window, the sea of buildings and city lights. I said I wanted to get her out of my system. Well, this ought to have done it.

And I figured out what I had to figure out down there.

And now I'm getting myself back together.

I head into the bathroom and get rid of the condom.

I splash water on my face.

What kind of place does she live in? Is it a hotel? Is she really on her way to Vegas? That's what they told me.

"And that matters why?" I drag my hand down my face, rough with whiskers.

Her cherry scent is still in my nostrils. Is it from more than her lip stuff? Body lotion? Perfume? I imagine her putting it on. Did she put it on for Dardan?

God, will she go back and find him now? Some other guy?

Something coils in my chest. I imagine keeping her all for

myself. A hundred percent mine. I would unravel her secrets and bathe in her scorn.

I splash more water on my face.

I'm being fucked up. I'll send her off and concentrate on my mission.

She's still in bed, doing things on her phone, when I get back out. I watch her, torn between sending her away and fucking her again.

She is mine for the night, after all.

The fact that I'd even think along those lines is why I need to cut her loose.

"Put yourself back together and get out of here. Now."

She sits up.

"That's right, your night-long sentence has been commuted to sex served."

It takes her a while to process this. "We're done?"

"You need an engraved letter of dismissal?"

"Can I..." She gestures at the bathroom like she's not sure if she can use it.

How new is she at this? Whores always use the bathroom on their way out. They use the bathroom and leave without a word. That's the drill.

I wave my hand. "Use it and get out."

She snatches up her skirt and panties. "One sec."

I turn to my phone. Orton has Zedd's corner guy, and they're coming over with him. Good.

I scroll through my other messages. I won't look at her again. I won't think about her lips or her freckles or her primness or her angry edge or anything, and then she'll be gone to Vegas.

Even if I want more of her spark and scorn and all that, I won't be able to get at her without a fuck-ton of hassle.

If there's one thing I've learned over the years, it's how to deny myself.

# Chapter Seven

EDIE

*Use it and get out?* What an asshole!

I look in the mirror, my heart pounding in my chest. My hair is wild, the pinup girl style long gone. My cheeks are puffy from his whiskers, and my neck... God.

I trace my fingertips over the pinkest part.

I had sex for money with an awful, horrible killer. But it was... overwhelming. All-consuming. The dark rush of it is still coursing through my veins.

Who am I?

I should be scared. Repulsed. This man paid to use my body for his pleasure.

Yet I can't stop thinking about his eyes. And his hands. And his chest—hard and strong and scarred like his hands. The way his cock bobbed up, thick and sturdy, a primal club wrapped in bronze skin and sinew.

The college guys I've been with would never just stand there with it out, looking me over. But Luka did exactly that, like a king surveying his domain, stroking himself, hardening more to take me.

I blink, lost in the memory of him hovering over me. The

moment felt electric. And then he entered me and got me off so intensely... it's like I was transported to another realm—a raw, uncharted realm of endless sensation.

And god, the look in his eyes after he pulled out of me, still hovering over me, like we'd shared something...

Even now, I can feel his dark pull. I want to go back out there. Is this what a junkie's first taste of heroin is like?

*Stop.*

*He's a dangerous killer—that's why things were heightened,* I tell myself.

*Cats purr when they're hurt as much as when they're happy,* I tell myself.

But those are just things I tell myself.

Right then, my phone flashes. I have the sound turned off, but it's ringing. It's Bender with my excuse. How long have I been up here? Two hours? I shut it off.

With trembling fingers, I use a pin from my clutch to close the front of my dress. I unroll my wrinkled poncho and put it over my head, thankful I brought it. I grab my cherry lip gloss and roll it on. The smell of it brings me back to myself a little bit.

I came into this sinister world to save my sister, and I got my head turned around, and it's over now.

He paid for the whole night. Or Dardan did, anyway. The folded-up money is still in my purse from when I slipped it in there. A thousand dollars is so much money. Do I get to keep it? Luka doesn't seem like the kind of guy to take it back. It's probably nothing to him, but I need it so badly.

And what will Officer Bender say? Will he take it away? Should I keep it secret?

Luka is wearing a hotel bathrobe when I walk out in my rain poncho. He's got another glass of whatever he was drinking before, and his gaze is fixed on his phone.

"Well... thanks," I say.

He looks up with the strangest expression.

Was that weird? Do hookers say *thanks*? I immediately want to take it back. Why would I thank him? He should be thanking me.

"I just mean... for saving me from that asshole down there."

"Don't kid yourself," he says all rumbly. "I'd toss you right out that window for a decent Lambrusco."

I stiffen my spine. Such an asshole! "Well, maybe you don't think it's a thankable event, but for me, it is. Not—" I wave my hand at the bed. "I just mean... being with you is probably marginally better than being with Dardan."

He crosses his arms. "*Marginally* better?"

"At best," I say.

"From what I could see, there was nothing marginal about your enjoyment. But I'll accept the thanks."

"I've changed my mind. It wasn't a thankable event at all. I retract the thanks."

"You retract it?"

Things feel wild between us. "That's right."

"You could barely keep that scorn going," he says. "So, I'll give you an A for effort but a D-minus for acting like you hated it. Not convincing."

"Being in a position to take advantage of an economically disadvantaged woman doesn't give you the right to define how I felt."

"Being in a position to take advantage of an economically disadvantaged woman? You mean because I'm the savage who made the top of your head blow off three times?"

"Two times," I say.

"Aha. Two times." He gives me a smug smile. "I'd call that thankable."

I narrow my eyes. "So full of shit."

His gaze sharpens. Does he think he looks hot? All squinty with his dark whiskers?

"Again, consider my thanks retracted." I head toward the door.

"Change of plans. You're not going anywhere."

I freeze.

"Come here."

I don't turn. What have I done? Can I ignore him and keep going?

"Don't make me say it again."

"You released me already."

"I'm retracting it."

Heat kicks up between my legs as I imagine him picking me up again and carrying me back to that bed.

Would he hold me down again? Of course, he would. And he would hold my wrists, too, probably... hopefully.

I would have nowhere to go, and he would make me feel everything again. Or maybe he'd escalate things.

I stare at the door, heart bongo-ing against my ribs as I remember his belt. He would come after me. Maybe tie me up. And then the belt...

"So this is what we're doing?" he growls.

Something heats inside me at his imperious tone. He thinks he gets to order me around? I shouldn't give him the satisfaction of obeying—I shouldn't!

At the same time... I'm nearly home free. Why would I jeopardize that?

I spin around. "What?"

He just sits there, one arm over the back of the chair, all lazy and superior, like every inch of the universe belongs to him.

He's offensive—he really is, thinking he can order me around.

"Was there some ambiguity in the phrase 'come here'?"

I force myself to take a few steps toward him and stop in the middle of the room, crossing my arms and holding my head high.

The way he looks at me... I want to punch him. Or maybe jump him.

He goes to a drawer, pulls out a box, and takes out a phone.

"You have a box of phones?"

"That's right," he rumbles like he's angry.

God, that angry rumble rubs me the wrong way, and it's not entirely unpleasant.

Luka rubs me the wrong way, like when you rub velvet the wrong way, and it stands on end, deep and dark. It brings out the intensity. The vibrancy. That's what he does to me.

I watch him punch things into the phone.

"Is that a thing criminals have?" I hear myself saying. "A box of standard-issue criminal burner phones? Is there a special criminal Costco where they're on sale?"

His gaze shoots up at me.

Why am I asking about phones? Why do I care?

"Sit down."

I sit on the edge of the bed.

He comes over and puts the phone in my hand. "The password is *green*. You staying in the Bronx or Manhattan or what?"

"W-why?"

"Answer the question."

"Manhattan."

"What's your name?"

"Honey."

"Real name."

I hesitate a second before blurting out, "Edie."

He gives me a hard look. Does he want my full name? He goes to another drawer and takes out a stack of money that looks like fifties. It's a lot of money.

"Two weeks," he says, setting it in my hands.

Shivers flow over me. I'm almost afraid to close my fingers around the stack. It's thousands of dollars. So much.

"This is double your full-night rate and some extra. For the next two weeks, you belong to me. When I want, where I want. I text, you come. There's nobody else. You understand?"

"Y-you're hiring me for two weeks?"

"Yes."

Frantically, I think about my school schedule. I have classes. Exams. Shifts on the Stafford cleaning crew.

"But I was just passing through to Vegas and… I have places to be…"

"Customers?"

"More like… obligations."

"In Vegas?"

"Obligations," I repeat.

"Break them."

"I can't."

"Is it the money? I'll buy you out of them."

"It's not a money issue."

"Is it a people issue? Your handler?"

"Nothing like that."

"What is it, then?"

"I don't know if I can always be available. That's all."

He takes a step toward me. "I'm not playing here. You belong to me now. Like I said, I text, you come. Don't make me send somebody to hunt you down. You and yours won't like it. And trust me, I will find you."

"B-but…"

"I just paid you for fourteen nights with a few grand extra thrown in. You're mine, same as that jacket there. If you try to hide, I'll find you. If you leave town, I'll find you even faster. For the next two weeks, you are mine and mine alone."

What the hell? This isn't right. He can't just do this! I grit my teeth, mustering up all of my hate.

"When I say come, you come." He lowers his voice to a rumble. "When I say spread, you spread."

Perversely, my sex swells with want.

A light appears in his eyes like he's feeding off my bottled-up hate. "And when I tell you to bend over, you ask me how wide I want you to pull apart your ass cheeks."

My jaw drops nearly to the floor.

"All that scorn is getting me hard." He sets a finger under my chin and lifts my face to his. "You can never stop looking at me like that. It is really working for me. You understand? Nod if you understand."

"It might not be possible—"

"Two weeks. No other man will touch you. If you so much as look in the direction of another man, I'll find out, and I will cut that man's balls off. And then you will answer to me in a way that you will not like. Are we clear on that?"

I swallow—hard. Why am I arguing? I'll go home, scrub off my makeup, change into leggings and an oversized sweater, and disappear into the faceless stream of college students, where Luka will never find me. He would never look in a college residence hall.

"We clear?"

"Fine." I clutch my stuff and rush into the elevator, stabbing the lobby button a million times.

I check the time. Two hours I was in there with Luka, but it feels like a lifetime. There are two calls from Bender and one text asking where I am, pointing out that my shift is up, though he doesn't seem overly concerned.

I text back:

on my way.

Finally, I'm back out on the street. It's three in the morning, but Middleton Road is lit like a circus.

I suck down the smoggy air in great gulps.

# Chapter Eight

### EDIE

My Uber speeds past bars and pizza places and slumbering construction sites.

I smooth my hair and pull my rain poncho tighter around myself.

Luka gave me two weeks' pay based on double my night rates. Did he see the thousand dollars Dardan paid me? That means he gave me at least twenty-eight thousand dollars. Could I possibly have that much money in my bag?

That kind of money would be life-changing to me. I could start eating normal meals again. I could give up some of my nights on the tower cleaning crew.

But I can't keep it—not that kind of money. It's probably drug money. It probably has cocaine residue on it.

He plans on calling me—on the phone he gave me. Just the thought of that makes me feel funny inside, like an invisible wire inside me is still connected to him. And he can tug it any time and make me come.

In every sense of the word.

Is it possible he's tracking me? I pull out the phone and type in "green" to unlock it. Sure enough, GPS tracking is enabled.

I switch it off. My heart starts pounding. Will he know? Of course, he'll know.

It doesn't matter. This thing is over.

I stare out the window, reviewing my mnemonic devices and reciting the names, dates, and places that I heard.

With every repetition, I'm clawing myself back to stable, secure ground where doing the right thing is the right thing. That's where I prefer to live.

But I can't stop thinking about the money. I could open a savings account and put it toward the life I want to build for Mary and me—a little house in a seaside town with a garden like we dreamed of when we were kids.

I'd get a job teaching high school and support Mary while she cleans up her act. I owe her at least that much for all she's done for me.

I shake the thoughts out of my head. Taking the money is not who I am.

---

It's after three a.m. when I arrive. The place is like a 1950s diner with chrome and sparkly red vinyl on the chairs and fifties-style neon stuff all over. These Bronx places are less crowded than the ones in Manhattan. No lines. No hovering. Open tables.

Bender is at a side table, hunched over a cup of coffee. He's a big man, a bruiser type with pale cheeks and hair in a crew cut.

He smiles when he sees me. "You made it!"

"I did, and I did what you asked."

"Good going. Coffee?"

"Ginger ale," I say.

He signals the waitress and orders. I can feel him looking at me strangely. "You didn't answer your phone."

"Yeah. I need a piece of paper or something."

He takes out a little spiralbound notepad as the waitress delivers my drink. I begin to write. Name, place, name, place.

I can feel him studying me. "You remembered all this?"

"I'm on a history scholarship at Columbia. I can memorize a few names."

"Fair enough."

I add all the details about Zedd, and then I stop writing. If he knew the rest of it, would I be in more trouble?

"Is that it?" he asks.

"No, there's more. But let me clarify—does the completion of this task absolve me of the charge of prostitution? Because you know that's not what I am. I want you to admit that you knew I wasn't a prostitute all along, that I was just looking for my sister."

"Yeah, that's our deal."

"And you'll help me find my sister now."

"Again. That's our deal."

"Is that a *yes*?"

"Yes," he says, annoyed. Like I'm playing schoolgirl games.

"Okay." I make a line and write "Luka Zogaj, Orton, silent man arrive." I start jotting down the stuff Luka said.

"Wait—Luka Zogaj was there?"

"He came and sat down after a while, yes."

Bender's sitting up at full attention now, just like the people at the table did when they saw Luka.

"Luka himself?" The way he says it, you'd think Bigfoot visited.

"Luka himself sat down."

"You're sure they weren't just talking *about* Luka?"

"I'm sure. They called him Luka. Tall—maybe six-two. Brown eyes. Dark hair. I thought he was going to kill Dardan right in front of me."

"Jesus Christ," Bender says.

I go back to the list I'm making. "He had a man named Orton with him. Orton is six feet tall with a shaved bald head and a big, bushy beard. And then there was a silent man who looked like a battle-hardened Nordic type."

"Storm," Bender whispers.

"So you know these guys?"

"Know of them. Did Luka say anything about his brother, Alteo, or what happened between them?"

"Actually, a little, yes."

Bender sits up, riveted. "He talked about it? What did he say?"

"This guy named Ghost asked him what his beef with his brother was, and Luka was like, 'If you guys are loyal to me, I'll make you princes. But if you're disloyal, you'll see how dark a man can go.' He didn't specifically speak to what happened with his brother."

"That's it?"

"That's it. The men were all very concerned, though."

"I bet," Bender whispers.

I continue jotting.

"So, nothing about being out on the boat with Alteo? Anything about a boat?"

"Nothing about a boat." I jot the rest down and slide the paper to Bender. "This is every name, place, caper, and more that was mentioned."

He reads it over. "Looks like Luka asked a lot of questions. Did you get a sense of what he was driving at?"

I shake my head. "Right there I gave you every name that was mentioned, every date and place that was mentioned, all of it. Unless you want, like, stuff about the Knicks."

He squints at the paper. "What was Luka's beef with Dardan?"

I swallow.

"You can't leave anything out, or our deal's off."

Bender's a cop... what if he had people there at the bar? What if his surprise is an act, and he had cameras there and saw me disappear upstairs with Luka? If I don't tell everything, he might not uphold his end of the bargain. My sister's whereabouts and my future career are on the line.

"Luka wanted... to be alone with me."

He looks at me strangely. "He wanted to hire you?"

My face flares red. "He did hire me."

He looks shocked. "You and Luka..."

I look him right in the eye. "In a hotel room, yes. So, I more than completed this assignment, I'd say. You told me I only had to sit there, and I ended up in a lot of danger. You put me in a dangerous, illegal situation that went way further than I agreed to."

He looks mystified.

"So..." I shrug.

"I'm sorry you had to..." He blinks. "How did he seem?"

"How did he seem? I don't know."

"You don't understand who this is. The tiniest scrap could be important. Was his mood happy, angry..."

A lot of words stream through my mind. Dark, dangerous. Extreme. Troubled. He likes my scorn of him. Sexier than any man I've ever met.

Coolly as I can, I say, "He seemed like a dangerous and mysterious man of few words who showed very little to people. Everybody was scared yet wanted his approval, but he barely gave it. Later, he seemed like a mob guy who wanted to have sex."

I grab a napkin and use it to extract Luka's phone and the stack of money.

"What's all this?"

"Luka's going to be calling me to come to him whenever. Maybe you can use it to find him or something. I don't care. You could probably run it for prints. I'm sure the money's drug money. Maybe there's blood on it. Or drug residue."

"Jesus!" Bender snatches the bills and the phone and shoves them into his pocket. He throws a twenty onto the table and practically drags me out into the cool night.

"What are you doing?"

"He could have geolocation turned on that thing. You want him to think you're a CI? You stopped at a cop diner! Fuck."

"Don't worry, I turned it off."

He glances at me, surprised. Like he didn't think that would occur to me. "It's off?"

"Yeah. He had it on, and I switched it off."

"Still. There could be a redundant one."

A chilly breeze blows down empty sidewalks. A light turns green, and cars speed by.

I jerk away my arm. "I can walk on my own, thank you."

"So he's calling you. When?"

"Whenever he wants. You'll probably find over twenty-eight thousand in that stack."

"He wants you back." More of a question than a statement.

I shrug.

He sends a text to somebody. "This way."

"Where are we going?"

"Meeting somebody. What's your class schedule like for the next two weeks?"

"What does it matter? Busy."

We're at a light. "Look... I need you to... keep up this act for just a little longer."

"What?"

"If he calls."

"Excuse me? No!" I say. "I can't."

"You don't understand—this is major."

"But I'm a college student, not a..." I look around. "A prostitute. He'll figure it out. He'll know."

"Did he figure it out tonight?"

"No."

"If he hasn't at this point, he won't."

"It doesn't matter. I can't—"

"You've gotten somewhere nobody else can get. This guy, coming back onto the scene out of nowhere, the thing with his brother, the questions, the rumors, nobody knows jack about him, nobody can get near him, and suddenly you're in…"

"His bed?" I supply.

He sucks in a breath. "Look, what I did for you last week, holding off on the charges…" He lowers his voice like the buildings might hear. "I could get in deep trouble for that sort of thing. And I was happy to do it because we're allies."

"And I paid you back. Per our agreement."

"Right. And look, I can probably get you that location for your sister, but what if I went above and beyond? Your sister hasn't been easy to find, which means she's deep into something. And I said I'd help you, but locating a person and extracting them? Those are two very different things."

"Deep into something? What exactly does that mean?"

"Look, we checked the morgues, so that's the good news, right? She's alive. But you have to ask yourself, why haven't you heard from her? She might have gotten herself into something she can't get out of so easily. She could be inside a cartel; she could be kidnapped, locked up under another name. Locked up abroad, in some sort of debt to somebody powerful. You go this extra mile for me, and I'll do the same for you."

"Oh my God. You think she's being held against her will? Is that what you think?"

"I don't know. All I know is that it will take more muscle than you have to go the extra mile for her. More of me breaking the law for you. Like I did with your arrest."

I swallow. "But I'm not a prostitute. You arrested me for prostitution, and you know that wasn't what I was doing."

"Regardless, now you're doing undercover work. You're helping the world. And the money—that's for you to keep."

My head spins with fear. Awe. Full-on shock.

"And I hate to say this, but even if you tried to hide, he would find you."

"In a city of eight million? In a Columbia dorm?"

"That's right. Come on." The light turns, and we cross.

Music thumps from a nightclub as people spill out onto the broken sidewalk. We sidestep the crowd and push on, past a pizza place, past a shuttered bank, until we stop at a bus stop bench. "We'll wait here."

"For what?" I ask.

He doesn't answer, just takes the money from his pocket and stuffs it into my bag.

"I don't feel okay about this," I say.

A van pulls up. He looks around, then goes to the window and hands my phone over. The van pulls away.

"What's going on?"

"That's tech. They'll pull over somewhere to clone it and check if there's redundant tracking and then bring it back to us." He sits on the bench and pats the seat next to him.

I sit.

"When Luka calls, you are going to show up. Two weeks. I'll do for you, if you do for me. In the meantime, you're gonna go out and buy yourself some beautiful things with that money."

"I can't! I can't do this! You know I can't!"

"Yes, you can," he says. "And there are some special things you're going to listen for. He was sent away as a boy. Where? Prison? Military school? Another family? Also, what did his brother do to piss him off so much? Figure it out. If you can get these answers, it would go a long way toward helping your sister."

"What if I have classes?"

"Figure it out."

I feel dizzy. And is Bender getting harsher with me?

"This whole thing... a person needs years of training for this type of work. I'm a college student, Bender. I listen to Taylor Swift."

"Wrong. A person needs instincts and common sense and balls, Edie. You went out on the street looking for your sister, and now you're making some real progress in getting to her by wheeling and dealing with the likes of me and Luka Zogaj. So, trust me when I say you have what it takes. You got over the hard part—you're inside. From the sound of it, he yanked you right into his orbit. He won't think to question you."

"It seems like... a lot."

"Don't worry. You're a natural."

I grip my bag tighter, knuckles turning white. I am worried, but not just about playing criminal informant—I'm terrified because when he looked at me, I forgot who I was supposed to be. I forgot my sister, my principles, my entire life. I forgot everything except how he made me feel.

# Chapter Nine

## LUKA

Traffic is sparse at this hour, and the air is thick with the lingering scent of rain. I pull up my collar, waiting for the car. The sidewalks are lit in patches by the faint glow of neon signs and scattered storefront lights. Horns blare in the distance.

*Maybe you don't think it's a thankable event, but for me, it is.*

*A thankable event?*

And then she wanted to retract her thanks?

I just completed a bloody takeover of one of the most savage clans in the history of the Albanian mafia. I have killers to find and scores to settle... and her right to retract her thanks is what I'm focusing on?

And what kind of whore talks to me like that in the first place?

I'll admit, I goaded her. Some dark part of me was hungry for her balled fists, her flashing gaze, and the way she lifted her chin when she was upset.

And God, the way it felt to be inside her, her defiance burning through me like a purifying flame.

Not that I need purification. I left behind concepts like dirty and clean a long time ago. Brute force is the only thing that matters now.

*Taking back her thanks.*

I check the GPS. It's off? Off?

I grind my molars together.

That won't do.

The town car slides up, long and sleek. I slip in next to Orton, across from a kid. Zedd's corner guy.

Orton unwraps a stick of gum. He's a terrifying bull of a man, crafty and cunning yet sentimental. He loves the old songs. He can dance the *Valle Pogonishte* better than anyone. He believes in the ancient lore. If this were olden times, he'd be burning heretics or joining up with the Spanish Inquisition.

When I seized power from my brother last month, Orton commissioned us a traditional Albanian man's brooch inset with a hound's head and carved from deep red carnelian for the Ghost Hound Clan. Such brooches are traditionally used to hold together vests or scarves, but we use them as tie clips.

This kid is fourteen at most. His wild gaze is fixed on me like I might tear out his windpipe at any second.

I put out my hand. Orton gives me a stick of gum, and I unwrap it. "You know why you're here?"

He stares at me, wide-eyed, teeth clenched around his black bandana gag.

I give him a version of the loyalty lecture I gave to the other guys as Storm drives us through the night, silent as a mountain.

"Some people think they're better off telling me what I want to hear when I ask them questions," I say to the boy. "Some people think it's safest to stick with their original story, like maybe they lied at first, and now they're thinking that hiding that lie is the only way out. Like once they've gone down that road, they have to stay on it." I pause here, nice and long. "Those people are all dead."

The kid nods. Storm tied the gag; I can tell from the lack of twists. Orton always twists a gag up like a rope.

I pull out a blade and slice the thing off. The story pours out before I can get to the zip tie binding his wrists. As I suspected,

Zedd thought he'd take advantage of the chaos surrounding the leadership change to cash in, and he strong-armed this kid into playing along, using money and a threat on the kid's dog as his carrot and stick.

Ten minutes later, Storm's shoving Zedd into the back seat with us.

Zedd puts the situation together pretty quickly and starts blaming the entire thing on the kid, which is very convenient and just more proof of his guilt.

Zedd denies it all the way to the Palisades. We park and walk to the edge of the cliff. I make the boy watch me put a hole in Zedd's face with my nine. Orton shoves his body over the edge and down into the river.

I turn to the kid. "Any questions?"

He shakes his head energetically.

Orton lights a match, lets it burn down to the end, and then throws it over the cliff and into the river after him. The match symbolizes extinguishing a life. Tossing it into water cleanses the sin.

Supposedly.

We drop the kid off at the run-down building where he seems to be squatting.

"Your brother would have killed the boy, too," Orton says when we're back on the road. "And the boy knows it."

I grunt.

"And now he's yours. You'll have his loyalty now." He turns to me there in the back seat. "You came for the vengeance. You stayed for the power trip."

I give him a look. "How much do I have to pay you to stop saying that?"

He's grinning. "You took the throne, and you like it."

"For now." That's all I'll commit to. I never wanted to follow in my father's footsteps long term, but I do like the power and all the rest of it.

"You send the girl home?" he asks.

"Yeah, but she's on the hook for two weeks."

Orton straightens, surprised. "You hired her for two weeks?"

"Yup."

He falls silent in a way that says *no comment.*

"What?" I demand.

"Just not like you, that's all. To want a repeat performance."

"I saw her, I wanted her, I took her. Now I'm keeping her a bit."

He toys with his relic ring now, looking thoughtful. The ring has tiny hinges on the side where it once opened, though it would've been long since fused shut, concealing its contents inside.

I don't do relationships—at least not in this decade—and I never fuck the same woman twice. Orton likes the people around him to be predictable.

I fix him with a hard look. "Got something to say?"

"It's just not like you."

I let the uncomfortable silence expand beyond what normal people can tolerate, daring him to say Sara's name. I know that's what he's thinking.

*It's not like you to get hooked up with someone since Sara.*

*Not like you to care about who you fuck since Sara.*

*Not like you to differentiate one pussy from the next since what you did to Sara.*

But he stays quiet. He concentrates on his ring, turning it on his finger.

The ring is a family heirloom that he managed to keep through our mercenary years, from bloody battles in sweltering alleyways to snowy hellscapes. I'm supposed to take it off him if he dies. He's supposed to take my St. Michael medallion.

He twists it again. Old rings like his usually contain family relics or clan relics—hair or bone or bits of burial shroud from The First, a mafia king who lived four centuries ago. Orton will never say what's in it. More superstitions.

The pseudo-uncomfortable silence stretches on. Orton can tolerate as much discomfort as I can.

"Right, okay," Orton finally says.

I grab my coat. I'll be the judge of what's like me or not.

# Chapter Ten

EDIE

I sneak into the suite I share with Odetta, clutching my rain poncho around me.

Odetta's sleeping—no surprise there, being that it's four in the morning on a Tuesday. In a few hours, normal students will be getting up and going to Butler Library to study, grabbing coffee and pastries at the Hungarian Pastry Shop, or hitting the fitness center for an early workout.

And here I am, just getting in.

Quietly as I can, I pull off the plastic rain poncho and strip off the ruined red dress, shoving it into the bottom of my dirty clothes bag like evidence from a crime scene. I stuff my clutch full of money under my pillow and take a shower that does nothing to wash away the electricity of Luka's touch still pulsing through me.

My body still vibrates with his fingers, his mouth, the intoxicating weight of him pressing me down.

I towel dry my hair, throw on a faded sweatshirt, and sit cross-legged on my bed. With trembling fingers, I pull out the money and count it under the glow of my desk lamp.

Thirty thousand.

My mind spins with what to do with it—lodging, classes,

credit card, food. My debt has been spiraling out of control, but with this huge windfall, things can turn around.

It seems illegal to have this much cash. Only criminals would have this much.

But I *am* a criminal—a criminal on a leash, and the other end is held by Luka Zogaj.

I google him, trying to get his history, or just any kind of information. There's nothing much but names and addresses of a lot of Zogajes. There is, however, a Zogaj family associated with the Albanian mafia clan known as the Ghost Hound Clan in a list on Wikipedia.

*Ghost Hound Clan. What the fuck.*

I peer over at Odetta, still sleeping. Whatever happens, I have to keep her safe from all of this.

I divide the money into four small stacks. I wish I had some sort of a professional hiding place like in the movies—a dresser drawer with a false back or a puzzle box or something. I settle for stuffing it all into a sock and shoving it into the back of my underwear drawer.

What if he finds out I'm a college student? Will that look strange? Or maybe not. College is expensive.

I don't want the ice cream I promised myself anymore, so I try to sleep, but I'm too jacked.

I tiptoe to the bathroom, fill a glass of water, and stare down at 113th Street. Nine stories below, blue Columbia banners flap from the row of streetlamps illuminating empty streets, parked cars, and shuttered shops. It's always bright here in Manhattan, unlike back home in the suburbs of Hartford, where night was actually night.

This is my fourth year here and my third rooming with Odetta. Odetta's in the history department, too—early Roman Empire—but she wants to do law.

I specialize in the medieval and Crusades eras. I'm going to do my thesis on Byzantine princess Anastasia Laskarina, who is thought to be one of the earliest female historians and the first known teen historian.

Learning about her as a young girl sparked my passion for history. I loved imagining her in her castle chambers or out on walks with her ladies, observing history brewing all around her. I loved to think about her with her journals, writing everything she saw.

I have a dream of writing a book focused on teenagers in history—not just those who shaped events but those who recorded their experiences firsthand. I want my textbook to encourage kids to observe, reflect, and think critically about their worlds.

This idea of mine helped me land a full-ride scholarship, but it wasn't bullshit I said for the scholarship. It's a plan I mean to carry through. Write the textbook. Be a teacher.

It's a plan that Bender could destroy with one word. Nobody will hire a teacher with a criminal record.

# Chapter Eleven

## EDIE

"There's the sleepy bird!" Odetta's beaming up from our favorite nook of the 98th Street library, extra cute in braids and the orange hat that she knit last week.

"Shh!" I slide in next to her. "I'm so glad you're still here."

"When did you get in?"

"Don't ask."

She pulls her book to her chest and leans in, grinning.

I told her yesterday that I was meeting a city guy, a businessman, in a restaurant. A friend of a friend, I told her.

"And? How was it?"

I sigh, remembering the way he took me over with his big, weathered hands and his dirty talk and his dark confidence.

"It was... intense."

She searches my gaze. "In a good way?"

I stare up at the stacks, stretching up into the dusty silence high above us. "I don't know. Intense in a different way."

"Hmmm." She's not sure what to make of this answer. "What did you guys do?"

"Had a few drinks at a weird bar in the Bronx and then hung out a little."

"Like hung out how...?" She wants the hot details.

"Yeah, like, we hung out."

"You kissed him."

My face goes red. I didn't kiss him. There was no kissing.

"You fucked him!" she squeaks.

"Maybe," I breathe.

Her eyes go wide.

"What?" I protest. "People do that."

"People that aren't you."

"Well..." I make a face. "Surprise?"

"Some city guy? Also, the Bronx? I mean, do you like him? Are you going to see him again? What's he like? Spill the tea."

"He's like... not even like the same species as us. And he's older."

She leans in. "How much older?"

"I have no idea," I say, pondering the strange timelessness of Luka. "Older."

"Silver fox older?"

"More like in his thirties older, but something about him makes the guys our age seem like children. Most of them—I don't mean Chad." Odetta's boyfriend, Chad, is a psych major who works a software sales job nights and weekends. A sweet workaholic.

She snorts. "No worries. I'm into it. Go on."

I wrap my arms around myself. "You know how when you're on a roller coaster, and you sit down, and the safety thing clamps down over your shoulders. Then suddenly, the ride starts, and you're climbing and climbing, and then you're dropping through space and flying and powerless to resist. Like maybe you're scared, but you wouldn't stop it, and it's not good or bad. It's more about... this experience."

"Intense and climbing and dropping through space and flying? Does he have a brother?"

"Stop it. You have Chad."

"Kidding!"

I shake my head. "Really, I don't know if I'd recommend this roller coaster. I don't even know if I'd recommend it to me."

Her eyes sparkle. "But you're going to ride it again."

I swallow. I might have to ride it again.

"You're going to ride it again," she repeats. "Because you can't stay away. You are powerless to resist. Or is he a one-time thrill?"

She's my roommate and my best friend, and I hate lying to her. I look at her straight on. "We'll see. He's not a good person, but he's compelling." That's the best piece of truth I can offer her.

"The Pied Piper was compelling."

"Exactly."

"Should I be worried?"

"No," I lie. "I'm good."

She sits back in her chair and regards me for a long moment. "You are blowing my mind right now."

I'm blowing my own mind.

"And you'll probably see him again. Because he's wildly compelling."

I'll have to, and anyway, he'll hunt me down if I don't, but I just nod.

"And you wouldn't have it any other way," she whispers. "Because of the climbing and dropping and flying through space!"

I shrug, wracked with worry. What if Luka calls during class or in the middle of the night wanting me to come to him? How long do I have to get to him in a scenario like that? And what if I'm in the middle of a test with my phone turned off? Will he send people all over Manhattan looking for me?

Would he be able to find me?

Will Bender come and arrest me?

Luka's phone is on vibrate in a zipped pocket in my purse, waiting like a threat and a promise.

# Chapter Twelve

## LUKA

They say there are only sixteen types of people. Everybody has a type they mesh best with, but what about the type that gets under your skin, the type that invades your every waking thought? And you get up in the morning with dream fragments of them at the edges of your mind?

My consciousness tends to be a very dense element, which is to say, nothing gets in, and nothing gets out.

Except for Edie, apparently.

But at least I slept. That's new.

I grab a coffee and respond to a dozen texts about a Bratva situation that's gotten out of control. I ping Storm and tell him to pick me up in an hour. Places to go, Russians to kill. Running this clan would be a lot smoother if my brother hadn't done such a shit job of management.

I wander to the window and look down at the people racing this way and that.

My new penthouse is in Esterford Tower, a glass monstrosity reviled up and down 237th Street for its cold, sterile look, but I like it.

I check where Edie is, only to remember she's turned off the tracking.

I clench my teeth, pissed off that she's done that and even more pissed off that I give a shit. What do I care where she is when she's not with me?

I shoot her a text:

> turn on the tracking.

The three dots appear. She's typing. Then the dots disappear before she's back to typing.

> That wasn't our deal

> Turn it on.

> You text I come that was our deal

I stare at the phone in disbelief. She's right, but I'm not in the mood for this pushback. And why won't she do it? Is she hiding something?

> Do I need to call you over here and put you over my knee?

> You text I come...is this texting for me to come

I frown. If I didn't have such a busy day, she'd be back in my bed so fast. I'd be schooling her on how you don't say no to me, and maybe on punctuation, too. And I'd make her tell me how she knows Arianiti. And she'd give me that scorn before consuming every inch of her. I'd make her tell me how much she hates criminals while I fuck her stunningly fuckable mouth. And would it kill her to use a little punctuation?

> Take a picture of your lips.

Dots.

Will she say no to that, too? Everything in me is standing at attention, not just my cock but all the deepest parts of me. I want her to say no, and I want to get into things with her.

This time she complies, and there they are, those frowny, unhappy lips that fit together in the hottest pout ever.

keep them ready for my cock.

I toss aside the phone and do my morning stretching routine, designed by a disreputable but brilliant doctor in Dubai to keep the scar tissue from hardening, right at the windows that soar up to the ceiling.

"Very you," Orton had said when he first saw this obelisk of a building. "You can see out, but nobody can see in. So fucking you. So on the nose."

He wasn't wrong.

I bought this place lock, stock, and barrel the day I arrived in New York, flush with millions that Orton, Storm, and I had pulled from a hidden nook deep in the Norilsk mines of Northern Siberia.

"I'll take it all, furnishings and everything," I said.

"You don't really want this stuff." The selling agent picked up a framed picture of a covered bridge. There was another with a horse and another with a woman waving from the Eiffel Tower. "You don't even know this person."

"I want all of it," I'd said. "Everything here."

"Wouldn't you want your own pictures? Imagine a vignette in the corner with treasured objects from your travels." She walked over to a shelf with lots of books and showed me how they were just cardboard boxes with sides made to look like spines. "I could give you the name of an interior decorator who'd handle it all to your tastes. Home decor is a way to express what's inside of you."

"How can I explain this?" I'd given her a hard look. "With some people, it's best that they don't express themselves."

At that, she gave me all of it.

I wasn't bullshitting. Expressing myself, whatever that would look like, surely wouldn't end well, but more than that, a home is a transaction, just like a relationship.

I go through my schedule, seeing that I can pull Edie in tonight. In the meantime, she has the day off.

What does a woman like that do on a day off? Does she shop? Read? Watch movies? Do spa treatments?

I try to imagine her in all of those scenarios, and then I remind myself it's just about the fucking.

Until a dark thought comes to me—what if she's not on vacation? What if she's taking clients secretly on the side? What if it's not up to her? She may operate through some kind of a handler or an agency.

Heat rushes up the back of my neck as I imagine another man ripping off her clothes. Another man putting his hands on her. Fucking her and getting all that scorn.

I told her I'd rip a guy's balls off if she did that. Did she understand I meant it?

If I could look into her eyes while I asked her, I'd know if she'd been with anybody else. That defiant fire in her gaze would flicker differently; her contempt is untainted when she looks at me, and it wouldn't burn so bright through a lie. She's mine—those eyes, that mouth, every inch of her body and what it does when I touch it. Mine alone.

Before I can stop myself, I'm texting her a warning. I hit send and throw the phone back on the chair.

No one touches what's mine.

# Chapter Thirteen

## EDIE

I have two important classes to study for on Sunday. Historiography of the Crusades, which explores how the history of the Crusades was written, and Comparative Proto-Indo-European Syntax.

Proto-Indo-European is the common ancestor of half the world's languages. It was thought to have been spoken in the Bronze Age, but nobody really knows.

I'm studying for that one at a table with a few other students from that class, laboring over identifying the roots of the word "farcical," when my phone vibrates. My Luka phone.

I don't want to look, but I have to. My heart pounds as I grab the phone and enter the passcode.

He wants me to turn on geolocation.

I tell him no because what else can I do? He can't know I misrepresented myself.

We go back and forth. He's not a man to take no for an answer, but somehow, he settles for a shot of my lips, which I do as discreetly as possible.

Just when I'm catching back up with the discussion of the roots of farcical, he texts again:

> Just to reiterate, if I find you have been with any other man, I will string that man up by his feet. The screams will be deafening, and the rivers will flow black with blood. The same goes for any other person who was involved in that transaction.

I suck in a breath.

Another message.

> Except you, of course. You, I will punish in a different way.

"You okay?" my table neighbor asks.

"Yeah. Just... a thing." I shove the phone back in my bag and force my attention back to my books.

Would he actually do those things? Exactly how dangerous is he?

And does he expect me to reply to that last message? I don't want to get into another exchange with him and give him the idea to summon me. But it might be worse if I ignore it.

I could do a thumbs up, but a thumbs up on that kind of message might be seen as patronizing. At least it would be by most people my age. But Luka is older, and he doesn't live by the phone.

And there's Bender to worry about. Bender will have seen the whole thing. He might be mad if I don't reply in some way.

I take out the phone, shoot a thumbs up, and quickly pocket it again.

Luka is out there thinking about me.

I get this strange charge, imagining him thinking about me.

I visit my friend Janey in her office at the student paper after that. Janey's a journalism major who went through all three years of French with me, and she has access to a super-high-powered database.

"Bonjour," she says, looking up from her cubicle. "Did somebody bring me cookies?"

"Oui." I set down the Cookie Madness bag on her desk.

She looks inside. "And what did I do to deserve this bounty?"

I pull up a chair. "It's what you're about to do."

"Is this about your sister? I've still got that flag out for any news of her. There's been nothing new."

"No, it's something else. I want you to look into a new name for me. It's a really long story about why I need it, but there's nothing much on the web."

"Okay." She spins around in her chair and taps a few keys. "Hit me."

"Luka Zogaj."

She freezes, fingers poised over the keyboard, before turning her head to look at me. "As in part of the Albanian mafia clan?"

"Yeah."

"And why would you want this?"

"I'd prefer if you didn't ask," I say.

"Yeah, but this is mafia stuff."

"It sort of has to do with my sister... in a roundabout way."

"Mob shit is dicey, Edie, and this is the *Albanian* mob. I don't have to type anything into this box to tell you the results—steer the fuck clear. If your sister is involved with them, this might be tough-love time. I hate to say it..."

"I just need to know how dangerous he is."

"Has she joined his organization?"

"Can I not say any more than that?" I pull another bag from my backpack and set it next to the first one. That cookie was for me to eat, but this is important. "All information is worth having, isn't that what they say?"

"No, not all information is worth having." But she types away all the same. A spinning wheel comes up, and she opens another screen. A list of publications comes up. Some look like they're off a law enforcement site; others are court docs or transcripts. She continues on, chasing links deeper and deeper.

"There's a ton on the Zogaj family but not much on Luka,"

she observes. "And he's the only Zogaj alive at this point, it looks like. Of the immediate family, anyway."

"It's my understanding that he's been out of the country."

"That would make sense."

She finds exactly one image of him: a class picture of him as a ten-year-old boy. He's standing with a dozen other boys, all in school uniforms, but I pick him out right away. He looks angry. "There's not much for Luka. Weirdly."

"What do you have on the family?"

She pulls up a few articles. It turns out they're a longtime Albanian mafia powerhouse stretching back to the seventeen hundreds, possibly earlier, and their clan is named the Ghost Hound Clan.

"Very dangerous. The father, Bernardo Zogaj, the late *kyre*— that's their word for don or king—was killed in a suspicious plane crash ten years back with his wife, Violetta. The elder Zogaj brother, Alteo, took over the Ghost Hound Clan after that and ran it with an iron fist, expanding operations across the Southern Hemisphere until he was killed in a suspicious boating accident— just last month, in fact."

"Lots of suspicious transportation accidents," I say.

"No shit." She taps some more. I wait, staring longingly at the cookie bag.

"Here's a transcript of court minutes that indexes Luka. It's not about him per se, but it suggests Luka was sent to an Albanian military school at the age of twelve. Hold on—" She taps some more and finds a different court transcript where somebody says he apprenticed in a crime family operating in Buenos Aires. There's another theory that he was sent to a reformatory of some sort. "Just a lot of rumors. Here's what I know: rumors pop up in the absence of information."

"How did the brother die? What exactly happened with the boat?" I ask.

"All I have is those three words—suspicious boating accident."

"Drowned?"

"Who knows? I'm sure it's common knowledge among the criminal set, but it's not like I have access to that sort of information. If you want to tap into the bad-guy rumor mill, you'd have to go to the dark web, but it's not something I'd recommend."

"Wait, do you think I could get a lead on my sister over the dark web?" I ask.

"I mean... unlikely? But anything is possible with the dark web. I mean, it really depends."

"How does somebody get to the dark web?"

She shakes her head. "You shouldn't."

"But there's an outside chance I could get a lead on my sister and get more information I need on Luka Zogaj... I have to find somebody who knows the dark web."

"No matter how fucked up your sister's situation is, you're not doing her any good getting yourself fucked up, too. You understand? This all feels like a hornet's nest that you don't want to poke."

"You know somebody, don't you? There're more cookies where that came from."

She sighs. "This isn't a cookies thing."

After a lot of prodding, I get her to promise to contact a kid named Darren from the computer science lab who can get onto the dark web.

"Darren is paranoid as hell, though," she warns me. "He'll only meet face-to-face through referral, and you have to pay him in bitcoin. He has this whole superspy way of doing reports. You'll see. I'll tell him to reach out to you."

# Chapter Fourteen

LUKA

Orton shows up at my penthouse looking upset. I lead him in, gesturing to a couch.

"You better be standing for this," he says.

"What's up?"

"There's a nasty little rumor going around. Somebody's saying that you're not a true Zogaj."

*Not a true Zogaj.* Orton lets the words sit between us, scowling all the while.

"Any idea who?"

"No."

I shrug. "People say all kinds of shit."

"They're saying you're not a true *Zogaj,*" Orton repeats gravely. "We need to shut this down. It's heresy."

"I'm more interested in whoever did the Tucumayo job," I say.

He follows me to the kitchen where I fix us both a black coffee with a splash of raki, an Albanian liquor of grapes and anise. Raki purists get mad when you put it in coffee, but Orton and I, we'd put it in anything over the years.

"I did get one possible lead on the hitters."

"Tell me."

We discuss Orton's lead. It's a good one. He's a gifted investigator.

"But the true-blood bullshit—to suggest you're a bastard!" Orton will not let it go. "Maybe that's who's behind the rumor, whoever did the Tucumayo job.'

"If it is..." I shrug. "Can't make a man sorry twice."

"*You* can," he says. "You can make a man sorry twice. I've seen it."

I go to the window and gaze out over the grimy rooftops. We were both seventeen by the time we got out of Tucumayo, and I definitely made a lot of people sorry.

"I find that trying to make a man sorry twice is the same as one very long sorry," I say.

Orton doesn't think it's funny.

"The bloodline thing," I add. "If they had proof, they'd show it."

Orton comes to stand next to me. "The proof cannot exist. It's not possible." This he says like a command.

"It's not *impossible*—" I say.

"No! It is impossible because there's no question. You're a true blood, end of story."

I say nothing. Orton is invested in my having a pure clan bloodline because he's invested in being my knight. That is his destiny—knight to a true *kyre*. It's a thing with him.

If I weren't true blood, he might be the first to kill me. It's just how he rolls.

Lucky for me, nobody's getting my DNA. I took this throne from my brother—or the man who everyone assumes is my brother—and I'm keeping it until I'm done with it.

Same with Edie. I'll keep her as long as I want, which will hopefully sink in with her.

"Do I look like a man who doesn't know a true Zogaj?" Orton grits out. "Do I look like a man who'd follow a fake? Your brother's a liar, that's all. He lied when he said you weren't a true blood."

Orton was much more upset than I was about my brother saying I wasn't a true-blooded Zogaj.

Personally, I don't give a shit about my bloodline, being that I hate my family. I hated them before they sent me to Tucumayo, and I definitely hated them once I was there.

"A father doesn't send his son to a place like Tucumayo for no reason," I remind Orton because I'm the kind of man who likes to call things what they are.

Orton sniffs. "The reason they sent you away was because of the prophecy. They were afraid it would come true. And it did, didn't it? You killed the kyre and took the throne."

"Most kyres get killed."

Orton harumphs, which means he'll hear nothing more of it.

And he really would kill me if I was a false kyre and not a true blood. For nearly two decades, we've been risking our lives for each other, but it's some supposed strand of DNA deep in my cells that keeps him loyal to me.

That goes for half the men I'm leading now.

The rest follow me from fear.

"I took the throne, and I'm keeping it, DNA or not. Tell me about tomorrow," I say.

Orton tells me how he'll be terrorizing a few of the people who might give us the details we need. Then we'll find the men we're hunting, and it will be done.

I'd just assumed I was a true Zogaj until that day out on the boat last month.

In those last bloody moments, my brother, Alteo, said I was a bastard and that my father paid a crone to deliver the prophecy that I'd kill him so that nobody would question why he sent his son away. He said my father didn't want people to know his wife had strayed.

Alteo's words could be true. Deep down, it makes sense.

But it's not like anybody's digging up bodies and running

DNA tests. Orton gets to believe I'm a true blood, and I get to believe I might not be my hated father's son.

"It's a fucking death wish," Orton says because he really can't leave it. "Whoever it is, they want to die because you'll come for them for saying that."

I look over the Hudson, following a tugboat making its way down the murky waters, waiting for Orton to say what I know he'll say. He doesn't disappoint.

"*With every prick, the spider's web tightens, thorn for thorn, blood for blood.*"

I nod. This is an Albanian vengeance saying that Orton repeats every chance he gets.

He wants to believe—he really, really wants to.

Sometimes, the things a man wants are no good, but still, he wants them.

# Chapter Fifteen

## EDIE

I'm curled up in my favorite chair in the study commons on the seventh floor of our residence hall that night, trying to focus.

Not easy when a mafia kingpin might summon me for sex at any given moment.

*Sex.* That one word seems too small and limited for what happened between us.

My mind spins with the image of him naked, strong and proud, prowling over me like a lion. The feel of lying on that bed, masturbating at his command.

How quickly he made me into a depraved person who likes wrong and twisted things.

I tell myself that woman wasn't me once and for all, and I focus on pulling together resources for the paper that I stupidly declared I'd write. The paper is titled "The Evolution of Byzantine Iconography in the 11th and 12th Centuries: New Themes, Styles, and Influences," but Odetta and I call it "Iconic Regret" because it's been such a bear to research.

I find myself in a dead end with too narrow of a search term, so I tweak it and try again.

The commons area is an enforced quiet space with lots of

overstuffed couches, tables, and homey lamps on side tables. Ruffles of colorful flyers adorn the row of bulletin boards along one wall, advertising jobs, clubs, services, and room shares.

What if Luka figures out where I am without geolocation? While a hooker college student isn't impossible, his guys would only have to interview a few of my friends to know that this isn't something I'd ever do. How long would it take him to figure out that I was planted by the police?

I remind myself he could have no idea I'm a college student. And that he hasn't texted yet. I organize my highlighted material, like that will help the chaos of my life right now, and, of course, that's when he texts.

I don't notice it at first; my Luka phone is on vibrate only. But then I get a call on my normal phone, which I do notice.

It's "Brenda," a.k.a. Bender.

My heart starts pounding. What does he want? Is something going on with my sister? I pull out my earbuds and answer. "Yeah?"

"You gonna text him back anytime soon?"

"Oh. He texted?"

"*He texted*? Yeah, he texted. He wants to see you tonight."

"I had my earbuds in."

"He texted twice."

*Fuck, fuck, fuck.*

"Hold on." I put my phone down and pull the burner phone out of the zipper pouch, and sure enough, new texts.

One text is from an hour ago. It's a Bronx address and a string of commands.

11PM tonight. Dress nice. Wait outside.

The other text is from five minutes ago, and it's a repeat of the first message with the words "confirm receipt."

"I see it," I say, gripping my phone, lost in a whirlwind of emotions.

"Are you planning on texting back? You want him to come looking for you?"

I set the phone down even as Bender's tinny voice goes on. I need to concentrate on what to say to Luka. I decide on short and sweet.

> Got it. CU then.

I pick up Bender again, pulse racing. "Done."

"That's an Albanian restaurant. How are you getting there?"

"Uber, I guess."

"Hail a cab and pay cash. Have the cabbie drop you at the Concourse station. Wait for him to leave and walk a few blocks to get another cab to drop you two blocks from the restaurant. And pay with cash. Got something nice to wear?"

"I'll have to see..."

"If you don't have anything, reuse the dress we set you up with."

"Okay." I don't tell him it's ruined.

"I don't have to tell you how important this is—for both of us. And your sister."

*Was that a warning?*

I swallow back the dryness in my mouth. "I got it."

"Keep your ears open like you did last time," Bender says. "You did real well, and he has no idea, or he wouldn't be calling you, okay?"

"But... wouldn't he be just as likely to summon me if he got suspicious? To see who I'm working for?"

Bender laughs. "You've been watching too many movies. That's not how it works. Now, in addition to keeping your ears open for any and all names, dates, and places, what is the specific critical information you're going to try to get?"

"I'm supposed to figure out where he's been all these years and find out why he killed his brother."

"Not just *why* he killed him, but why he killed him the way he killed him. Get any of that intel, and you'll have a lot of goodwill from me. A *lot*."

"What if he wants me to turn on geolocation?"

"You handled it perfectly before—it wasn't the deal you made. Guys like him don't beg and wheedle. If he didn't trust you, you wouldn't be there."

"So you say."

"Though he may have you followed. Simply out of curiosity, if nothing else."

"What?"

Bender goes on to give me instructions on how to lose a tail on my return home—like it's no big deal. "Change your pace, use reflections, make sudden turns, enter crowded places, use public transport, get off at the last second..."

My head is spinning by the time we hang up. How is this my life right now? Eleven at night is usually when I'm reading in bed, if not sleeping, but the Lukas of the world start their day at night, I guess.

I go back to work, reviewing my highlighted stuff, but the words swim senselessly in front of my eyes.

Will I get sucked into his whole dark depraved vortex again where I was panting for him like a dog in heat? It was wrong, so deeply wrong. Panting for a killer. Coming for a killer. Desperate for him to pull my hair and all the rest.

So wrong.

If only he'd lost interest. I could keep the money, and Bender would still have to help me with Mary because I did my part.

It's here I get a new idea: Could I *make* Luka lose interest in me?

He liked it when I seemed prim and angry. When I looked at him with scorn. *Don't act like you like it,* he said.

So... what if I went with the opposite? What if I acted infatuated with him instead of hating him? What if I were to smile sweetly instead of frowning and glaring?

The more I think about it, the more I think that this could be the key. Luka loved when I turned on the whole haughty thing.

I'll be a pliable playmate. Unopinionated. Happy to oblige.

Could I pull it off? Of course!

Maybe then he'd decide I was a bad investment and move on.

And Bender won't be able to do anything about it because Luka would have rejected me.

He'd still have to help me with my sister because I did everything he asked, didn't I?

I just have to act nice. Bland. Obsequious. I can do that.

*Dress nice.*

Did he like the sexy red dress? Well, then, I'll find the opposite of that.

An hour later, I'm window shopping on the Upper West Side.

I stop at a vintage store with a pale pink dress in the window— so pale, it's nearly pearl, with a tiny stitch detail along the bodice.

Odetta always teases me that my favorite color is pastel. Like that's a bad thing. I love the calm serenity of pastels. The elegance of pale salmon. Buttercream. Light blue. And this pale pink is the prettiest thing I've ever seen. It's quiet. Simple, with a small collar. Maybe even a bit prim and not at all sexy.

This is not a dress to be lusted over or even noticed in. How much would Luka hate it?

I grin. He said to wear something nice, and this counts as that.

I go in and try it on with kitten heels. I put my hair in a ponytail and walk out to check the mirror. A shiver runs through me.

It's the perfect Edie dress. And he'll so hate it.

# Chapter Sixteen

## EDIE

I tell the second cabbie to drop me off on a Little Albania side street a block from the restaurant, just as Bender wanted.

I pay in cash and walk the rest of the way, passing a shuttered shoe shop and a tailor's storefront that looks like it's been around for generations—the kind of place guys like Luka probably go to get suits made.

I imagine him standing on a stool like a movie mafioso, squinting into the distance while an old man measures his powerful arms. His squint would deepen as he broods over his dark empire. His dark brows get these little wings in the middle when he squints, but they stay pointy on the outer edges. And, of course, his devil-angel eyes would stay wrongly gorgeous.

The restaurant turns out to be on one of those below-the-first-floor spaces where you have to go down a couple steps. There's no sign, but it's clearly a restaurant, judging from the red canopy and candlelit interior.

I head down and pause in front of elegantly carved dark wood double doors. There's a menu posted on the side window above a picturesquely drippy candle.

I clutch my small pink purse in both hands.

I ate two packs of ramen noodles before I left so I wouldn't be hungry. I'm going to just be fake and smiley and not even give Luka the satisfaction of feeding me properly. And most of all, if he thinks he's getting the scorn, he can guess again.

This date will be unsatisfying to him in every way. Maybe he'll send me home before anything else even happens.

The door to the place opens, and I straighten. It's the man who seems like a soldier. Storm, I think they called him.

And then Orton comes. "Gimme the bag."

I hand over my small clutch, and he goes through it. Phone, makeup, and a small wallet. Mints. He pockets the phone and hands the bag back.

"Hands on the wall."

"What?"

"Do it."

I turn and put my hands on the wall. "I'm not armed."

He snorts like that's ridiculous. Like, even if I were armed, it wouldn't do shit. Then I realize he's looking for a wire. Recording devices. Maybe that's why he took the phones.

What can they do about the giant recording device between my ears? That's the one they should worry about. That's the one Bender is counting on.

He looks hard into my eyes. "I've been with Luka over twenty years. He sees everything. Understand?"

I nod.

"You wanna know what happens when Luka sics Storm here on somebody stupid enough to fuck with us?"

I look over at Storm, who glowers at me in his special ice-mountain-man way.

"I'm not up to anything," I say softly, hoping he doesn't sense my fear. I'm desperate, suddenly, to get to Luka.

"You wanna know or not?"

"No."

"Good answer." Orton leans in. "Because if you knew, it would fucking haunt your dreams. Let's go."

He leads me through a candlelit sea of hushed voices and soft clinks against crystal.

Booths are built into the wall along the sides and the back, all spaced far away from each other and private.

Nestled into the far back corner is the most shadowy booth of all, but it's not shadowy enough that I don't see Luka's impossibly beautiful eyes.

He stands.

I stop some ways away from him, feeling nervous.

He's in another of his perfectly tailored black suits, shirt brilliant white against the dark fabric—all power and deadly elegance. His heavy gaze slides from my pale dress with the sweet bodice detail to my bare legs and my white kitten heels and back up.

It seems like forever that I stand there. Is this some kind of inspection? Like I'm a piece of meat? I'm overtaken with the instinct to narrow my eyes in disgust, but then I remember.

I'm bland tonight. Nice. I put on a vacant expression. Very Stepford wife.

He says, "Your dress. It's..."

*Hah!* He doesn't like the dress!

But I don't smile. Instead, I tilt my head like a pleasant little robot. "You don't like it? You said nice."

He swallows with seeming difficulty, still staring.

I try to think of something else boring to do, some other way to be the opposite of what he wants. And then it comes to me—I told him my smile was my own the last time we were together.

*Be careful what you wish for, mister,* I think as I form my lips into a big, wide smile, like I'm pleased to be on display in my nice dress. Like I admire him. Adore him.

His gaze darkens.

I brighten my smile.

Thoughts seem to flow behind his eyes, and then he sits down and crooks his finger. *Come.* That's what the finger means.

He doesn't even say it. Just the finger. *Come.*

The booth is large and filled with maybe seven guys. And they're all looking at us.

I force myself to put one foot in front of the other. I stop in front of him, keeping my big, fake smile.

His cruel, beautiful lips twist into something that's definitely not a smile. "Closer," he commands.

I step in closer, right between his legs, close enough that I can feel his breath on my neck and the power and darkness that roll off him.

His whisper, when it comes, is unbearably intimate. "Look at me."

I look down and meet his dark gaze with my big, fake smile, hoping I'm managing to keep the emotion from my face.

"I like the dress."

My pulse thunders so loudly in my ears that I'm barely conscious of the gentle press of his knuckle against my belly.

Slowly, he draws it upward, my entire being swirling along with it. I'm a melted confection, slowly stirred by his traveling knuckle as it continues up my rib cage, between my breasts, up my neck, and finally to my chin.

He stands again, keeping his knuckle right there.

I clench my sex as he lifts my chin so that I'm gazing up at him.

My pulse is on overdrive. My panties are wet with arousal. I swallow, thinking of all the good guys I've dated. The sweet picnics and silly jokes and long talks about classes.

Those are the guys for me—not this awful brutish one.

And he wasn't supposed to like the dress, dammit!

His knuckle nudges my chin higher. My chest rises and falls under his gaze.

"God, baby, you're right there for me. I love how you're right there." With that, he releases me and pulls out a chair. "Sit."

I sit. He pushes it in behind me like the gentleman he's not and sits beside me at the end of the booth.

"Look alive, buttercup," he says with a glint in his eye.

I give him a blank stare like I don't understand.

*Boring, boring, boring*, I think. I will not be eating. I will not be drinking. I will not be enjoying any part of this night.

A waiter sets down a basket of warm herbed bread with a plate of roasted peppers and feta, and it all smells so good I want to die.

Luka smiles. Like he knows.

# Chapter Seventeen

## LUKA

The waiters descend with more food and a gin and tonic for Edie.

"Drink, eat." I set a piece of rosemary bread and a slab of feta on her plate.

"Not hungry." She gives me another one of her fake smiles, all wide green eyes and cherry lip gloss.

"You knew you were coming to dinner, but you're not hungry?"

She shrugs, expression vacant.

I take a strand of her hair between my fingers. What's going on with her?

Orton discreetly presses the guys for information about something that happened years ago, back when my brother, Alteo, took a bigger role in the family. Alteo would be forty now if I hadn't killed him.

Only Orton and Storm know I'm here for vengeance. You never show your hand, and you never reveal what's important in life.

My brother ordered the Tucumayo killing. That's why he died. But there are still actual killers to find.

Everybody involved in her death dies—that was my vow to

Sara all those years ago. I don't care who they are; they die. Ultimately it's my fault, of course, and a lot of indiscriminate killing won't change that, but that's one of the good things about being all-powerful—the shit you do doesn't need to make sense.

As luck would have it, I'm good at running this clan. One month in, and they've never been stronger. Never richer.

*You came for the vengeance, and you stayed for the power trip.*

I catch her staring at the bread, practically drooling over it. Oh, she's definitely hungry.

I take a piece for myself and load it up with cheese and peppers. I let her watch me take a bite. I dab the corners of my mouth. "You're missing out."

She smiles and shrugs.

I grit my teeth. I know when a person's hungry. They'd keep us so hungry in that place.

God, why does her hunger feel like a three-alarm fucking fire? If she wants to deny herself, who am I to interfere? If she wants to play cat-and-mouse with where she lives or what she's doing during the day, why do I care?

But the bland act? No.

I settle my hand onto her thigh and hover my lips over her ear, warm and electric. "I will break you of this so hard."

"What?"

"Don't play dumb."

She pulls back with a frown as though she doesn't understand.

There are five other men at this table besides Orton and me. My top brass. Two of them were my brother's top guys—the only ones out of his whole crew I deemed trustworthy. The other three I handpicked.

They know to ignore us.

Storm eats alone at the bar because he rarely joins the group; he's too far gone to be anywhere but on the fringes.

I turn back to her. "I will find you. You think I can't?"

She pretends to be confused.

West pockets his phone. "Florian's coming. He's shook up about something."

I exchange glances with Orton. *What now?*

Florian arrives a few minutes later, looking stressed. He puts his palms down on the table. "Bloody Lazarus might be *alive*."

I straighten. "Bloody Lazarus? Not possible. He got blown up. There were witnesses."

"And did they find his body?" Florian says. "No."

"Because it was incinerated," I say. "Aleksio and his brothers saw it themselves."

"They never found the body, though, did they? Nobody found that body. This is Lazarus we're talking about."

Orton narrows his eyes. "Bloody Lazarus? Are we talking about that psychotic enforcer for... who was it?"

"Aldo Nikolla, the Chicago kyre," I say to him. "Lazarus and Aldo did a big, bloody massacre twenty years back, just before I was sent down to Tucumayo. You were already down there, but man, it was fucked up. They slaughtered the Chicago Dragushas and took a lot of territory. Two decades of darkness and violence. And then the Dragusha boys came back for vengeance..."

People fill him in on the more gory details, which ended in Lazarus being incinerated in a Hummer "with enough C-4 to take down a football stadium."

"Well, apparently, Lazarus survived that incineration," Florian says.

My East Side guy, Cards, isn't convinced. He thinks it's bullshit.

Orton sits back. "I've learned not to believe a man is dead until I see the body and maybe poke at it."

"Did somebody actually see him? Did somebody talk to him?" I ask. "Who is this coming from?"

"Aleksio Dragusha," Florian says.

A hush falls over the table.

"There was a murder out in the Poconos with Lazarus's signature," Florian continues. "Aleksio went down there himself. Got some criminologists or profilers or whatever involved. They're all pretty sure. I didn't get all the details, but..."

"Fuck," somebody whispers, speaking for everyone.

Lazarus is back?

Cards's expression darkens. "Nobody wants Lazarus dead more than those Dragusha boys. There will be blood."

I can feel Edie's interest. It's strange. I turn to her. "You got something to add?"

Her eyes widen. "No! This guy sounds... twisted."

I grunt. The chat rolls on with people saying where they were during the war that broke out after the Dragushas were hit all those years ago.

We fall silent as the second course arrives.

"Eat. Go ahead."

Edie tries a compliant smile. "I'll gladly do whatever you say."

I settle my hand onto her thigh and lower my voice. "Don't play a game you can't win."

"What? You wanted me to smile last time."

"You think you can play a part with me? Hide from me? I'll find you."

"I'm right here."

I slide my hand down before gathering the silky fabric and pulling up her skirt, exposing more and more skin under the table. I lean in, and in a low voice only she can hear, say, "I'll find you so hard."

She blinks, keeping up the bland look. "I'm here for whatever you want."

"No, you're not. You're trying to deny me it." I slide my hand higher.

Her chest jerks with the sudden intake of air when I hit the edge of her panties. She widens her eyes. "Whatever you say."

I don't like this. I don't like it at all, but the next course is here. "Byrek," I say to her. "Thin layers of phyllo with cheese, spinach, chicken, and pumpkin. Delicious." I remove my hand from her thigh long enough to load a bit onto her plate and then mine. "They make an incredible red sauce."

"Really not hungry."

Yeah, right. She's not *hungry*; she's full-on ravenous.

Shouts come from a table up front. West is tussling with one of the diners near the door.

A man stands.

West grabs something—a plate, from the looks of it—and marches out the door. He comes back empty-handed. More people are standing now. More shouts.

The guys are looking at me expectantly. My brother would've gone ballistic at a guy acting out. He didn't like anything to be out of his control. All those years I didn't see him, but I know what he was.

"West's a big boy," I say. "Free to be as fucked up as he wants to be, as long as it doesn't affect the clan."

Kress the Shadow smiles. The guys approve. Guys like this don't take to a short leash.

West comes back looking outraged. "Bringing circle cookies into an Albanian restaurant?"

"No!" Orton barks. "What? No!"

I stifle a groan. *That's* what it was about?

"I told them to take them out of the restaurant, but..." West shakes his head. "Feeding circle cookies to their kids just days before Good Friday. *Here* of all places!"

He and Orton bond over that while Florian grumbles darkly.

I look over at Edie. She's curious as hell, but she doesn't want to ask because she's desperate to play her game.

"It's not exactly common knowledge," Kress the Shadow says.

"There's a menu," Florian says. "They can choose from that. They decide to bring in outside food, and it's circle cookies?"

"Circle cookies," I growl, just to fuck with Edie. "What the fuck?"

The waiter comes back. "I'm so sorry, Mr. Zogaj. If I'd seen they had such cookies, I'd have taken them out myself."

"Of course," I say. "Comp their dinner and get them out of here."

Edie's watching the side of my face. If she wants to know, she can ask.

The waiter comes with sides and more fresh bread. Dishes are passed. People help themselves.

"Stuffed peppers with bechamel sauce." I dish some onto her plate that's still loaded with uneaten food.

"Thanks."

I dig in.

Edie's taken to staring at a painting on the wall—a man atop a majestic horse. He wears a white embroidered shirt under a colorful vest. His pants are tucked into knee-high leather boots, and his woolen cloak is slung over his shoulders. Behind him are ancient stone walls and distant mountains.

"The Albanian Alps," I supply.

"Mmm," she says with that fake smile. She doesn't fool me. She wants to know about the cookies.

I take a bite of the peppers. They've outdone themselves today. "Delicious."

As if on cue, her stomach rumbles. I shouldn't care—I really shouldn't. She's just a *kurvë*. She'll spread her legs for me, so what do I care if she's doing her best imitation of a blow-up doll?

But she's my *kurvë*, that's the problem. Mine.

I swipe a finger in the pale sauce and bring it to her lips. "Open."

"No, thanks."

I lean in. "Not a request."

"What if I'm allergic?"

"Are you?" I ask.

She hesitates.

Holding her gaze, I press my finger between her lips.

# Chapter Eighteen

## EDIE

My sex clenches, and I allow my lips to part just a little.

He slides his finger in. "Suck."

Halfheartedly, I suck. I get a hit of pepper and nutmeg.

It's good. So good.

It's like a microcosm of our relationship. Something delicious that I'm trying not to like. And what's up with the cookies?

Our gazes lock.

He pushes in his finger further, invading my mouth, holding my gaze. The feeling shoots clear down to my sex.

It's so hot it feels like it shouldn't be allowed in public. But we're in the dark corner of a restaurant with nobody watching—not even his guys.

The pad of his finger settles onto my tongue.

With his other hand, he gives my thigh a squeeze and then slides his palm up toward my core.

Rough fingers push up under my panties and explore the softest, most secret part of me while his other finger owns my mouth.

It's a shockingly erotic invasion.

I fight to control my breathing as my sex blooms with heat. It's as if my mouth and vagina are connected in some forbidden way that only Luka knows, being the monster he is.

And I want more and more. And more. It's all I can do not to suck his finger like a little demon and arch greedily into his hand.

God, who does he think he is to do this to me? Make me want these things?

I'm on the verge of losing the battle to keep my mask of blandness in place, to stay unaffected, un-outraged, un-turned on, but thankfully, Luka pulls out the finger, leaving me secretly aroused. Breathless.

He looks at me strangely, like he might have been lost for a moment.

But that's impossible. This is not a man who gets lost.

He picks up my fork and puts it in my hand. "You'll eat."

"If that's what you want." And I want to—I really, really do.

"You'll eat." He turns back to his own plate, to the conversation.

And I eat. It's all I can do not to inhale everything in sight.

The peppers are perfectly done, stuffed with rice, onions, tomatoes, herbs, and some sort of meat. The phyllo pastry dish is madness. I put some cubes of cheese and some olives on a piece of bread and eat that. He's right—it's warm and delicious.

So delicious.

Is this how my sister felt? Sucked down a rabbit hole of erotic and culinary temptations?

I take seconds of my favorites. Thirds of the pastry thing.

"Good?" Luka's voice knocks me out of my orgy of consumption.

He's watching me with that predatory amusement that makes my skin heat.

"It's okay."

He leans in. "I love the way you think you're so above this. So indifferent."

I squint at him like he's not quite making sense.

"You just go with that. It'll just be all the more enjoyable to crack you open and make you beg."

"Whatever you like. Happy to oblige."

He just looks amused. "No, you're not."

The talk at the table rolls on. They're back to Lazarus and trading Lazarus stories. What I'm gathering is that his signature, his calling card, is to add something weird and fucked up to the murder scene. One time, he apparently killed somebody in their bathtub and then made a hospitality fold on the spatter-soaked roll of toilet paper like they do in high-end hotels—that little triangle fold at the end of the roll. Which is nothing short of bizarre.

Another time, he ripped out a man's intestines while he was still alive, watched him die, and placed a Daffy Duck Pez dispenser in each hand. They begin to describe the scene in extreme detail.

"Enough!" Luka looks over at me. Is he worried about my sensibilities?

He shouldn't be. I'm a medieval historian; it takes a lot more than disembowelment—which was a common practice well into the nineteenth century, usually for high treason—to upset me.

Though, adding a bizarre and whimsical detail to such a scene is just unhinged. I need to get away from these people.

"Get a message to Aleksio that our resources are at his disposal," Luka says. "Aleksio and I knew each other as kids, and the Poconos are in my backyard."

One man makes a call, speaking in a Slavic language that's probably Albanian.

"The Dragushas will want blood," someone else says while he's on the phone, and everybody is staring at Luka to see what he'll say. "Lazarus could bring hell."

Luka pops an olive into his mouth and chews leisurely, as though his only care is if the olive is up to his evil standards, and then he dabs the sides of his mouth. "Let the Dragushas have their blood. Let Lazarus bring his hell. Let there be chaos. We'll revel in it and turn it to our advantage. We'll use it to be stronger."

The men beam at Luka. They love his brand of big talk.

"We'll skewer the fucking world on the ends of our razor-sharp teeth," he adds.

The men are so into it, I'm surprised they don't all kiss his ring and roll around on the table in orgasmic pleasure.

I have to admit, it's... weirdly impressive.

Is this stuff he learned at his military school? How to rally the troops?

Also, *on the razor-sharp points of our teeth*? Janey said their clan is called the Ghost Hound Clan. Was that Luka cleverly working in their name? A hound with big teeth? It's so old school.

This whole experience—the nice suits, the luxurious meal, the casual violence—is like I'm in another world.

A bad world, I remind myself.

I'm not impressed.

*Not impressed.*

This man killed his own brother in such a brutal way Bender won't even tell me.

Luka turns to me then, his voice dripping with brutality. "Let any man come after me or mine. I'll rain hell on him like he's never seen."

Something like pleasure crashes over me. I shouldn't love this kind of talk—I shouldn't.

It's just that nobody's ever rained hell for me. Nobody would even consider it.

Luka just watches me. His devil-angel eyes are dazzling in the candlelight, and bits of silver twinkle in his inky hair like sparks of forbidden energy. He's older than me and a zillion times more dangerous than any guy I've ever met, and he'd quietly rain hell on anybody who came after me.

I should look away.

*This is not strength; it's evil,* I tell myself. *Look away,* I tell myself.

I can't. I won't.

His gaze is a palpable thing. Even without him touching me, I can feel it. It's like he knows things about me. I'm used to being the bookish girl in the corner, unnoticed, unremarkable.

Nobody ever saw me. Until him.

His heavy hand returns to my thigh. Excitement bolts through me. My breath shallows.

"Let any man come into my territory or come after my people," Luka growls, sliding closer to my quivering core. "Let him touch a hair on the head of anyone here, to even *think* of taking what's mine..." He doesn't bother to finish the sentence.

He doesn't have to.

He's talking about me. His hand is electric with energy. I want him to touch me everywhere.

Dimly, I think I should distract myself. Eat some more, maybe, but I can't think about my belly when my clit's throbbing and his hand is so close to the needy ache between my legs.

I reach for my drink. I'm concentrating so hard on steadying my trembling hand that I fail to navigate properly and catch a wineglass, tipping it over.

Wine splashes across the table and onto the front of my pale pearl dress.

I jump up.

"Oh no!" I gasp.

I'm more upset than I should be—on the verge of tears, in fact. I'm upset about the dress, but it's more than that. It's the danger and the stress and the way Luka is stealing my soul.

I raise my gaze to his. "It's all ruined."

# Chapter Nineteen

### LUKA

I give her a napkin, and she blots the dress, blinking back the tears.

"It's just getting worse."

"We'll get you another dress," I say.

"It's one-of-a-kind," she blurts out. "I love it, and you can't fix it. Nobody can fix this."

She's going to cry. Women's tears don't generally affect me, but for whatever reason, I can't tolerate Edie crying. I will not have it.

"I got it," I say.

"How?"

I turn her by her shoulders and point her at the restrooms. "You're going to go in the ladies' room and take off the dress and wait for me."

"You're going to make me wait naked in a bathroom for you?"

"Yup."

She blinks at me.

I wait. "Is that a no?"

She grabs her purse and heads off.

I make a few phone calls. A tray arrives with a large silver bowl, a kettle, and a small flask. I bring it to the ladies' room and knock.

She cracks the door.

"Let me in."

She steps back, clad in a simple white underwear set. It's just like that dress, sexy with a little bit of a good-girl edge--without even trying.

I like it, but I'm not here to fuck her. Not yet.

"Let's have the dress." I set the tray down on the hutch. The ladies' room here is nice enough to have actual furniture in it.

She hands it over. I stretch the fabric over the silver bowl. "Hold it like this, stretched."

"What are we doing?"

"Do as I say."

She stretches the fabric over the bowl. I take the kettle and begin to pour a stream of boiling water over the delicate, stained fabric.

"Shouldn't you use cold?"

"Cold's for amateurs." I continue on, pouring in a pattern, back and forth, back and forth, working my way down the stain, which begins to disappear.

"What the hell," she says, momentarily dropping the blank act.

She moves the dress to stretch a different part over the bowl, and I erase that part, too.

"How does a guy like you know a trick like this?"

"We all know this trick, Edie."

"A lot of wine spills?"

I keep up my precise operation until it's gone.

She raises her gaze to mine. "Why are you doing this for me?"

"Hold it up for me to see."

She holds it up for me, trembling. "Wow. Thank you."

There's a knock at the door.

"Yeah?"

A woman's voice. "Polkov."

I hand the wet dress out, exchanging it for the garment bag labeled Polkov's Dry Cleaning.

"She'll finish it up for you. This is something in your size. No guarantees on style."

"What kind of dry cleaner is open in the middle of the night? Did they open special just for—"

"I care for what's mine," I say.

"That's very kind of you."

"It's not about kindness."

She pulls off the plastic bag. The dress is simple. Pale blue. Her size, best I could guess. And I asked for a soft color. I suddenly don't like her in the loud colors.

"This is a really nice dress. Wow. Thank you—that was so kind."

"Kind? We're in a transaction, not a relationship. Your ass is mine to use as I please, and you crying doesn't do it for me."

"Oh, I'm sorry. You're right; making sure my dress wasn't ruined isn't kind. You don't have a good bone in your body."

"That's right."

"You learn that wine trick in military school?"

I slide my finger over her cheek, and she comes alive with a shiver. Her whole body is probably goosebumps. "Somebody's been googling me."

"A girl likes to know who she's dealing with."

I study her face. A different man might think she's here gathering information. Maybe she is gathering information. It doesn't matter. I'll be gone in a few days.

"It wasn't a military school, and the trick isn't for wine."

And there it is—that edge of judgment as she processes that bit of information and realizes it's for blood. "Oh."

"Tell me again what you think of criminals."

"We're not doing that."

"Come on," I say, pushing off her panties. "You hate me, don't you? I'm an awful man who takes whatever he wants without paying. A beast who hurts the good people of the world just because he can. And now you belong to me, and I'm gonna make you come again, and I'm gonna make you crave me, and there's not a goddamned thing you can do about it."

# Chapter Twenty

### EDIE

His cock is a steel bar against my mound. I gasp as energy throbs through my pussy, my belly.

He presses his hands to the sides of my hips and guides my panties down. Electricity shivers over me.

"You hate how I make you feel."

I gasp.

He kneels in front of me, my panties now at my ankles and then off, and touches his finger to the seam of my bare pussy. "Trimmed is fine, but I would ask you to shave yourself before I see you again."

I huff in protest, but nothing matters anymore because he's found the ache. He's touching me there.

It's not enough for this man that I'm half naked and powerless; he has to take everything.

His fingers are on the outside of my lips, pressing like he's plumping out my clit.

I stifle a cry as he slides his tongue between my legs and licks, a long, hard, ice-cream-cone lick that nearly turns me inside out.

I grab onto the sink. I vaguely remember something about

acting bored. I've failed miserably, but no way will I let him make me come. I start a recitation of state capitals.

*Bangor, Maine, Madison, Wisconsin.*

He licks again.

*Springfield, Illinois.*

I focus on my surroundings. It's nice as restrooms go, with a rug over dark marble tiles and a candle on a small, low cabinet next to the sink under a photo of an old bridge.

It's no use. No use. He's burrowing his tongue into some hidden nerve center deep inside me. He has me, and he's merciless, and he's right that I can't hide from him.

He's chasing down my orgasm like a lion going after prey.

A few more brutal licks and I can't stop it—my soul explodes with pleasure. I'm spinning, flying, trying desperately not to show it, but I'm shuddering in spite of myself. He slows his licking, then stops completely.

He presses a kiss over my mound and then my belly as I try desperately to collect myself. I think I have by the time he's looming over me, so smug and evil.

I try to look blank. I even put on a dazed smile.

"You'll want to stop doing that. That fake face."

I furrow my brows like I don't understand.

"Fine. Go with it, then." He grabs me by the ass, sets me on the sink, and pushes apart my legs. "Hold yourself open for me. Spread and glistening. Not one centimeter together, you understand?"

I bite my lip. He's evil, and I shouldn't want him inside me. "Whatever you say."

He fits my hands to the sink, urging me to hold on.

*Tallahassee, Florida, Carson City, Nevada,* I think as I hold my legs apart for him. Behind him, the dry-cleaner bag flaps like a surrender flag.

"You think you can hold yourself apart and above, but it never works. Nobody escapes." The sound of a zipper.

I hold myself open for him. The cool air kisses the heat of my sex. *Sacramento, California, Santa Fe, New Mexico.*

I'm yearning for him to fill me—dying for it. It's the worst thing and the best thing ever.

I hear the crinkle of a foil wrapper, recognizing the motions of a man who's rolling a condom over his cock.

He studies my eyes as he presses his fingers to my clit. I nearly come again, just from that.

"Somewhere along the line, somebody messed with your head and left you high and dry. Probably your daddy."

I suck in a breath. Who does he think he is? He's sort of right, but who cares?

He spreads my juices around and around, watching me like he thinks he knows everything about me.

I bite my lip as he fits his giant cock to my sex, a warm bulb nudging between my legs, smooth and hard.

"I'm your daddy now," he says, entering me slowly, stretching me over the sink and working me how he wants.

I hate him, hate him, hate him. Also desperate for him.

"That's right," he says, watching my eyes, pushing into me, filling me. When he's fully seated inside me, he tweaks my nipples, soft and then harder. "Show me how you feel about that."

"I don't know what you want," I say, channeling my hate into boredom as he stokes my arousal. "You want me to come? Is that it?"

"I don't want you to just come," he grates in my ear. "I want you to come *undone.*"

"Unlikely..."

My words die on my lips as he thrusts into me. He changes his angle and hits something deep. I almost lose it, but then I'm back. *Austin, Texas, St. Paul, Minnesota.*

I hear the clink of glass behind me.

What else did he bring with him?

"What are you doing?"

"It's a surprise."

*Such a horrible person,* I think against the delicious feeling of him rocking inside me. *Horrible.* I keep it to myself, of course, because he'd love it if I said it aloud.

Then I feel a slick finger at my asshole, sliding up and down, oiling me from behind.

I gasp as he fits a fat fingertip to the opening of my asshole.

"How about now?" He grabs my ass cheek and pulls the flesh aside before pushing in an oily finger.

I suck in a breath as he penetrates my asshole with his hard, slick finger. I'm panting. I've never felt anything like it. It's... good.

"How about now... what?"

"How do you like criminals now?" he asks, fucking me from the front with his cock and behind with his huge finger.

The feeling of it blows my mind. Pleasure ramps up inside me like chaos. He's going to make me come again, dammit.

He curls his finger inside my asshole as he pushes in with his cock. He's fucking me ever more deeply, ever more slowly.

I can't think of any new capitals; I can't think at all.

*Colorado...Denver? Boulder?*

My asshole widens uncomfortably as another massive finger enters me. He's a monster, pleasuring me beyond my wildest dreams.

"Eyes on me," he demands.

I look up, fighting to maintain a neutral expression, but maybe it doesn't matter. Maybe it's too late. Maybe I'm too into it.

"You'll take what I give, won't you?" he rumbles. "Because you're mine."

I close my eyes. *Mine.*

He pushes his fingers deeper, stretching me, his breath hot and ragged.

The men at the table worried about war, and Luka came back with his big talk. Right. At this moment, I think he could make chaos itself his bitch if he wanted. I think he's relentless. I think he's bulletproof.

"Eyes on me," he whispers.

I open my eyes, but I'm not all here.

I'm thinking about medieval Norsemen and Viking invaders. Dirty, violent men who take what isn't theirs, who don't care one bit about civilization or crashing through castle walls with their brute force.

I'm thinking of the warfare of that era, the way killing meant you looked into a man's eyes as you plunged a broadsword into his breast.

That's how Luka is fucking me. Exactly like that.

"Mine," he whispers, invading my gaze with his. It's unbearably intimate, the way he looks at me now.

Nobody has ever looked at me like that. All my life, I've been the unremarkable mouse in the corner, noticed by nobody. Finally, somebody does notice me, and it's this guy—this monster.

He's slowing, taking me on a ride with him, building powerful sensations in me, a secret tidal surge. He has me right where he wants me, plunging in and out while he watches me lose myself to him, to the forbidden pleasure of him.

He said I'd come to crave him, and I do crave him, but that's not enough. He wants to bring bad things out of me.

*You'll take what I give, won't you?*

Who even says that? Anger burns in me because seriously? He thinks he owns me. He thinks he owns the world.

"You're a monster," I say.

"There you are," he whispers, still fucking both of my holes. "There you are."

I snort like I don't care. Like I don't have a death grip on the sink.

His voice is a rumble. "You didn't stand a chance—you never did."

"Dream on," I gasp as the pleasure blooms through my core. "You don't know anything about me, and you never will."

"I know you're lying to yourself right now, acting like you hate me, but you are right down in the gutter with me. You're enjoying being fucked by a dirty criminal heathen, and if I stopped right now, you would beg for it."

He's perverse and evil, and he won't rest until I'm down at his level. But I'm not at his level and never will be. I glare openly at him now with naked scorn. It's too late. It's all too late.

Something essential in him seems to relax. Because he likes the scorn.

*Fuck.*

"Nothing's fair, is it, Edie? Especially when you hate the man who's about to make you come."

I grip the sink harder, bearing against the invasion of his fingers and his cock.

"Look at me like that again." His voice is hot and hard in my ear. He pulls away and watches my eyes.

I look at him like he wants. It's the only true thing in me.

"Yeah, like that, baby." He's moving differently now. There's something wild about him. He rocks against me, movement less measured, breath ragged. "Just like that."

He was so in control before, but he might just be the one coming undone now.

He repeats the words a few times, becoming less intelligible each time, as though the words themselves are breaking apart into bits of debris, breaking up and floating away.

That's the last thought I have before I shatter in an explosion of feeling. In unstoppable waves of bright sensation.

He shoves into me once more with a cry, burying himself as he presses his face to my neck, using it to stifle a soft grunt of ecstasy.

The waves slow. I'm riding them. Loving them.

Did we just come together?

I'm panting. Shocked. I'm so conflicted; I hate him, but the way we just fucked... I need to touch him. I need some human contact.

Tentatively, I set my hands on his shoulders, and right then, I don't know what anything is. I just know that I can't float alone in space.

# Chapter Twenty-One

LUKA

She starts to get down from the sink.

I clamp a firm hand over her thigh.

"Stay right there," I growl.

She looks outraged.

I run warm water over a towel and clean her.

She seems surprised, but this is what I'm doing. "You got something to say about this, too?"

She shakes her head.

Gently, I pat her pussy. "You sure? No bullshit about this, too?"

"It's nice," she says.

"You tell yourself whatever you want," I say.

"I'm going to tell myself it's nice, then."

I pet her pussy with a dry towel now.

"When I make you come while you hate me," I say, "it takes a little bit of your soul, doesn't it?"

She narrows her eyes, processing what I just said. "Literally— you are so deranged."

"We established that a long time ago. But I think you are a little bit, too."

She sniffs, chin held high, and grabs the cloth from my hand. She finishes up while I put myself back together, and then she hops down and throws it in the towel basket.

"Ready?"

She hesitates. Something's on her mind—I can tell from her expression. How is it I've come to read her expressions so well?

"What?" I ask.

"The cookies! I have to know. You have to tell me."

"What about the cookies?" I tease.

"Come on! What was so offensive about them?"

I give her a confused look, trying not to smile.

"It looked to me like that guy was about to kill somebody over cookies. And you're all like, yeah, those cookies."

"You know what they say about curiosity and the cat."

"Oh, come on." She grabs my shirt and tugs on it playfully. "You have to tell me!"

I roll my eyes, enjoying her curiosity in spite of myself, drinking in the way the pale blue dress kisses her curves. "It's an old Albanian superstition. Cookies in the shape of a circle are bad luck during somber or dangerous occasions. You would never serve them during funerals, for example, or the day a person dies, or when you're marching into a dangerous battle."

"I've never heard of that."

"The idea behind it is that the circle symbolizes a cycle or repetition."

"Wow." She nods. "That's why he mentioned Good Friday being soon. The death of Jesus."

"Exactly."

She studies my face. "Do *you* think they're bad luck?"

"I think if you think something's bad luck, then it will be."

Her gaze sharpens. "So when you were all, 'Circle cookies, what the fuck!' at the table, you were playing along with your guys?"

"That was more for you," I say.

"Oh my God!" She gives me a playful push.

I laugh, chest light and free, like something in me unwound. And this is when I know that things have gone far enough. "We're done."

She blinks, studying my face.

"For the night." I drag her back out. The guys are talking sports again. It wasn't even an hour that we were in the bathroom, but it seemed like longer. Like we went on a journey in there.

She grabs her coat. I tell her to text her address to the dry cleaners, and they'll send it.

She stills, clutching her purse. She doesn't want to reveal her address, it seems, even for the dry cleaner to send her dress. "I'll pick it up later," she says. "Polkov, right? I'll google them."

"For fuck's sake," I say.

"What? Why can't I pick it up?" She turns to me with a big frown. "Is Polkov Dry Cleaners a secret, criminal dry cleaner? Are they located next to the criminal Costco?"

"I brought you here. All that happens is my responsibility— mine and mine alone."

"Oh, I should've known; it's a *mine* thing. The standard-issue criminal mindset. Mine."

I step in close to her. "You got a problem with it?"

"No, but Johnny Law does."

"*Johnny Law.* Who says that?"

She snorts. "I do."

I'm about to demand that she tell me, but I can feel Orton tuning in to our conversation now.

Good God, since when do I have ridiculous banter with a hooker?

And since when do I give a shit what people do or where they go on their own time? Where they live or how they know Arianiti's eagle? I forgot to make her tell me about that one, but that's not what this is.

I send a guy to hurry them up, and I hand her my black Amex. "You will buy some more dresses."

"B-but—"

I lower my voice to just a shade off of menacing. "Buy more dresses and outfits like that one, but don't get too attached to them because I am going to be destroying those fucking outfits, and I don't want drama about it."

"But you already paid me."

I give her a warning look.

"Okay, okay, okay." She pockets the card, watching me expectantly, waiting for my next command. The whole fucking thing is getting me hard.

"Use the card or else."

"Understood," she whispers. Orton returns her phone.

I tell Gianni to drive her home, and I watch her walk off with a feeling I don't like. Why am I acting like this?

I join my guys. We hash out some personnel problems.

Gianni texts me when he drops her off—at a pizza place in Midtown.

What the fuck? A pizza place? After *that* meal?

And who the fuck lives in Midtown?

I'm fucking annoyed now. Is she more of a distraction than she's worth? Yes. I should cut her loose. It's not me to be fussing about people like this.

Eventually, it's just Orton and me at the big empty table, with Storm up by the door. The ghost who's not quite here, his favorite position to play.

"Got intel," Orton says to me.

"Talk."

"The Tucumayo hitters weren't ours. Weren't even Albanian clan."

"Who told you that?"

"Florian. He took me aside and told me privately. I'll double-source it, but the info seems good."

"Florian's got his ear to the ground," I observe.

"Sure does."

I'll be glad if it's true. I don't like to think that the men I've inherited would slaughter an innocent young girl. Bloodbaths I'm fine with, but young kids who aren't in the game? There, I draw the line. It's a matter of honor. *Besa.*

It also says that my brother went out of his way to hire somebody or somebodies outside the clan. Hitters he knew would do a vicious job.

"Florian says there are lots of rumblings about our quest to find the Tucumayo hitter or hitters," Orton continues. "You gotta think whoever did it knows we're after them now."

I set a fork on its tip, rotating it minutely, watching the reflection scatter through the tines. The last thing you want when hunting a hitman is for that hitman to know you're hunting him.

Orton pushes a plate of baklava toward me. "You're a target now."

"It was always just a matter of time," I say. "They won't come at me personally—not at first."

"No, they'll throw something at you to figure out what he's up against. Nobody knows what you're made of. You should keep Storm around you."

"I'll think about it."

"Don't be fucked up. Keep Storm with you. They're gonna test you."

"I don't need a bodyguard."

Orton drains his raki.

I press my fork into the triangle tip of the baklava, oozing with honey and spices. The baklava here is unmatched. Edie would've liked it. I should've made her stay for it.

As if hearing my thoughts, Orton taps his own fork on one of the glasses left at the table. "Want me to run it for prints?"

So he held back Edie's glass. "Nah."

"You don't know who she is."
I take another bite. "She's nobody to me."
Orton stays silent, eyeing the glass.

# Chapter Twenty-Two

## EDIE

I'm reading in bed the next morning when Odetta bursts in, fresh from her Etruscan seminar, with two large mochaccinos and some residence hall gossip, which she imparts in her fun, dramatic Odetta way.

She really is a good friend. This is what somebody who cares about me does, I think. Somebody who cares about me doesn't push me around and treat me like a possession.

"So?" she says once we've exhausted the subject of how bonkers some people can be. "How was your dinner date?"

I marvel at the question. It was a level-nine DEFCON, stay-in-your-pajamas-for-a-week date.

I take a sip. "It was... intense."

"Yeah? Where'd you guys go?"

I describe the restaurant and the extravagant foods, though I leave out the gory dinner chat.

"And afterward?" Odetta gives me a sly look.

"You think I'm this cheap? One coffee and I'll tell all?" I wish I hadn't asked it that way, though, because I'm cheaper than she knows. A man can buy my soul. "We ate dinner. I met a few of his friends, and then I came back home."

"No... your place or mine?"

I shake my head.

"How very old-fashioned."

"He is kind of old-fashioned," I say. Suits and ties. Death and honor.

I sit back and stare at the ceiling. We put adhesive glow-in-the-dark stars all over it the week we moved in. It feels like years ago.

I sip my coffee. Boys shout outside the door. There's a sound on the hall wall like a dodgeball ball hitting a flimsy wall.

I spend most of the day studying for my Indo-European exam in the commons. I'm armed with a full supply of suckers and high-lighters and my best headphones. I need to make some progress.

Odetta and her friend Brittany join me after a while, and it helps to have them there, studying right in front of me, reminding me that I'm still a normal girl.

Even so, I can't get Luka out of my mind. One moment I'm memorizing Latin word roots, and the next I'm back in that bath-room with him telling me to look at him. Or I'm back in that restaurant booth with his heavy hand on my thigh, anchoring me to the heaven and hell of his dark control. And then in that restroom again with him swiping a soft, warm, wet washcloth between my legs, tending to me in a way that spins me up with too many feelings.

I'm grateful that I have Latin in the afternoon because it's such a bear—really old and nobody actually speaks it. The perfect way to get me out of my body and into my head, which is where I need to be.

I hurry down the steps, repeating verb declensions, and nearly jump out of my skin when a guy wearing thick glasses and an over-sized Packers windbreaker comes up to me. "Edie?"

I clutch my book to my chest. "Yeah?"

He lowers his voice. "Janey says you've got some queries for the dark web."

"Oh!" It's Janey's dark web friend. "Darren?"

"At your service."

Darren has the type of frizzy hair that you can't really part, but he's used a lot of product in an attempt to make it part because dudes just don't know things.

He gives me a sheet of paper. In hushed tones, he explains that the top number is an account number and gives instructions about depositing enough bitcoin into it to buy an hour of his time. He tells me what it is in dollars, and it's not a ton of money.

"You in?"

"Yes."

He hands over a small pad of paper. "Write your questions here in the order of priority."

"Okay." I stare down at the pad. "Mostly, I'm looking for information on my sister. I could email you the details—"

"No emails. Write them down for me."

I write down her full name—Mary Francesca Carson—along with her birthdate, last known address, and all the details that I think will help him find things out about her.

He takes a look. "Missing person. That won't take the whole hour. Got any other questions for my leftover time? My minimum is an hour. You're paying for it anyway."

I take back the pad. I should let that be the end of my questions, but I can't help it.

*Information about Luka Zogaj, the new leader of the Ghost Hound Clan, specifically regarding his brother. How did he kill his brother? Why would he kill his brother in such a way?*

I pause before handing it back, tapping the pen on the pad. It's not that I'll tell Bender, but I want to know. I *need* to know. I hand it back. "Just if you have time."

He reads it and laughs. "The Ghost Hound Clan. Now we're cooking with gas."

"Yeah?"

He smiles. "I'll get you everything gettable on your sister and everything out there on Luka Zogaj and his brother. Nobody will give you better service than me. Nobody will be more thorough." He tells me to meet him around the corner from his residence hall. He'll hand me a copy of *The Elements of Style* by Strunk and White, and my answers will be on a sheet of paper folded inside.

"*The Elements of Style?*"

He shrugs. "It's a book you'd borrow from me, and it's easy to get a shit ton of them because they get updated so often. You could probably find a hundred of them in the dumpster outside Beacomb Hall right now if you looked."

Odetta and I are back in our room that night sharing a big bowl of popcorn and watching the latest installment of *Love is Blind*, a show where people talk to each other from different rooms without being able to see each other.

It reminds me of me and Luka in an odd way. We don't know everyday things about each other, but we've hooked into each other deep down. I get his sense of humor. I know it pushes his buttons when I seem to judge him for something. I know he's possessive and powerful and dangerous and a good leader who hated his brother enough to kill him. I know he's got major commitment issues, what with his insistence that our relationship is nothing more than a transaction—he uses that word enough!

Odetta says something about the show, and I realize I've spaced out, thinking about Luka. I can't seem to stop.

They say focus acts like a magnet, narrowing your world to the object you're concentrating on. That's why people tell you not to focus on the negative things in life.

I know this, but I can't stop focusing on Luka.

I'm careening into him, and sometimes it feels like careening into pure, delicious obliteration.

# Chapter Twenty-Three

### EDIE

I get my Brazilian wax down on Broadway after Latin, paying with his credit card, of course. I've always trimmed down there, but it feels completely different to be bare. Clothes feel different against me, too, like a constant reminder of him.

Maybe he wants that.

A wave of something strange ripples through me, hot like hate but not as extreme.

I buy expensive jeans and two cute tops at Madewell and then get the most splurgy flowered dress ever from the "new arrivals" rack at Anthropologie—in two colors in case he destroys one of them—plus a necklace-and-earrings set, and a jeweled bumblebee hair ornament for Odetta. I throw in a brown velvet newsboy cap. Score!

They aren't exactly mafia-call-girl purchases, but they are things I'd buy in normal life if I actually had money.

What's he going to do if he doesn't like them? Fire me?

The total is sky-high—to me, anyway. I hand over Luka's credit card feeling like a thief.

I walk out loaded down with bags, still keenly aware of the wax job.

A few hours later, I get a text from "Brenda."

He wants to meet in Central Park after my last class. He actually sends me a map with the route I'm supposed to walk, setting off from the building where my art history class is at four fifteen, which is ten minutes after it ends. The map takes me through crowds and has me double back twice.

It's all so cloak and dagger.

Does he think Luka might know where I live? The idea makes me feel a little sick, but it's more about the look on his face if he discovered I was talking to the cops than his retaliation, which is an example of misplaced priorities if ever there was one.

I remind myself what I'm doing all of this for. My sister. Our future.

I swipe out of the app with Bender's map, pull up Zillow, and check for small two-bedroom homes near the Connecticut coastline with a hiking area as a way to get my head back on straight. I pick out a sweet, yellow one-and-a-half-story with white window shutters. Mary and I could plant flowers along the front walk. Daisies.

That afternoon, I set out according to the extreme directions. It's a nice April afternoon—bright sun and cool, crisp air. Light jacket weather. The after-work joggers are just coming out, and moms push babies in strollers.

I walk slowly, pretending to do things on my phone, but really, I'm watching the pavement in front of my feet.

I head into Central Park, imagining daisies. And Mary getting clean. And me getting a teaching job in a quaint little school.

A ways in, I pass a man on a bench who I'm ninety percent sure is Bender wearing a ball cap and a red shirt with some kind of insignia. But I keep going like the instructions said. I get to the spot Bender marked, which turns out to be a small pool with a large metal turtle in the center. The turtle spouts water from its back, and people stand on the edges, watching the water crash down. A girl in a school uniform throws a penny.

I dig around in my backpack and find a penny to throw, but then Bender's sidling up next to me. I hold it in my fingers, waiting for him to begin.

I suppose it's a good place to meet. A lot of people really do stand around staring at the water, and the splashing would ruin things for somebody trying to record conversations from a distance.

I really want to ask if this is a standard-issue clandestine meeting fountain, but he wouldn't think it's funny.

Luka would think it's funny. He might try to act all stern, but I already know his eyes crinkle a little when he likes something. Not to be confused with his full-on bad-guy eye narrowing.

Bender is just standing there acting like a stranger, not saying anything, so I decide to go for it. I step up onto the stone edge of the fountain, lean over the black-painted rail around the water, and throw the penny into the area with the other pennies, making a wish for my sister to be safe.

"Are you *trying* to draw attention?"

"Other people are throwing pennies..."

"And don't look at me."

I turn back to the fountain. "It's not like he even knows I'm a college student."

"Don't be so sure. How'd it go?"

"Wait—*don't be so sure?* What does that mean? Do you think he might know who I am?"

"I think you really don't want him to find out."

"Fine. No more pennies," I say.

"So. Last night. I want everything."

I've thought about this moment carefully. How much I'll say.

I've decided to breadcrumb him, giving him just enough to make him think I'm all in. Mafia gossip seems safe. Things that would be likely on the dark web or news articles seem safe. Things an observer could figure out. But private or important things about Luka that could be traced back to me? That's where I draw the line.

I tell myself it's for my own safety. Somebody has to look out for my safety, and I'm getting the feeling that Bender doesn't give a shit.

"He was holding court at that Albanian restaurant where we met."

"Of course. It's his place," Bender says.

"His place... that he owns?"

"He's a powerful Albanian kyre," Bender says like that's an answer. "Who was there? What did they say? I want everything, start to finish, and don't think about leaving anything out."

I stare at the spray, not loving Bender's harsh tone.

"There were six men besides me and Luka. Different men this time, except his friends Storm and Orton. He and Orton have known each other for twenty years."

This seems to interest Bender. "Did he reveal where they met? Where they were?"

"He didn't say. It was Orton who told me while he was checking me for a wire." I relate what he said about Luka hearing all and seeing all.

"I sat down, and the only other name I got of the people there was Florian, this guy who came later, full of bad-guy gossip."

"Let's hear it."

"People are starting to think some guy named Lazarus is alive."

"Hold on—Bloody Lazarus?" Bender looks pale.

"Yes, Bloody Lazarus, the enforcer for one Aldo Nikolla. Very violent."

"They think he's *alive*?"

"Not all of them. Some think it's bullshit. The man apparently got blown up in a Hummer. Lots of C4. But his body was never found."

"Jesus Christ. What does Luka think?"

"Luka was hard to read. He didn't discount it. They said that Lazarus disemboweled a guy and put Pez dispensers in his hands."

"Lazarus did what?"

Bender doesn't know about the disembowelment? I'm happy to deliver on that count. I treat him to the goriest details ever—the pain, the blood, and how long the human intestine is, courtesy of things I learned in my Medieval Crime and Punishment seminar. Some of the people back in those days were really off the chain and invented truly wild punishments. It's fascinating—it really is. To me, at least.

He stares at the fountain. "Jesus."

"I know!"

"What else?"

"People were obsessing about Bloody Lazarus for the rest of the night. Also, Orton likes to poke at a dead body to make sure it's dead. He made a phone call, but it was in another language."

"You know who he called?"

"No. Also, people are wondering if Aleksio's out for vengeance. Like there could be blood on the streets."

"What did Luka think about that?"

I think of the way he seemed to relish it. The vision he provided for the men—that they would skewer their enemies on their razor-sharp hound's teeth. The darkly exciting way he dared the world to come after what's his.

"He didn't seem that worried. His attitude was kind of like, 'Bring it on.'"

"Really?" Bender seems surprised.

"That seemed to be the gist."

Bender presses me for more specifics. I supply some of them, and then Bender stares glumly at the fountain. He seems unhappy about Luka being powerful and effective. Like it's a personal affront or something.

I stare at the insignia on his shirt, a Norse-style Thor's hammer design, thinking about the parts that felt private and special between Luka and me. *Let any man come after me or mine. I'll rain hell on him like he's never seen.* And the way he looked right at me when he said that. Like he'd fight for me.

But Luka reaching out to Aleksio Dragusha? I won't tell Bender those parts.

"After that, there was sports talk and food talk."

"Nothing else?"

"We ate. I spilled wine all over my dress, and it was a complete mess. I went to the bathroom to try to clean it up. When I came out, he sent me home with Gianni, and I had him drop me at the Midtown pizza place—"

"What? He simply sent you home?"

"Yeah. I walked in and then put on a hat and walked out with a group of people like you told me, and I took an Uber the rest of the way."

"He fed you and sent you home? You didn't go back to his place or back to the hotel?"

"I was covered with wine, and there was possibly some freakishly violent killer come back from the dead..."

"But you said Luka wasn't worried."

"I'm telling you the events. Freakish killer. Spilled wine. He sent me off and stayed to talk to Orton. This is literally what happened. We did not leave together."

Bender stares at me for a long while. "I can see that you're a careful girl who considers all the angles. You don't want to get too deep into this, and I can appreciate that."

"I'm telling you what happened."

"I understand. But you should stop to consider that I might be careful, too. That I might consider all the angles. That I might even have somebody on the inside, and I'm evaluating your truthfulness right now. You might consider also"—he leans in close—"what effect your omissions might have on your sister."

"My sister is why I'm doing all of this!" I burst out.

Bender stares at me, and my heart is pounding. Did Bender

have somebody watching? Did he know we were in the bathroom forever?

He says, "It's awful what a depraved man could do to your sister…"

"What are you saying? Do you know where my sister is? Is she in trouble?"

"Not from what I can tell. But understand me when I say if you're playing games with me? If you're holding back with me? Not good. You want me in a mood to help you with your sister because wherever she is, she needs us to find her. She needs you to give a hundred and ten percent to me on this project of ours."

My pulse whooshes so hard it's deafening. "I'm doing my best. I was in the restaurant with him. I spilled wine on myself and was in the bathroom getting it out for a while. Then he sent me home."

"Okay, then." Bender draws a black cloth from his pocket and wipes the screen of his phone. "Think about what I've said. I'll be in touch."

---

Three hours later, I get another text. It's a Riverdale address and a time: one a.m.

I text back.

Dress code?

Did you do what I told you?

Yes.

Dress code unlocked. Isn't that what you kids say?

I stare at the last message. Is Luka making a joke? It seems outrageous that he'd make a joke.

Give me an address. I'll send a car.

No need.

There's a shocker.

I send him the face-with-tongue emoji.
He sends me the frown face.
I stare at my phone. Are we bantering now? Is that what we're doing?
I shove the phone away.

# Chapter Twenty-Four

## LUKA

Running a clan isn't like managing some fucking corner store. It's messier, more complicated. One bad call can destroy everything we've built, turn allies into enemies, or put my people in the ground. Mistakes don't end with a bad review—they end with blood.

You need more than instincts—you need a predator's vision and a fierce bullshit detector. And the meetings—Christ, the meetings. Always in the dead of night, in the backrooms of businesses where real power moves in shadows.

I don't mind. Each meeting establishes my dominance. Shows who sits at the head of the table.

I stride out of one such meeting from the back of an electronics store on 156th Street, having just straightened out the Russians and their Bitcoin problems. They came in loud and left quiet. Problem solved.

Dardan follows me out with a few other soldiers, their eyes never meeting mine directly.

Dardan approaches after the Russians disappear. "I hope you enjoyed yourself the other night."

I fix him with a stare.

"The girl? Honey?"

In one fluid motion, I close the distance between us, my hand finding his throat before he can blink. His eyes widen as I apply just enough pressure to remind him of his mortality. "Never mind!" he chokes out.

"She's not for you," I say, voice like ice.

"Didn't know—"

I tighten my grip slightly. "Now you do."

I release him, and he stumbles back, hand at his throat, fear and respect warring in his eyes. The others look away, pretending they saw nothing.

Storm waits in the shadows where I positioned him, a lethal sphinx ready to pounce at my command.

"Let's roll."

We set out walking, my stride purposeful. The weird fury at Dardan still pulses through me. The thought of him even looking at her makes my blood boil. I didn't know she was yours, he was going to say.

Storm cocks his head at a sound in the distance, then dismisses it with a barely perceptible shake of his head. We continue, comfortable in our silence, the city parting before us like we own every inch of concrete we cross. In many ways, we do.

Orton and I first liberated Storm from a terrorist bunker near Moldova. He was chained like an animal, but even restrained, you could see the killer in him. We weren't being merciful when we freed him. We were recruiting excellence. That's what separates a true kyre from the pretenders—recognizing raw talent that can be molded into something lethal.

I've got a midnight meeting with a financial guy a few blocks up. The kind of meeting that happens off the books, where the real millions are made. After that, I'm seeing Edie.

The smart play would be to send her away. In this business, she's a liability. A transaction, not a relationship. But some things aren't about being smart.

We round a corner, my territory unfurling before us.

"Heard a rumor today," Storm suddenly says, breaking character. He's a ghost most days, silent as death.

"Yeah?" I don't break stride.

"Somebody saying you're not a true blood Zogaj."

"Let them talk." My voice is casual, but my mind is already calculating who needs to disappear.

"They're looking for your DNA to prove it. Someone wants your throne. I don't like it."

"Nobody gets my DNA without losing their hands." I scan the street as we walk, marking potential threats, escape routes, vantage points. Always calculating.

"But if they do? And if the testing goes a certain way that we both know it could go?"

We cross to the unlit side of the street, darkness enveloping us.

Storm knows what my brother said before I put him in the ground. He's not superstitious like Orton. He's not even Albanian. But he sees the world as it is.

"There are people who will feel moved to kill you," he points out.

I laugh, the sound hard and cold. "People always feel moved to kill me."

He slants me a glance. *Orton*, he means, as well as half the Ghost Hound Clan. "If somebody gets your DNA, we gotta shut that shit down, even if it means moving on some lab. It's a hit on you, same as if they had a gun to your head."

All of this chattiness is unlike Storm. I stop walking, turning to face him fully. "If somebody steals my DNA and brings it to some lab, I will fucking burn that lab to the ground with everyone inside it. Nobody takes my throne until I'm good and fucking done with it. Understood?"

Storm nods, a ghost of a smile on his lips. He's seen me take over entire garrisons singlehandedly. Watched me put down a revolt with nothing but a knife and my reputation. An American lab wouldn't stand a chance.

"Still." He takes a sandwich bag from his satchel and tosses it toward a garbage can.

And misses.

He stops, retrieves it, and throws it in properly. This small disruption in his usually perfect coordination sounds alarm bells in my head.

"You okay?"

He grunts. "Just... off."

My senses go on high alert. Storm is violence personified. If he admits weakness, something is seriously wrong.

"Off how?"

"Just... off," he says, his usual economy of words failing to mask the gravity.

A block later, he sits heavily on a bench. This is a man I've seen take three bullets and still complete the mission.

Fuck.

I call Orton and order our doctor dispatched immediately, my tone leaving no room for questions. I pocket my phone and sit next to him, watching the street for threats. "How bad is it?"

"Pulse elevated. Lethargy. Slight loss of coordination. Dizziness." The battlefield report of symptoms.

I examine his eyes. "Pupils look normal." But his brown hair is dark with sweat, and the night air is cool. "Doc's on the way," I say, my voice carrying the certainty of a man whose orders are never questioned.

He blinks, seeming to have trouble focusing.

"Fuck," I say, already planning retribution against whoever is responsible.

"Go on to the meet. I'll wait," he says.

"The fuck you will," I snap.

The doc arrives within minutes—as he should when I call. His men bundle Storm into a car while the doctor hangs back with me.

"You think he was drugged?" I demand.

"Or bad fish. A seizure. Or a million other things."

"Find out which. Keep me posted. Every detail."

"Need a ride, boss?"

"Nah." I need to walk is what I need. Need to think about who might be making a move and how many bodies I'll need to drop before sunrise to remind this city who the fuck is in charge.

I continue on to the bank, past the neon glow of restaurant signs and nail painting places. The air is thick with the rich scents of South Bronx at dinnertime—fried meats, garlic and rosemary, curry and cumin.

I go further east, my footsteps commanding the pavement beneath me, not even flinching when that familiar prickle crawls up my neck— somebody's watching me, following me. Sixteen years in combat zones teaches you to smell fear and danger like other men smell perfume.

I deliberately slow my pace, a predator toying with its prey, turn a corner and melt into a shadowed doorway.

The footsteps approach and hesitate. Then stop. This person knows I've made them. Professionals recognize professionals.

I wait, heart steady as a metronome.

I'm surprised when they start up again, coming toward me— amateur move.

I wait until they're close enough to smell their aftershave, then explode from the darkness. One fluid motion and I've got him in a vise grip, my Glock kissing his liver.

"Drop it." My voice is crushed gravel.

He shakes his head, gasping for air. I tighten my hold. Not enough to send him to sleep, just enough to remind him who's in charge of this conversation.

A two-tone Smith & Wesson hits the pavement.

"Who?" I don't waste words.

"Dunno." His voice trembles.

"Don't fuck with me." I bring my lips closer, my breath hot

against his ear. "You came to my neighborhood. You breathe my air. Now, who sent you?"

"I—I don't know," he gasps.

"There are two ways this ends. You tell me here, or I take you somewhere nobody will hear you tell me. Choose." Something dark and hungry rises in me, something I've been trying to cage since talking to Dardan. I should have fucked him up is what I should have done, but she's not mine.

I sense the other one before I see him—a sixth sense honed in blood—and shift the man in my grip just as a shot cracks the night; the human shield jerks and goes limp in my arms.

Amateur hour's over.

I drop him and move through the shadows, circling back toward where the shot came from. The hunt is on, and I'm never the prey.

Somebody breaks into a run. I give chase.

I catch a glimpse of him as we turn onto a street crowded with civilians, all laughter and chatter, oblivious to our deadly game. He's big—built like a vault door—dark jacket and dark cap. Looks Albanian.

He cuts through a deserted office courtyard. His mistake. In the open, with no witnesses, he's already mine.

I'm on him before he clears the other side, slamming him against a half-built cinderblock wall with enough force to crack mortar. "Who sent you into my backyard?"

He surges at me with practiced combinations—military trained—and sends my piece flying. Doesn't matter. My fists were forged in hotter fires than this.

He lands a few hits, and I return with concentrated fury, fists finding his face, his ribs, his throat. The satisfying crunch of bone and cartilage is poetry under my knuckles.

That's when I feel the others approaching.

A setup.

They took out Storm to isolate me. Their first and final mistake.

Pure adrenaline floods my system as two shadows materialize, metal glinting in their hands.

The guy I just demolished is still clinging to consciousness against the wall. I grab him by the collar and drag us both behind a dumpster, finishing what I started with mechanical efficiency before relieving him of his weapon.

I lean around and fire at the closer shadow. Miss. Unacceptable.

The equation changes. Survival becomes the only objective. They're flanking me—professionals who've done this dance before.

My instincts take command. I fire where they don't expect, making them retreat. I fire again and catch one square in the chest. The odds improve.

Now we're even, and even is all I've ever needed.

Sirens wail in the distance, but they can't drown out the whisper of shoes on gravel that betrays his position.

I glide through the darkness, head throbbing from that earlier blow, and launch myself at him. The impact alone is enough to steal his breath.

We're face-to-face now. He's bleeding badly, but he'll live long enough to talk. "Just you and me now. A name. Give me that, and you walk away."

He shakes his head, loyalty still binding his tongue.

I regulate my breathing, focusing through the fog threatening to claim me. If I black out, he wins. "Tell me. Do të mbaj besën," I add in Albanian, invoking an oath older than either of us.

His eyes meet mine, recognition dawning.

"Nobody will know. The money stays yours. This employer of yours—he's a hornet in your hat," I say, invoking one of our oldest warnings. "You know what happens to men who keep hornets close."

Something breaks behind his eyes. "Killian," he whispers.

"Irish?"

"Yup."

I relieve him of his weapon and disappear into the night. I check my app and see West isn't far. I ping him for extraction and settle into the shadows to wait. Our encrypted system connects us like a family should be connected. Storm adapted it from battle-field tech.

Five minutes later, West is pulling up in front of me. He throws me a towel as I slide in the back. "What the fuck? Someone made a move?"

"Somebody sent a boy to do a man's job. Just drop me at the Milaga. I'm late for a meeting."

"We need to round anybody up?"

"Nah." I blot the blood. It's a lot, but I'm more worried about my head. "The boys are sorry, and the man's straight up in my sights. Works for me."

West likes this. I can tell it even in his driving. He's showing off a little, speeding down the Bruckner Expressway, crossing lanes like it's Formula One.

The bleeding stops. I'm coming back.

"Heard something fucked up today," he says. "Probably a rumor but..."

"What?"

"Some motherfucker messed with your dad's gravesite. I sent somebody to check it out. I was gonna verify the damage first, but here you are."

"Mmm." I fix my cuff links. This shirt is ruined. "Lemme know when you know."

"Will do." His demeanor tells me that he's heard the rumor about me not being a true Zogaj, and I can also see that it's the furthest thing from his mind that it might be true.

"I know you weren't the biggest fan of the old man..." he says.

"No, I wasn't. But you don't fuck with a man's gravesite."

"Fuck, no," he agrees quickly. "Bad move."

# Chapter Twenty-Five

## EDIE

The Milaga is an ornate historic hotel in the South Bronx, much nicer looking than the Belmoreland Arms, where this whole thing began.

A doorman in a red suit and cap comes out from under a red awning and opens the door of my cab for me.

"Thanks," I say, stepping out.

Orton is suddenly there. Where did he come from? "Luka's delayed. Come on."

"Hello to you, too." I follow Orton into a bright, elegant lobby. There are flowers everywhere and fashionable people I'd like to spend more time looking at. We pass a large roped-off area laden with gifts and a marvelous fountain on the way to the ornate elevator.

The elevator doors clank closed and it begins to move. The inside of the elevator feels like a metaphor for my situation—enclosed by gold filigree walls, rising upward, but there's definitely a chance I could start plummeting down.

The elevator ride takes forever, and I feel like Orton's looking at me weirdly. Like he can see my nervousness.

Well, I am nervous. And the silence feels awkward. "So... are all those gifts down there for me?" I joke.

"Saudi wedding, probably. Saudis love this hotel."

"So none of them are for me?"

Orton frowns at me. "Why the fuck would you think that?"

"Just joking around."

"Don't."

We ride the rest of the way without a word.

Luka's suite is on the eighth floor—the top floor.

"I'm in 802 down the hall," Orton says, pushing the door open for me. "Knock if you need something, but it better be life or death."

"Wait. How long will he be delayed?"

"He'll get here when he gets here." With that, Orton leaves.

"Thanks, jackass," I whisper, closing the door behind him.

I wander around the huge, luxurious suite, marveling at what looks like very expensive art on the walls, and there's an amazing view of Manhattan. I run my hand over the velvet couch back, making streaks of deep indigo in the royal blue fabric.

I'm trying to focus on anything but what's ahead. Anything but the feel of his hands on me. The brutal way he takes me over and makes me feel things I've never felt. The way he makes me lose myself.

I'm hyperaware of the kiss of my linen dress against my body. Of the coolness of the air as I suck in nervous breaths. And, of course, the Brazilian wax.

What if he is delayed for hours? I force myself to make the best of it, pulling out my phone and doing some reading about how everyday medieval households worked—cooking, cleaning, expenses.

At first I can't focus, jumping at every hallway sound, but I eventually lose myself in this obscure text I was lucky to find digitized.

Direct source material from the late 11th century is rare, especially when it's about common people. Anastasia Laskarina, the Byzantine princess and first teen historian, mostly recorded politics and rulers, though she did document village fears from her maids' stories—crop failures, plagues, and especially the Pecheneg invaders.

These nomadic fighters terrified both peasants and royalty alike. They'd burn olive trees and grapevines that had stood for centuries and consumed stored food before moving on to destroy neighboring farms. Pure waste. They could have sustained themselves for years if they'd left them intact.

I grab a bag of chips from the minibar, not caring if Luka's hospitality extends to snacks. I eat the whole bag of Fritos, my own little rebellion for making me wait for him in the middle of the night.

I burn through the Sun Chips and the mini-Pringles after that, staring out at the light on the other side of the Hudson River. There are small clusters of people down below, going home after a night out, probably, and not appreciating their free choice.

I'd be asleep in bed by now. That would be my choice.

I nearly jump out of my skin when I hear the door unlock.

Orton opens the door and steps aside to make way for Luka.

I gasp at the sight of him, all beaten up and bloody. His clothes are ripped, and his eye is so puffy it's nearly closed. "Oh my God, what happened?"

Orton shuts the door and points in the direction of the bedroom. "Leave us. Close the door."

I walk into the bedroom and shut the door. I sit on the bed and wait some more, clutching my phone. I can hear them arguing in low tones.

I hear the sound of water running. Are they cleaning him up out there? Angry voices. Arguing? Talking about somebody they mutually hate?

A door slams. The bedroom door bangs open a few minutes later, and there he is.

He stops at the foot of the bed, swaying like some sort of brute, bruised and battered and wild. A savage invader looking over his meal.

I'm more keenly aware of the Brazilian wax than ever. My heart pounds. Waiting.

His face is red and puffy in places, though the blood is washed off, thankfully, and he's changed from his bloody designer suit into a new dark shirt, buttoned up and tucked into gray slacks.

The bottom part of him is a fashion plate, but his face is pure beast mode.

With shaking hands, I turn off my phone and put it aside. "Are you okay?"

He seems to be processing the question. For all that he's beaten up, he looks beautiful, angelic eyes shining through his monstrously battered face.

"Luka?"

He points at a spot on the bed in front of him. "Need you to...."

"What happened?"

He points.

I scoot forward slowly. When I get near, he touches my hair and strokes a hand over it, movements clumsy, like a bear trying to be tender.

I let out a ragged breath, unsure what to do with the heat surging through me.

He grabs my hair, twisting it in his grip.

I gasp, thrumming with forbidden excitement.

He just holds my hair, twisting it more tightly. It's not pain so much as delicious intensity.

"Need," he breathes, swaying. "*Need.*"

*Yesssss,* I think.

He pulls me off the bed and makes me kneel down in front of him. "Take me out."

I press my hand to his ridge, hard as a stone. He groans and grips my hair harder.

The carpet is soft against my knees—a wicked counterpoint to the way he holds my hair.

I grab him through his pants. He growls like a beast.

I fumble with his belt, pulling it open.

He has both hands on my head now, one fisting my hair and one stroking it. It's like he's moving from a purely primal impulse.

I pull his underwear down. His cock springs up, hard and majestic. I grab him at the root and squeeze.

He makes a strangled sound that I find deeply gratifying. I hold him tightly and lick the shining bead off the tip of him.

"Yes," he breathes.

My pulse races as I press my lips over him and take him into my mouth. I shouldn't be so into this with him so dramatically injured. It's perverse, really—this man should be recuperating.

But I love him like this.

I give him a hard suck, and he groans, tightening his hold on my hair and using it as a rope to maneuver my head how he wants, like I'm a puppet to use for his beastly pleasure.

I glare up at him. He fucks my mouth with an unforgiving, unrelenting rhythm, nearly choking me with his cock because he's a bad, bad person.

I seriously can't believe how savage he looks, unbound by the laws of man and beast and even gravity.

"Fuck yeah," he growls.

I'm sucking harder, turning up the intensity. Not that I'm into it, I tell myself. It's just that things are getting intense.

Rough calluses slide over my cheek. "Eyes. Scorn."

When did I close my eyes?

I open them and give him the scorn he craves—easily. It's all right there. My desire and my revulsion for what I'm turning into are all mixed around in a brew of lust I don't even want to understand.

He tells me to touch myself, and it's like I'm rubbing out an ache, rubbing and rubbing while he fists my hair. He's made me into a base and senseless creature, masturbating while choking on his cock.

And the truth is that if he asked me to stop, I don't know if I could. His harsh enchantments have gotten the best of me, and I need to get off—just like this—with his unforgiving fist in my hair.

"Fuck," he gasps, coming into my mouth.

His rhythm becomes more animal, something dark and timeless, a primitive, punishing force.

His other hand spreads across the back of my skull, palming it and forcing my face fully into his cock, keeping and holding me there, choking me as his cock pulses.

I don't know if it's the shock of his brutality or what, but an orgasm explodes in me like a stormy ocean of pleasure crashing over my brain, crashing and crashing, consuming me.

I don't understand how it keeps going, sweeping me in and out, drowning me in pleasure.

Dimly in the corner of my brain, still pulsing with electricity, I'm aware of him petting my hair roughly like he has paws instead of hands. Petting my hair, swearing softly, "Fuck, fuck, fuck, fuck."

He's out of my mouth. He pulls me to him, my forehead against his warm, slightly furred belly.

And I'm spinning.

Finally, he lets me go, clambers up onto the bed, and collapses.

I stand up, dazed, wiping my lips and cheeks.

I go and clean myself up, then come back to Luka lying on the bed, eyes closed.

"Luka?" I whisper.

No answer.

Shit.

Did he pass out?

I crawl over next to him and touch his cheek in one of the few places that doesn't seem to be bruised. I've heard of men sleeping after sex, but this isn't that.

I shake him gently. "Luka."

He's not rousing. I pat his cheeks, and he groans and pushes me away. That's when I notice a huge gash on his head. What the hell?

"Hey," I say, slapping his cheek harder. Clumsily, he pushes away my hand.

Clumsy movements, slightly slurred speech.

"You're really injured!" I exclaim.

Nothing.

"You could have a concussion."

He mumbles something that sounds like, *You should see the other guys.*

"Did you actually just say, 'You should see the other guys?'"

No answer.

I lift his right eyelid, then the left.

"Hey! Your pupils are really huge," I whisper. "And they might not be the same size."

I try to compare them again—not easy with him fussing. I grab my phone and look up what to do for a concussion.

One of the main things is to avoid activities that raise your heart rate.

Awesome.

# Chapter Twenty-Six

## LUKA

I doze off for what could be just a moment, or maybe it's an hour, before I hear her voice. "Oh my God, you're barely even conscious right now! I'm calling nine-one-one."

I open my eyes and clap my hand around her wrist. "I got my own doctor. Don't need him."

*He's busy. With Storm.*

"You literally have a traumatic brain injury and who knows what else."

"I'm fine."

"At least let me get Orton."

"I'm gonna sleep. That's all I need." I turn over.

"You need medical attention."

"How do you know Arianiti's eagle?" I ask.

"That's your question? Luka! No! You need medical attention."

"How?"

"You're hurt." A gentle hand on my shoulder. "Don't be a big bad gangster."

"Is that an upgrade from a dirty heathen criminal?"

"No, you're still a dirty heathen criminal, but don't you wanna live to be a dirty heathen criminal another day?"

The worry in her voice sends a ripple through my chest.

"I'm gonna sleep. You're relieved of your duties."

"I feel like I should call a doctor. You need one."

"Did you not hear me? You're dismissed."

"I'm un-dismissing myself."

"Can't... un-dismiss yourself." I pull myself onto my elbow and point to my pants. "Bring me my phone."

She gives it to me, and I hit the button for Orton and hand it over.

I hear her talking to Orton, stressing how dangerous a concussion can be if it goes untreated.

I let my eyes drift closed while she argues with Orton.

At some point, the call ends, and she announces that Orton is not a good friend to me. "You have a concussion. You need somebody to wake you up periodically."

I groan. "That's not a thing."

"It's completely a thing! A hundred percent a thing. You're supposed to be woken up every three hours. I saw it on TV."

"TV, huh." I'm lying on my back next to her as she recites information from websites on her phone. She's going on about hydration. Limited exposure to bright lights. No loud sounds. Something about ice.

There's a silence, and then I'm conscious of a gentle hand on my forehead, like a hallucination from some other life.

She's wrong about the sleep thing, but I don't care anymore.

"And no sex."

"Uh-oh," I say.

"It's not funny." She busies herself arranging sheets around me, but then... "Wait. What is this bruise?" Busy fingers unbutton my shirt. She gasps at whatever she sees on the side of my rib cage. "Did you two just scrub off the blood and call it a day? This is how you treat injuries? Just wash the blood off and you're good? God."

"...not real injuries," I manage.

"Oh, not real injuries? Okay. Yeah, not real. Nothing to see here." She's mumbling about keycards and pharmacies. She seems to be leaving.

The next thing I know, bags are rustling and she's pulling off my shirt, gently urging me up and down and over.

*There, there, good...*

Then she's stroking something onto what I'm gathering is a gash on my chest.

It was a fuck of a fight. We did a lot of damage to each other. Pushed each other into a lot of things.

She moves her fingers tenderly over the spot that burns the most.

My mind floats back. I suppose our nanny must have patched us up. Or did she? I see her towering over me, always angry. My older brother, ranting and smashing things.

And then Tucumayo. Nobody would've bandaged me there.

Even Sara wouldn't have thought to bandage me. She was more of a marveller, gazing wide-eyed at various injuries, more shocked than helpful, though she was a victim herself, and we were young. We were like mice in those places, forever finding holes to hide in.

Edie lifts up my arm, movements gentle. I shut my eyes against the pleasure of it.

Fingers pressing something onto my chest. Edie. She's dressing it, probably. Bandages. It comes to me that I'm not thinking straight. I'm disoriented. If Storm or Orton were here, I'd add that to my list of symptoms.

The smell of antiseptic pulls me back in time, back to a field hospital in Sri Lanka, bandages fashioned from ripped clothing. Crude fishing-line stitches, soldiers trying to get each other well enough to travel. The dust and the stench and the punishing sun out the window. Shouts from broken-down Jeeps. The dust. So much dust.

"What about the dust?" she asks.

I open my eyes. The curtains are drawn. The room is pleasantly dim. She's holding something cold to my head.

Was I talking out loud?

"Who was shouting?" she asks.

"Nobody."

"Sit up all the way and drink."

I take great gulps, and it seems to wash the dust from my mind. She takes the glass and arranges pillows behind me. Gentle fingers slide over my bicep. "Does this hurt?"

"No."

"Let me get this all the way off." She urges me forward and struggles with my shirt.

I'm still in the dust and sun. Then, the mossy walls.

Her gasp breaks through the haze of my memories. "What is this?"

Fingers trace along my back. Tracing crisscrosses.

It's Edie, touching my back.

I need her to stop, but I can't quite bring myself to make her stop. I try to think of how to get the scorn back.

"What happened to you?" People have seen those scars, but nobody has ever dared to ask.

Edie's different.

"Bad-guy stuff."

"Was this the not-a-military school?"

I force myself to open my eyes, to glare at her with all the hell inside me. "Leave it."

# Chapter Twenty-Seven

## EDIE

Luka sleeps on his side, breath slow and steady, eyes shut tight behind dusky lashes. Even in his sleep, his body curves toward me, one arm thrown protectively across my waist. The most dangerous man I've ever met, and I feel safer with him than I ever have before.

The moonlight streams in, kissing his cheekbones.

I can't stop thinking about those scars.

Luka got those scars young—you can tell by the way they're stretched. His body wasn't fully grown when he got them. Where was he?

Each mark tells a story of survival. Of strength. I traced them with my fingertips and felt him shudder beneath my touch—not from pain but from the rarity of a gentle touch without judgment.

I slide my hand over his scruff, and his face seems to soften. I try to radiate calm vibes, but it's hard not to be angry on his behalf.

I slide my palm over his cheek again, moving along the direction of his whiskers. His cheek is soft when I run my hand down like that.

He still wears some kind of medallion—the one that I noticed the first day—and I take the opportunity to examine it. A winged warrior with a sword. It's the archangel Michael. Fighting. Perseverance. Just like Arianiti.

I go back out to the living area and grab a ginger ale from the minibar. I set my timer for four in the morning, grab a hotel scratch pad, and try to get back to work in the hours that I have before waking Luka.

According to Janey, Luka was sent somewhere at the age of twelve, and my guess is that's where he got the scars—from a whip, I'm thinking.

Rage fills my chest and heats my face. How could a person do that to a kid? How could a parent allow it? And whoever did this, are they still hurting children?

Janey said there was talk of a military school or reformatory. Could that place still be in business? Because they shouldn't be! They should be shut down, and whoever runs it should be arrested.

Punished. Severely punished.

I pull myself together and try to sink into my studies, managing a bit of reading, and I even get some good stuff for my thesis—supporting evidence I can footnote. I copy the citations onto a Google Docs file and make some notes for inserts.

Sometimes, I pause to sit with him and watch him sleep, feeling like I'm existing outside of time, outside of my classes, outside of the world. Just Luka and me.

When my phone tone sounds, I grab a towel and the ice bucket and create a makeshift ice pack. According to one of the sites I found, I'm supposed to hold the ice to his forehead. The cold will help wake him up and also address the swelling.

I shake him gently. "Hey," I whisper.

Nothing.

"Come on." I shake him again.

Grudgingly, he opens his eyes.

"I'm supposed to wake you every three hours."

"Says who?"

"The internet." I touch the ice pack to his forehead.

He pushes it off. "Get out," he growls. He's tired. A tired bear. Google said he would be. He rolls over, away from me.

"You need this on your head for five minutes every three hours."

He makes a growly sound, and it tugs at my heart.

"Hey."

I stroke his cheek, and he takes a deep breath like his nervous system might be calming. He'd never let me touch him like that during the day—he'd probably chop off my hand—but he's allowing it now.

I rest my hand on his cheek, cupping his cheek, while I press the ice to the injured spot on his head. You can feel the bump. You can see it.

Yet my touch seems to be settling him.

It's so strange having this man, this killer, so vulnerable by my side. And I'm calming him.

It's a kind of intimacy I'm not used to.

And he really, really is a killer. There's no way he's not. It's possible he even killed people within the past twenty-four hours.

But this is where I want to be.

After a few minutes, his breath evens like he might be falling back asleep.

"You can't fall asleep for three more minutes. Doctor Google's orders."

He protests sleepily.

"If you don't like it, maybe you shouldn't have gone around fighting."

*Grumble.*

"Three more minutes." I do the cheek-stroking thing again, and it works again.

Did somebody try to kill him? Will they try again?

A bullet in his head would solve a lot of my problems, but as I slide my hand over his hard, velvety beard stubble, it hurts my heart to think of it.

"Two more minutes, and you can sleep again."

I shift the ice pack and stroke his cheek.

He's a brute, yes.

But right now, he's my brute.

# Chapter Twenty-Eight

LUKA

She's sleeping when I wake up, phone near her hand as if she was clutching it until the last moment of drifting off. Her delicate features are serene, her hair in a messy halo around the pillow.

Memories of her caring for me flood back. The way she felt. Her hand on my cheek.

What the fuck.

Apparently, the bullet that grazed my skull took out a chunk of my senses because what was I thinking, letting her stay?

I look around the bed and see she's been writing something on a pad of hotel paper. Taking notes?

I lean over and squint at the little scribbles—a few lines about broom making and a list entitled "fireside/hearth implements" followed by "andirons," "tongs," "trivet," "cauldron," and "spits."

Brooms and hearths? What is this, Halloween shit?

I should wake her up and throw her out, but I guess she did stay up playing nursemaid all night, not that I needed it.

And who knows, maybe I'll fuck her again. I tuck her in and leave.

I take a shower, fix myself coffee, and call Orton.

He's over in a flash with an update on Storm. Somebody drugged him, but he'll be fine in a day or two.

"Also? Aleksio got back to me. He appreciated the offer to assist and is convinced Lazarus did the Poconos killing and that he's still alive. And he wants to send Razvan after him."

"Razvan Bektashi?"

Orton nods.

Razvan is a notorious Albanian hitter who moves unseen in the darkness like the gears in a clock, a lethal hunter who can change his appearance so effectively that nobody knows what he actually looks like. He's picky about his jobs, too. He would've never taken the Tucumayo job, for example. He would never go after a young girl like that.

But Lazarus? Everybody wants Lazarus dead.

"Razvan Bektashi," I say, impressed.

"That's where we come in. Razvan wants a face-to-face with Aleksio somewhere neutral, ideally in New York, being that Lazarus's last known location was upstate. Aleksio thought you could facilitate."

I nod. That I can do.

Sounds come from the room. She's stirring awake. We switch to Latin, a language we were forced to learn in Tucumayo.

"*Debemus id hic facere,*" I say. *We should do it here.*

We love the Milaga Hotel for meetings. So many exits, so many hideaways. It's a fucking rabbit warren.

I send him back to his room with instructions to work it out with Aleksio, and then I order up a pastry cart.

Not five minutes later, he's back with the meeting arranged.

He shares the plan in Latin: They'll secure the perfect room, provide detailed maps showing both official and hidden exits. Five of our men will be positioned discreetly, while Aleksio will bring his own security—including his brothers.

Will Razvan send people to do scouting? There's simply no way to know. There's very little known about the man aside from his eerie competence and deep reverence for Albanian customs. Like Orton, he's the type to throw a match after every kill. Probably big on the prophecies, too.

"It's good that we are doing this," Orton says.

"*Pueri a mortuis revocati*," I say. Everyone needs a friend. Especially boys back from the dead.

Orton leaves without a word. The door closes behind him.

She comes out, finally.

The sight of her wearing my shirt... *fuck*. My chest tightens as animal instinct floods my veins. I want to whisk her off her feet and carry her back to bed. Shut out the world so that it's just the two of us. We'd fuck and feast and fuck some more. Maybe later do crossword puzzles or something stupid like that.

*What. The. Fuck.*

*Just the concussion talking.*

"Time to go," I say.

She doesn't listen, of course. She's eyeing my face, all concerned. I know what she sees—fat lip, big, angry bruise on my cheekbone, goose egg on my head.

I point at the door.

"But your face—let me put some salve—"

"Nope."

"It's on the bedside table. It'll help reduce the swelling."

I stalk right up to her. "You may think because you played nursemaid and saw some scars that we have some sort of connection. But we don't have a connection; we have a transaction."

Hurt flashes in her eyes, but she doesn't make a move because it takes more than this for a girl like Edie to back off.

"You gonna make me throw you out in nothing but my shirt?"

"Fine." She puts her clothes back on and comes out all ready to go, but she hesitates, wringing her purse straps. Of course.

"What?" I demand.

"I need to know. Whoever did that to you... to your back and all that. Were they ever held accountable? Did they answer for what they did?"

*The scars.*

"What do you care?"

"What do I care?" She looks incredulous. "Because of what they did to you, that's what. That happened when you were young. Was it at the whatever school?"

"Look, Edie, shitty things happen all the time. A lot of really shitty things are happening to a lot of people this very second. There's nothing to be done about it."

"But this shitty thing happened to *you*," she says. "It happened to you when you were young, and it's not okay."

"Go." I point at the door, voice hard.

"No," she says, defiant. "I need to know if they ever answered for what they did to you. If it's some institution still operating, they need to be shut down. If it was a person..." Her eyes flash with conviction. "They should pay."

"And you'd be the one to hold them accountable?" I ask, incredulous.

"I would."

"How exactly would you manage that?"

"I'd find a way." Her voice drops, fierce and determined. "I'd make them pay. Don't think I wouldn't."

My pulse races. *She* wants to avenge *me*? Something deep inside me turns upside down, the ground shifting beneath my feet. I let her touch me in that bed, but it was nothing compared to how she's reaching into me now. Suddenly I need her back in my bed with an urgency that stuns me—a hunger almost stronger than the vengeance I've sworn.

I shake myself out of it.

I don't do relationships. This is a transaction. It can never be more.

"If you must know," I say casually, "they did, in fact, answer for what they did. You're right that I was a kid. I was sent to a school for bad kids down in the jungles of Tucumayo. Very old-fashioned and Draconian ideas of things. All iron rods and fire and brimstone. You know Tucumayo?"

She shakes her head, expression unreadable.

"It's a tiny jungle principality between Suriname and Brazil, and there's a notorious reformatory there. Bad kids were sent there from both North and South America, and there were a dozen adults in charge. I slaughtered them all—the adults, that is. Not the kids."

She straightens. "Excuse me?"

"Well, I slaughtered *most* of the adults, let's say."

Her eyes widen—in horror, probably.

Good.

"At one point, I let Orton and a few of the other kids out of their rooms, and they worked out some of their own fury on the adults. It was quite the bloody scene." I turn to the breakfast cart and select a scone, but really, I'm back there, standing over Sara's lifeless body just hours before I went wild with some berserker force. I had nothing to lose, and all the sadistic, grim-faced schoolmasters who I'd naturally blamed for her death didn't stand a chance.

Silence. I'm sure she's been rendered speechless by my little report. Well, sometimes you need to bring out the big guns.

I break the pastry open. "Needless to say, if you repeat any of this to anybody, you'll get a firsthand demonstration."

"Did you find a gun or something?" she asks.

"I had a bag of rocks at the end of the rope and a whole lot of fury. A few I killed with torches that I ripped from the walls. A bit of accelerant, and I burned them alive. You never heard such yells."

I concentrate on my scone. I can feel her vibrating with intensity. I always feel her.

"The head schoolmaster I killed with my bare hands. I ripped his windpipe from his neck while I looked him in the eyes. It takes a good deal of finger strength to grab a man's windpipe through his throat, but I was seventeen, and I'd done my fair share of finger pushups." I turn and force a smile. "A horrific and painful way to die, but it's not an injury you come back from, let's just say."

She's watching me thoughtfully. No revulsion. No fear. She simply crosses her arms. "Good."

"Good?"

"Yeah. Because if you hadn't done it, I'd want to go down there and make them answer for it myself." Her voice goes soft. "For what they did to you."

Something unwinds in my chest.

Because what the fuck? She... approves? What part of this is she not understanding?

I lower my voice. "Do you know what it feels like to take a man's life with your bare hands? To feel their blood run over your hands while the light goes out of their eyes?"

"N-no."

"It feels fucking amazing."

Edie sharpens her gaze.

It's the revenge that feels amazing, not the actual killing, but this is no time to split hairs. "I once gouged a man's eyes out with my thumbs. He was still alive while I did it. He was alive and fighting for his life—"

"Okay, okay, okay, I get it."

"Get what?"

"Is this a thing where you're trying to get me to be disgusted and horrified with you? You want the scorn back, is that it? Your precious scorn?"

"It would be a lot better than maudlin Mother Teresa."

"Yeah, you'd like that, wouldn't you?" she says. "God forbid anybody gives a hoot about you. Wanna know what I think?"

"A *hoot*?"

"I think scorn is your comfort zone. You're the badass who nobody gets to care about. Case closed."

"This is what you think?"

"Yes. And you killed all those people, but here you are telling me all the graphic and bloody details because I dared to have some freaking compassion for you. The eyes, the yells. I think it's a smokescreen you're putting up so that I can't see the broken-hearted kid who deserved better."

I bark out a laugh that I'm not at all feeling. "Okay, then. Well, it's a good thing I don't pay you to think, isn't it? What do I pay you for?"

She frowns.

It's a low blow, but she's not in Kansas anymore. She needs to see that and that she's not dealing with some brokenhearted kid, either.

This is not a relationship.

"Do you remember what I pay you for, Edie?"

She narrows her eyes and there it is. The scorn. And I do like it. She's very fuckable when she's got that scorn going.

"Do you remember?" I repeat.

"You pay me for my body, but you have no say over my thoughts and emotions."

"Your thoughts and emotions." I snort. "Not a fan."

She glares. The scorn's really rolling now.

I hold out a hand. "Let's have that phone."

She stiffens. She understands what this means—that phone is our only line of communication.

"You were a good lay, but it's gone on too long."

"You don't mean that."

"Hand it over."

She hesitates, then she pulls the phone from her bag and throws it onto the couch.

"That works," I say. "You're officially free to go to Vegas now."

"Excellent," she says.

"Just keep quiet."

"Unlike some people, I'm good for my word." She spins on her heel and leaves, shutting the door behind her.

I have the impulse to go after her and demand to know what she means by "unlike some people." Demand she give one example where I wasn't good for my word, something I happen to pride myself on.

I have my hand on the knob when I finally stop myself.

Because what the fuck? Why do I care?

This is not a relationship. It's a transaction, and that transaction is over.

# Chapter Twenty-Nine

## EDIE

I zigzag my way home, superspy-style—subway to crowded store to different subway line—keeping my head down and my face arranged in a don't-talk-to-me scowl that masks the trembling chin and burning eyes underneath. The city blurs around me as I focus on just one thing: nobody gets to see me fall apart. Not here. Not yet.

We had a connection—something raw and electric and real. I didn't imagine it; I couldn't have. The way he looked at me when he thought I wouldn't notice, how his voice would soften when we were alone. I know he felt it, too. And yet he cut me off so coldly, like severing a limb without anesthesia. But my pain goes beyond rejection—I'm haunted by what Luka must have endured as a child. Those scars weren't just physical; they told a story of suffering no kid should ever know.

And then he sends me away forever.

I get it. I went too far with the brokenhearted kid comment. But really, what sort of parents would send a boy to such a place? And then leave him there? He probably was a brokenhearted kid at one time, but he definitely isn't one now.

I pass a donut shop, the air thick with the scent of sugar and fried dough, and keep on walking, scowl in place.

Well, this is what I wanted, isn't it? For him to reject me? The bland-and-boring act didn't work. No, it turns out all I needed to do was show some genuine understanding and compassion. To actually give a shit about him.

My phone shows a zillion texts from Bender.

He wants to meet, of course, in the same part of the park where we met before, and he has my class schedule, so there's no way I can put him off.

We set the meet and I go to classes, barely making my eleven fifteen art history course.

I settle into the dark auditorium that smells of sour candies and body spray and try to concentrate on the pottery fragments that flash up on the screen.

*You were a good lay, but it's gone on too long.*

Luka went on a bloodthirsty rampage and enjoyed it, I remind myself. He's practically a mass murderer.

And I slept with him. Scratch that—I loved sleeping with him. And if I'm honest with myself, I'm glad he yanked out that man's windpipe with his bare hands.

The guy deserved it from the sound of it.

The slide on the screen switches. Another pottery fragment from a famous excavation of the catacombs below Rome. I try to focus. I was excited about this area of knowledge because of the way it showed a transition of style.

Now I feel... empty.

I slide my finger over my chin and a tender, nearly raw area—a whisker burn. I'm back in bed with his coarse whiskers against my skin and his thick fingers between my legs, getting me off.

*Do you know what it feels like to take a man's life with your bare hands? It feels fucking amazing.*

I'd be tempted to think it was a wild tale except for the scars and the fact that he and Orton spoke in Latin when they were planning the Razvan meeting. Latin is exactly what a strict and retrograde school teaches. And clearly, they believed in extreme forms of punishment.

I decide not to tell Bender any of it. No way will he know what was said in that room. The original Lazarus gossip seemed like public knowledge, at least for these Albanian clan guys, but planning a secret meeting? I won't tell.

The school stuff feels private, too. Like a secret he told me, even if it was part of an angry outburst designed to drive me off.

It's so Luka. He doesn't get close to people. Everything needs to be a transaction, and as soon as somebody gives a shit, he goes feral.

No, Bender doesn't get any of it, and I don't care. I've already given him more than he could ever have dreamed. And Luka and I are done now, and it really is for the best.

I sit in the darkened room looking at slides of Roman pottery, but I feel him all over my skin.

The student next to me scribbles furiously. Damn. What am I missing? I lean over, trying to read what she's writing. I can't see. The professor drones on. I start writing whatever he says. Usually, I can tell if it's important. Now I can't.

I scribble senselessly.

# Chapter Thirty

### EDIE

Bender is at the fountain when I get there at one, but he ignores me.

I fish in my pocket for a penny, fingers trembling slightly as they close around the cold, worn metal. For a moment, I just hold it, rubbing my thumb over Lincoln's faded profile. Then I toss it into the water. I don't wish for him to come back to me or for the ache in my chest to subside. Instead, I close my eyes and wish for Luka's scars to fade from wounds to memories. For him to know happiness, even if I'm not there to see it.

The penny sinks out of sight.

He sidles up, not even looking at me. "You're late."

"I came as fast as I could." His map today was like a maze around random blocks and through a random store.

"What happened at the hotel?"

"It was just a hookup. And he doesn't want to see me again. We're finished."

"Did you do something to turn him off?"

"Excuse me? No. He was just like, this is over. From what I've heard, he doesn't have repeats with anybody, and I saw him three times, so I think I should get a reward."

"Anything to report?"

"Not really. We don't discuss mafia business."

"So you can't think of anything of note."

"Like what?"

"How about the fact that his face looked like a punching bag?"

My heart nearly jumps into my throat. So they're following him?

"Isn't fighting, like, an everyday thing for a guy in the mafia?"

"Don't play stupid. He was attacked. That's something of note."

"Sorry." I frown at the fountain, not loving how mean Bender's gotten. Or maybe the chummy ally bit was the act.

"Did he say anything about who he fought?"

"He said, 'You should see the other guys,' and had a bad concussion. That's why I stayed."

"Guys plural? More than one?"

"Yes."

"Any significant injuries?"

I think about the old scars. But that's not what Bender's asking about. "I'm not a nurse, but he was pretty messed up. Cuts, bruises, the whole head injury situation. Acting out of it."

"Too out of it to fuck you?" Bender says.

"Excuse me?"

"You heard the question."

"I don't find such details germane."

"Listen to the schoolgirl. *Germane.* Well, I find such details quite germane."

My heart is pounding. "Why?" I ask, even as I'm wondering why I should care. Is the hill I'm gonna die on?

"I'll decide what's important," he says.

I sniff. "Well... it was a prostitution hookup. That involves sexual activities."

Bender frowns like he's unhappy to hear that Luka could be injured and still want to have sex. Does he see himself as being in some kind of pissing contest with Luka in addition to wanting to arrest him?

"What did you discuss?"

"Not much. I'm hardly a confidant. Orton came by in the morning."

"What did he and Orton talk about?"

"It was hard to hear. I was in the other room."

Bender regards me suspiciously. "But I bet you heard a little bit, right? Being that you know how important it is to help me out. Anything else about Lazarus? Did he reach out to Aleksio?"

My belly feels queasy. Is this a test?

"Is there a plan? A meet?"

Does he know about the Razvan plan?

Whatever flicks across my face, Bender notices.

He grabs my wrist, coming in closer. "You know how long I've been a cop, Edie?"

I try to pull away. "Let me go."

"Go ahead. Take a guess. How long?"

"Please!" I try to pull away, shocked, but he just tightens his grip. He's so strong; it's like he's crunching my bones.

"The answer is that I've been a cop long enough to know when somebody's lying. You know something about a meeting. Your eyes just told me so."

"W-what?"

"You think Luka's gonna be angry if you reveal what you heard? That ain't nothing compared to what I'll do to you if you don't give me what I want."

My heart races. "I don't know—"

The way he's looking at me, it's like he knows I know. He twists, sending a jagged bolt of pain up my wrist. "Wrong answer."

"Ow! Please—"

"You're gonna tell me all about whatever's going down, or I will snap your little wrist, and that'll be the least of your problems. It will be the least of Mary's problems, too."

My mind swims with pain and fear. "Please."

He twists harder. "I will see that she suffers extra."

"Ow, please! I'll tell you!"

He lets up a tiny bit, and I hear myself blurt out the time and place of the Razvan and Aleksio meeting.

"What else?"

"Nothing!"

He tightens his grip.

My lips move, but I can't think. I can't form words. I'm in a blind panic. "Nothing!" I manage. "They spoke in a weird language…"

He seems to decide I'm telling the truth, which I am, and he eases off a bit more. "What language?"

"A weird one. Not normal like French or German." Which is true of Latin.

"Albanian? Did it sound Slavic?"

"I don't know Slavic languages."

He finally releases my arm. I cradle my wrist against my body, head spinning, unable to process that he's suddenly treating me like a criminal.

"You have to find out what language he spoke," he says like everything's normal again. "That could be the key to finding out where the fuck he's been all this time. It could lead you to travel conversations, and you could ask how he's so fluent—"

"He doesn't wanna see me again," I say. "He even took back my phone."

"He took the phone? The one he *gave* to you?"

"Yes, that's how much he doesn't want to see me."

"Fuck!"

I wait. My wrist is on fire, and I'm petrified he'll grab it again.

"It's just a twenty-dollar phone. Why take it from you? Why not just… never call again?"

"I don't know. But he told me to go to Vegas. We're done."

"No, no, no, no. You can't be done. You still have time left on your contract with him. We have to get you back in with him to discuss languages and get his story and see why they're meeting. And I need you to get a strand of his hair. Then we'll be done."

"Wait, what? You literally want me to cut his hair?"

"No, I need you to pull it out or find a strand still intact. With the little white thing at the end of it."

"Pull a hair off of his head? He doesn't want to see me anymore, and you want me to yank out his hair? How does that not get me killed?"

"You don't have to yank it. You can get a hair off a comb or a pillow. People shed 'em all the time."

"He made me give back the phone!" I protest. "He's through with me!"

"I don't care." He scowls for a moment. "Oh! Here's what we do. We're set up at his restaurant, where he holds court two or three times a week. We'll let you know when he's there, and you'll just show up."

"That'll be completely suspicious."

"He's a good-looking guy. Maybe you have a thing for him."

"I don't think that's how prostitutes work."

He levels a hard stare at me, and my blood goes cold. "I understand you're getting straight As. A smart girl like you, you're gonna figure out a way to make it happen. Coax out what you can about this language he and Orton spoke and whatever else, get the piece of hair, and then and only then will our deal be done."

"*Will* it be done? I've fulfilled my end of our bargain, and you keep changing the rules."

"I do, don't I? Tough luck, you're not in a court of law here. You're in the Wild West, and I own you. You understand that? Your life is in my hands, and when I say jump, you jump. And you know why you'll keep jumping? Because I guarantee you, the alternative will be worse."

"I'm not so sure about that anymore," I say.

"You ever played poker, Edie?"

"Does it matter?"

"Let me tell you about my cards. One card could be sending you to jail for prostitution, which you have definitely been doing. One card is the men I control who are holding your sister. They have her in a cage, and she's safe for now, but that cage has a door. And the men on the other side of the door have knives—"

"You're holding my sister? You know where she is?"

Bender doesn't tell me. Has he known where she is this whole time? Or is it all bullshit? I stare miserably at the fountain while he continues telling me the horrible things that bad men might do to my sister, clearly delighting in it. I have no way of knowing if any of it's true. I have no power against this man. I *have* been working as a prostitute. He probably even has proof.

I want to weep.

"Here's another card," he continues. "I could put you in a cage, too. I was keeping that card a secret, but I think I know you well enough now that I can tell you about it."

"What?"

"You. Think of it. A cage, just like your sister's and men with knives. Even now, nobody knows where you are. Or I could just go ahead and put the word out that you're a snitch. I could put it exactly where it would get to Luka. How do you know I don't have a few photos of us together already?"

"You have photos of us together?"

"What makes you think I'm working alone? There are thousands of cops in this town, and every one of us wants Luka. There's nowhere you can run from us. Every police car. Every cop on horseback."

"So this goes on until I'm dead."

"Don't be dramatic. You're more capable than you want me to think, and you got closer to him than you let on. I'm just asking for a couple more favors."

"He said we were in a transaction—a transaction he's done with."

"Is he, though? Because I keep thinking about him taking that phone away. It's just a piece of trash to him. He'd never re-use it. And you're right about him never fucking the same woman twice. But he's seen *you* multiple times." He pauses and shows a horrible smile. "I find that very interesting. You know what else I think? I think he took the phone back because he wanted to remove the temptation. Like an alcoholic getting rid of bottles of booze."

"No," I say.

"Yeah. Yeah, I think this is gonna work. Unless you fuck it up. And you don't wanna fuck it up, do you?"

"He doesn't want to see me again!"

"Well, he's gonna see you again, isn't he? You're gonna make it happen. I'll text you when he heads to the restaurant next, and you are fucking showing up there, you understand? You tell him you miss him and beg him for one more date."

"He's gonna know something's off."

He leans in. "Better do a good job like I know you can, then. You'll be reunited with your sister, and everyone will be happy. The only way out of this is through."

# Chapter Thirty-One

## EDIE

I walk home, wrist throbbing, mind blazing with panic. I feel like there's nowhere to run—just danger around one corner and more danger around the other. My only instinct is to hide. Somewhere small. Somewhere dark.

How could I have let Bender bully me into telling him about the meeting? How did he know I was holding back?

What have I done?

A cop car slides by, and I'm sure they're looking at me.

I spot another police officer up ahead.

Are they all watching me?

I turn a corner in full freak-out mode. My heart is pounding so hard I think I might have a heart attack.

*Deep breaths.*

*Deep breaths.*

I stop and pretend to look at my phone. I don't know what to do or even where to go.

For one wild second, I think about coming clean to Luka, begging his forgiveness. I have this fantasy of Luka going after Bender—grabbing his hair and ripping out his windpipe—because nobody fucks with what's his.

But I'm not his anymore. Worse, now I'm a snitch.

What if he gets arrested? What if he goes to prison?

*Needless to say, if you repeat any of this to anybody, you'll get a firsthand demonstration.*

It was pretty clear what he meant by that. I'd get a firsthand demonstration of the slaughtering if I repeated anything I heard, and I definitely repeated things I heard.

I've seen enough movies to know if anybody's getting their windpipe ripped out, it's me.

*To choke the life out of somebody, to feel their blood run over your hands while the light goes out of their eyes. It feels fucking amazing.*

If only I could time travel two months back when my top three concerns were how best to bump an A-minus up to an A, if Chelsea boots were still in, and whether I had enough money to get a day-old turkey sub sandwich at the cafeteria.

Now, it's the bloody, horrific death at the hands of a man I may or may not be falling for.

*Think,* I tell myself.

First things first: my wrist. I buy an ice pack and a wrap at a Duane Reade. I'll tell people I tripped and fell and sprained it. I add a Butterfinger for self-care.

I head back up the dirty street, still freaking out that I told what I heard. Hating myself for it.

What if I were to warn Luka anonymously? Maybe I could send a message to his restaurant. Or like a courier with a message specifically for Luka. But how do I know Bender doesn't have people at the restaurant? If Bender were to intercept it, he'd know it was from me, and I shudder to think what would happen. Bender's dangerous; that much is clear.

I could send a message to the hotel, but Bender likely knows about that, too. He's obviously been following Luka. He could have somebody on the inside of Luka's organization. Maybe even Orton. Or Storm.

I have no reason to trust anybody at this point.

Crossing paths with Bender and his partner that fateful night when I was searching for my sister out on the streets—*not a thankable event*, I think miserably.

I pass a bakery window full of cakes and pastries and cookies, thinking about getting another self-care treat. Maybe a whole self-care cake. But getting hopped up on sugar definitely isn't what I need.

But then I slow my steps and back up to the bakery window. There, alongside double-chocolate chocolate chip cookies, is an engagement display. It's like a bouquet of engagement cookies in the shape of rings. Ginormous engagement cookies in the shape of rings and displayed on sticks as part of a massive cookie bouquet.

I set back off, mind spinning. Luka's crew completely freaked out when they saw those circle cookies. Wouldn't a meeting between potentially warring gangs be a somber or dangerous occasion? I could send them that bouquet.

But... would it be too obvious? They could go to the bakery and figure out who sent it. They'd want to know.

Then again, they don't have to actually be the recipients of the ring cookie bouquet... they just have to catch sight of it.

I'm thinking about all those gifts for the wedding party in the velvet-roped area of the lobby. Orton said Saudis love that hotel for weddings. If a giant bouquet of circle cookies could be placed behind the reception desk, that might do the trick.

It would for sure do it.

I have to be so careful, I decide. I pull a Bender and walk through one of the residence halls' courtyards and back through a Duane Reade. I see why Bender likes making me walk through this store; there are a lot of exits.

I buy a bright blue cap, stuff my hair into it, and go out a different exit, doubling back to the bakery, where I order three of the most massive and ostentatious ring bouquets they have for the meeting in two days. "I want these bouquets to be resplendent. I want them to just be so gorgeous, completely the ring theme. Just sparkling rings, really big and bright and bold."

She shows me pictures, and I give a few ideas, stressing that the rings have to be super prominent, and then I fill out the paperwork, directing that they be sent to the Milaga Hotel. I pay in cash. "The hotel desk will know what to do with it."

"I need a name or a room number. It can't just be to the hotel."

I pretend to look at my phone, but really, I'm trying to remember how many floors there are. There are eight floors. I look up and smile. "Room 914."

I give her my information—most of it fake.

"And it's to be delivered at exactly 1:30 p.m." The meeting is at two, but I'm thinking mafia men come to things early.

"A delivery time guarantee is extra."

I'm more than good with that. I add two chocolate chip cookies to the order and head back home, giving myself a pep talk about how my plan will totally work.

Somebody in Luka's crew has to spot the cookies—those bouquets are big and obvious, and the ring cookies are literally on sticks. I went for the most over-the-top ones—how could they not see them?

I tell myself that it's a good plan. Mafia men will be posted and vigilant all over the hotel. Luka told me how superstitious they all are. I'm counting on it now. I just need one of the men to see the circular cookies and freak out like West did back in the restaurant. The other guys will surely back him up, just like they did at the restaurant. They all supported that one guy's read of the situation. Surely that's enough to ruin the meeting.

Best of all, Bender will think it was because the cops were recognized. And how would that be my fault?

There's still the problem of showing up at the restaurant. Bender said he's only there a couple times a week... which means

I'd have to be staking out the place. How would that not be obvious?

Lovelorn stalker stuff, that's not me, and Luka would know. Luka gets me in a way other people don't.

It's strange to realize that.

Also strange that I actually miss him. Luka is like nobody I've ever known, even though, yes, he's a killer by his own admission. A very bad man who scares other very bad men, a guy who hires prostitutes, a man who killed his own brother in some unspeakable way.

Even so, I miss him. It's more than the sex, though that is shockingly good.

I inhale the cookies, replaying the night.

The way that the scars lined up suggested he was whipped by somebody who really enjoyed it. Luka grew up under the control of complete monsters until something happened and the tables turned, and he killed them. He wanted me to be horrified by what he'd done, but I wasn't. How could I be?

Luka said he was quite the good little boy at one time but that it turned out to be a farce. Is that what that place did to him? Made it so the only emotion he responds to is scorn? Well, he certainly doesn't like compassion. Show him one ounce of compassion, and he pretty much freaks out. Takes the phone away.

I shouldn't have pushed him. I don't generally push people, but everything with Luka is different. We vibe together—deeply. Wildly.

This makes no sense because he's a mafia don or whatever you call it in Albanian, and I'm an aspiring schoolteacher who has a thing against criminals. But Luka feels like my people in a way I've never experienced.

Our outsides don't match, but our insides resonate.

At least on my side.

I loved being with him. Whether we're fucking or just sitting there, it feels right. I can't stop being endlessly fascinated by him and caring about him and wanting good things for him."

But he's done with me. And technically, it's for the best.

The absolute best-case scenario would be for me to show up at the restaurant, he sees me standing there, and he makes one of his guys throw me out before I even get a chance to talk with him.

That would absolutely be the best-case scenario.

It's a hundred percent what I should want.

A million percent.

Maybe that's how it'll happen. Maybe things will be okay in the end—it's not impossible.

I wave at Odetta, who's commandeered a window table, feet up and earbuds in.

She's in a faux fur vest with brown yoga pants and pink platform sneakers, one of her go-to awesome outfits. When she sees me, she sits up and pops out the earbuds. "Finally!"

"I had to stop at a drugstore." I hold up my arm.

"Oh my God! What happened?"

"Don't text while walking, kids." I sit down and pull out my art history textbook one-handed. "It's just a sprain, though."

"Did you ice it?"

"Right before I got here."

"Fuck."

"It's fine," I lie.

"You sure?"

"Of course." A sprained wrist is barely on my radar as a problem at this point.

"Chad did an ice-heat-ice-heat thingy for that sprain he got in dodgeball. I think Jenna down the hall has a heating pad."

"Maybe I'll try it." I pull more stuff out of my bag and plop it down. "Is Chad working this weekend? Because I could really use an eighties rom-com night."

"Friday late shift. Let's do it!" Her eyes shine. She loves eighties rom-com movie nights. "Meanwhile..." She goes back to her studies.

So we'll have a rom-com movie night... unless Bender makes me go to the restaurant.

I pull out my iPad. Getting started on schoolwork right away after class is my secret to success, and hopefully, it's the secret to getting my mind off the vortex of danger that is my life right now.

Odetta opens a bag of corn nuts and positions them under a folder. You're not supposed to eat or drink in here, but the powers that be look the other way if you don't make a mess.

"Barbecue," she whispers.

Gratefully, I take one.

# Chapter Thirty-Two

## LUKA

Orton and I lurk beneath some scaffolding while we wait for Killian, who should be returning from his frozen yogurt run any minute.

"I get that he's retired, but vary your fucking schedule," Orton says.

"No shit."

I should be hungry for this kill. When I took down my brother, I was vibrating with energy and bloodlust. The catharsis was off the charts.

And this man is as responsible for Sara's death as my brother was.

But now it's like I can't get it up, metaphorically. I touch my St. Michael medallion.

*Focus.*

"There he is," Orton says.

I follow his gaze to Killian Arthur Shaw, a lanky fifty-some-thing walking toward his building. He's wearing wire-rim glasses and a Yankees cap, but I'd know him anywhere.

We watch in silence as he heads inside.

I thought I was avenging Sara's death all those years ago when I killed the schoolmasters. That's why the kills felt amazing; I wasn't bullshitting Edie about that.

But it was my fucking brother and his hired Irish hitters. Seven years older than me, rich as a king, next in line to rule the Ghost Hound Clan, and he still had to go after what was mine.

Death was too good for him.

And now this one will pay, too.

I nod to Orton, who moves to cover the fire escape. I cross the street and use the key my soldiers acquired. Positioning myself at the L-shaped corner near his door, I listen for the elevator. The whine of the motor. The ding. Footfalls on the carpet. A key sliding into a lock.

I fly around the corner and push him into his place, knife at his throat. He tries to fight. I flip him around, twisting his arm and smashing his chin against the wall. The dead look in his eyes tells me he knows he's done.

"Twenty years ago, you and Declan O'Malley killed a girl in Tucumayo, but you messed her up before you killed her."

"Those were the orders," he pleads.

"And now my blade's making the orders."

I try to summon the rage by thinking of Sara's face, but the image that flashes is Edie in Vegas, men's eyes following her, men's hands reaching for her. The thought of another man's hands on her makes something primal surface inside me—something I can't control. She's mine. I'll kill any man who tries to take what was mine. I end him with one brutal slice.

He drops, clawing at his throat.

Orton comes in and lights his match, letting it burn down, before dropping it in a glass of water on the guy's bureau.

I wish I could feel something. Victory, maybe. But I just feel tired. My bed has felt wrong without her in it. Too large. Too cold. I haven't slept properly since she left.

We debrief later at a neighborhood bar on Trevor Street, one of those old-world jobs, small, dark, and dank with light-up clocks advertising beers they stopped making in the eighties and drunks at one end who practically have names on their barstools.

And multiple exits.

"One more to go," he says, meaning one more kill and the vengeance will be done.

"One more," I say.

He wants to talk about the future.

This is new for him. The three of us have never been ones to make plans for the future. We're about episodic plans—surviving this or that assignment, landing the next job.

Orton was one of the few American kids down in the St. Neri reformatory in Tucumayo and an Albanian American at that, which struck us as quite the coincidence until we figured out that my family had probably heard about the place from his family. Most of the other kids were from Central and South America, with a few Europeans and Asians thrown in.

Orton was a cunning loner with an explosive temper. *Furioso*, they called him. I was *monstruo bello*—beautiful monster.

We were friendly due to our shared language and shared hatred of the twisted schoolmasters who ran the place with their scholars' robes. These were men who would punish kids by putting them in the hole, which was a literal hole lined with cement in the deepest part of the seminary. It was dark and scary and lonely, and we all got put down there at some point, except for Orton, who managed to avoid it due to his terror of confined spaces.

But one day, there was an incident where a kid was stealing bread from the kitchen. Everybody knew who it was—a red-haired boy named Ricardo—but us boys stuck together and didn't tell on each other. That was the culture.

The schoolmasters lined us all up, and the head schoolmaster announced that Orton had been the one to take the bread, a lie that was obvious to all. Orton went pale. I knew he wouldn't handle it, so I stepped forward and announced that I took the bread. I'd been in the hole a couple weeks before, and I felt like I'd cracked the code of it. And you had to stick together in that place.

Still, it was impulsive.

"You can't," Orton whispered because, obviously, I wasn't the one who stole it.

I gazed right at the headmaster. "And it was delicious."

That sealed my fate: I wound up in the hole for yet another week.

Once I got out, Orton stayed by my side whenever possible. He's one of those guys who can't get enough of the crones and their prophecies, and I soon discovered that some famous Albanian crone had told him that he would be a knight to a *kyre* one day. She said he'd roam the world with this *kyre* and come into wealth beyond his dreams.

Albanian crones love to use promises of wealth because the word "wealth" is so flexible. It could be wealth in terms of love or wealth in terms of money or health or anything.

Orton was all in. "You're a Zogaj—part of the bloodline descended from The First. You have the mafia king's blood, a natural-born kyre, and the fact that you took the punishment for me is a sign that you are my kyre."

"It's a sign that I'm a stubborn asshole who loves pissing off those guys," I'd said.

He wasn't having it.

Orton always points out whenever a crone's prediction comes true.

I always point out when one doesn't.

In spite of our differences, we were fast friends after that, though it was an unbalanced friendship being that he sees himself as my knight.

Some drunks get into a fight at the other end of the bar.

"You know we can't go back outside," Orton says, and he doesn't mean outside of the bar. He means back out into the field as mercenaries.

I grunt. He's right, of course. That type of balls-to-the-wall soldiering is a young man's game, and we're in our mid-thirties. We got out mostly intact. No small thing.

He's silent for a long time, then, "We have this now. I know that you don't want to follow in your father's footsteps—"

"No, I don't."

"But from where I'm sitting, you're good at this," Orton continues. "Alteo sucked as a leader, but you have a gift. The men see it, too. We're making money. You like being king."

"And I'm not going anywhere—for now," I say.

"Why just for now? That's what I'm talking about. What about long term? What if you said, 'I choose this life?' It's a good life, don't you think?"

"Not that you're biased."

"Yes, I'm fucking biased," Orton says, "but that doesn't change the fact that this right here is good. What are you gonna do, move to a beach and take up watercolors?"

"Maybe."

"Fuck you. You'd kill yourself after two weeks of that." Orton stands. "I gotta go."

"Wait."

"What?"

"You still have that water glass from the other night? Edie's glass?"

Orton furrows his brow. "Are you changing your mind about the prints?" I can tell from this that he kept it. Of course, he kept it.

"Go ahead and run them. Let me know what you find."

"Is there a problem?"

"Just get me a report on her."

# Chapter Thirty-Three

## EDIE

I get a Snapchat message from Janey that Darren has a "book for me," which is his superspy dark-web way of letting me know he did the research I ordered.

Is it possible he could have located Mary? It's probably too much to hope, but I can't help it. Good things do happen sometimes.

I head out to his residence hall and wait at the bus stop across the street, per the instructions. A few minutes later he comes strolling up, acting all surprised to meet me, a real Oscar-winning performance.

"Hey, I have something for you!" He digs in his backpack and produces a copy of *The Elements of Style,* the familiar tan-cover edition with big black letters on the front.

"Thank you!"

He lowers his voice. "You'll find my notes tucked inside of there, but I'm going to fill you in on some of the narrative right now."

I nod.

"The last known address of your sister, Mary, is in Newark, in the South Ward."

I straighten up. "Is that a current address?"

"No, sorry. When I followed up, the place had turned over two times, and nothing was forwarding. I'm guessing you know about the arrests, the last one for solicitation in November?"

"Yeah."

"I poked around for known associates, but they've dispersed. If someone's on the streets or couch surfing or whatever, it doesn't always end up online, even on the dark web. People still need a reason to write about it."

I nod. If *only* she were couch surfing. I suppose it's possible.

"You also asked for the down-low on Luka and his brother. The details are there, but long story short, he got good grades in school, no juvie rap sheet. The teachers seemed to like him well enough. He had one brother—Alteo—who was seven years older than him. At the age of twelve, Luka gets shipped off somewhere. Nobody knows where, but the consensus is an Albanian military academy. You'll see three citations."

I nod.

"The odd thing is that when you check into it, you can see that there are no military academies in Albania. Unless it's an unlisted military school, which isn't impossible, but it's unusual. Why not list it?"

"Right."

"So he's gone from the picture all those years from the age of twelve to today when he's thirty-seven. That's twenty-five years he was a ghost. What kind of military school keeps you twenty-four years? Was he in jail? Farmed out to another family? There's a good deal of speculation on message boards, and I stripped some of the chat for you that framed the leading theories. There's also a rumor of another brother, which I'm currently following up on. At any rate, approximately one month ago, he burst back onto the scene and promptly took his dear old brother out for a boat ride. Though, one assumes the brother didn't go voluntarily."

"Okay," I say.

Darren glances up and down the street. "The details are a bit extreme—"

"I want them."

"Fair enough. So, they're on this boat ride where he kills his brother and *gouges out his eyes.*"

"Excuse me?"

"Gouged them right out, probably with his thumbs."

My blood races. "Is this for sure?"

"Nobody out there is disputing it. Luka Zogaj kills his brother, gouging out the man's eyes, and throws the body into the water. Seabirds had pretty well ripped into the corpse before it was recovered, but the medical examiner was able to determine that it was a human-caused injury. They could tell by the cleanliness of the damage—if seabirds had pecked out Alteo's eyes after death, the damage would've been more ragged, with uneven tears and peck marks on the surrounding facial tissue."

My blood races as I remember his words, how he told me he'd gouged out a man's eyes once. He wasn't making it up. It was just his own brother.

A chill goes over me. "Any word on... why he'd do such a thing?"

"What reason could there ever be to gouge out another man's eyes? I'm gonna go with being a sadistic madman."

He has a point—what reason could there be? But deep down, I think Luka must've had some reason... right?

"Here's where it gets interesting," he continues. "The eye-gouging was foretold by a two-decades-old prophecy that stated the youngest Zogaj boy would kill the king and gouge out his eyes and ascend to the throne. As king."

"Foretold? Seriously?"

"According to an analysis by a longtime commentator on all things Albanian clan, the prophecy was originally understood to mean that young Luka would kill his father. Most people think it's why he was sent away wherever he was—to protect his father from him. Fast-forward all these years, both parents are dead, and older brother Alteo is running the clan. Luka comes back from being missing and kills Alteo, gouging out his eyes and becoming king. So ultimately, the prophecy came true; only the unlucky winner was his brother."

Darren goes on about prophecies, telling me how superstitious the older generation still is and that this has carried down to some of the younger ones. Apparently, there are still crones in the old country cranking out prophecies.

I'm still reeling. He did that to his own *brother*. Why? Luka is a lot of things—brutal and intense and violent—but he's also smart and deliberate. I've seen it. And he's not a sadistic madman, so I don't think I have that wrong. Maybe I don't know his favorite color or his birthday or anything surface-level like that, but I know his scars. I know his heart.

"There's a bit of time left on your clock," Darren says. "I want to follow up on one more detail I uncovered, but that's all for now."

# Chapter Thirty-Four

## LUKA

In the days leading up to the Dragusha-Razvan meet, a few rooms at the Milaga are rented by men who look like tourists. One wears head-to-toe athleisure with clean white shoes, and another has an "I Heart NY" cap, but their eyes give them away. A man knows his kind.

Scouts from Aleksio. Maybe Razvan, if he has scouts. Doubtful.

The afternoon of the meeting, Orton and I sit at the coffee bar on the far side of the lobby, shooting the shit with a barista, who will make any kind of coffee you can dream up—and who will look the other way when Orton puts in a splash of raki.

We're doing more than keeping an eye on things; sitting out here is a way of being transparent. Aleksio Dragusha and Razvan Bektashi are coming to our house, after all, so it's up to us to demonstrate a certain amount of visibility if not vulnerability.

Albanian clan manners.

Aleksio's probably been here for a while, but we would never recognize him. After all those years on the run, the man knows a thing or two about lying low.

The meeting is to start at two in the lavish third-floor meeting suite—very private and plenty of ways to get in unseen—a favorite for smaller, under-the-radar events like this. We've named this one the New Horizons group, and anybody who goes to the desk to ask where the New Horizons group is meeting is given the key card.

One hour.

Another man comes in with the look of the Chicago mob. He scans the lobby while he waits for them to process his card. He sees us but he doesn't show he sees us.

A woman working on a laptop across the lobby has Storm worried. Business suit, sleek blonde bun. After his last sweep-through, he texted me that she didn't feel right. West chimed in from the other side of the lobby:

Agree. Too on-the-nose biz traveler. Cop?

People are on edge because we don't want Razvan to spook, and this woman feels wrong.

Orton and I are quietly discussing whether to send West over to hit on her when we get a text from him. It's just one word:

FUCK.

"What's West upset about?" I mutter under my breath, risking a glance his way.

"What the fuck," Orton suddenly says. I follow the line of his vision and see a pair of delivery people up at the reception desk, each holding a massive bouquet. But these are no ordinary bouquets; they're large, cellophane-wrapped cookies.

And those cookies are in the shape of diamond rings.

In other words, circle cookies. Lots of them.

"Christ," Orton says. "If Razvan sees that? He is gone."

"No shit. A man like that? He's careful and old-school. He'll be in the wind. All these weddings," I add, knowing it doesn't matter. The damage is done.

The Athleisure guy is on his phone, whispering urgently. He gives us a dark look and beelines for the door.

"So he *was* a soldier," I say.

Orton's on his feet. "Let's get outta here."

"Easy there, cowboy." I slide a few bills across the coffee bar and get up slowly.

As if on cue, Florian walks through the door, proceeds to the desk, and stops short, frozen in his tracks. He pulls out his phone and presses it to his ear, pretending to get a call, before he spins around and walks out.

We head out.

"Circular cookies and a possible cop in the lobby. What the fuck?"

Orton frowns. "Let's reconvene elsewhere." That's code for linking up at the Trevor Street bar. He really is spooked.

"Gotcha," I say.

# Chapter Thirty-Five

## LUKA

Orton slides onto the stool beside me with a scrape of wood against linoleum. The bartender barely looks up before setting down a glass.

"I assume you got a picture," I say, voice low.

"Already sent it."

No need to say where. The facial recognition guy—our inside man—will run it. A Fed we have in our pocket.

"This is some fucked-up bullshit," I mutter.

Orton grunts in agreement, his fingers tightening around his glass.

A cop. At our meeting.

It shouldn't have been possible. We put this together fast, and only a handful of people knew.

Someone leaked. That's the only answer.

My guys were vetted the way I vet everything—blood loyalty, tested in fire. Aleksio's crew is hardened—men who've lost everything to stay by his side. And Razvan? He's a ghost. No face, no name, just a whisper in the right circles. He's careful.

We drink raki and talk business, but something else gnaws at the back of my mind.

"Circle-shaped cookies in the lobby. An hour before our meeting. That's too much of a coincidence."

Orton scowls. "What the fuck good is a message from the unseen world if we don't see it?"

"A bouquet the size of a Range Rover isn't exactly subtle. It's a fucking neon sign screaming to cancel the meeting."

"The spirits use whatever tools are available. You got a problem with it? Take it up with the Bogomils."

The Bogomils were Albanian mystics; their ancient cave church is shrouded in lore to this day, though the Bogomils themselves are long gone.

I set down my glass. "Find out who sent the cookies."

He exhales sharply. "Seriously?"

"I wanna know."

He thinks it's a waste of time, but he'll do it.

"It's too something," I say.

"Everything is too something."

I smirk. "I'll put that on your gravestone."

"Yeah, you do that."

His phone vibrates. He checks it.

"Aleksio thinks Razvan might be open to giving it another try."

That surprises me. Did he not see the cop? Maybe Razvan never made it that far inside. Maybe the cookies kept him out.

"You extended my apologies?"

"From all of us."

"See about rescheduling."

We talk dates and places. Obviously, not at the hotel.

Orton starts working his phone, and I work my drink, letting the alcohol burn as it goes down.

My thoughts return to Edie. The sharp glint of her green eyes. Her stubborn scorn. How badly she wanted to despise me but could never quite bring herself to.

Doesn't matter. I'm done with her.

Orton's phone dings. He checks it. "Fingerprint results for your mystery lady."

"I don't wanna know. She's nobody."

"Edie Maureen Carson," he reads, slowing, squinting. "Age twenty-three. Born in Hartford, Connecticut."

"In the system. There's a surprise." The fact that he can get anything off her fingerprint means she's in the system.

"She's in the system, but she doesn't have a record." Orton scrolls, then stops, eyes narrowed at whatever he's reading. "She's a college student?"

I frown. "Edie?"

"Columbia University as of eight months ago when she was fingerprinted as a condition for campus employment. Master's program. There's not much more than that. I forwarded it to you."

"A college student?"

"Knew she wasn't right," he mutters.

Moments with her replay in my head. The way she'd suck in a breath at the slightest touch like an innocent and untouched maiden. Her sometimes nerdy choices, so out of place. Her berry-scented lip gloss and clean soap that were so different from the perfumes I was used to.

The naive act. But it wasn't an act.

Edie Maureen Carson. A fucking college student.

"What the fuck." Why walk into my world that night in that red dress? Why sit down with a man like Iron Jaw Dardan, of all people? Even a sheltered virgin could take one look at his cold, dead eyes and know he was trouble.

Fuck. I drain my drink and bang the glass down.

College is expensive. Is that why she did it? For the money?

I think back to the hungry way she watched the food, how her eyes would follow each dish, how she'd unconsciously lean forward when the warm scents of rosemary bread and spiced meats wafted past. The way she cradled the stack of bills I gave her that first night, eyes wide like she'd never seen so much money in her life.

"We should send someone to talk to her." By talk, Orton means a very enthusiastic warning not to tell tales. The girl sat with us and saw our operations.

"She's got nothing that isn't public knowledge," I say.

"She misrepresented herself."

"She's got nothing," I grit out.

Orton holds my gaze a bit too long, then looks away. He knows when not to challenge me. He takes off soon after, but I stay to deal with a few emails. Business to handle. People to manage.

An hour later I'm searching her name in the Columbia Academic Commons. It's a lot of student stuff—honor roll and extracurriculars. Reviews of professors—all of them very positive because Edie would be like that. She's the girl who sits in the front. Never misses a day of class. I find three research papers she wrote and dip into one, telling myself I'm just going to see what the fuck is so important that she's writing her papers on, but I end up reading all three of them from beginning to end. Edie is obsessed with medieval castles. The day-to-day activities of peasant women. Old languages. Bloody battles fought with swords forged in fire.

That's how she knew Arianiti's eagle.

A college student.

I was right to send her away. Best call of the week.

***

Two days later, I'm strolling onto the bustling Columbia campus. My tech guy has come through with her class schedule and daily habits, not that he had to hack into much, being that the kids today put everything out there for the world to see.

I linger in a shadowy nook near a hot dog vendor off from the pathway she'll take from art history to the library where her study group meets.

The late afternoon sun bathes the old brick buildings in a warm glow, and students mill around everywhere. Soft, young faces. Stupid ideals.

These kids have never seen a man die, never had to fight their way out of a jungle prison.

The hot dog vendor is popular, and the kids have elaborate orders involving baked beans and pickled carrots and even pineapple. One of them storms off, personally offended when they find out the guy's out of crumbled bacon bits. A fucking tragedy in their pampered lives.

Then I spot her.

She's wearing a fuzzy beige sweater and jeans with a light blue bucket hat, her light brown hair curled loosely around her shoulders. No trace of the seductress in the red dress. This is pure Edie—backpack slung over one shoulder, laughing with a friend as they walk. She probably has that cherry-smelling lip stuff on.

This is who she is. What the fuck was she thinking, stepping into that bar?

A group of college boys pass by her, and one of them—tall, preppy type—clearly checks her out. Something dark and possessive coils in my gut. These innocent, doughy boys have no idea what she's capable of or what she needs. They'll never appreciate her sense of right and wrong or the way she'll go to war if you fuck with her people.

Not that I'm her people.

These college kids are her people.

I follow at a distance as she heads into the library. Through the windows, I watch her claim a spot near the stacks, spreading out books and notebooks with careful precision.

She tucks her hair behind her ear as she reads, biting her lower lip in concentration. That mouth.

I think about the way it felt against my skin, the way she gasped when I touched her and tried to pretend she wasn't unraveling under my hands.

I thought it was an act. I fucking ate it up.

I sit there a while, watching her through the windows like the predator I am. Memorizing her movements, the way she takes notes, how she absent-mindedly twirls her pen when she's thinking.

Getting my fill.

And then it's time. I head back out the gates and down the two blocks to where Storm waits in the Range Rover.

"Let's get out of here."

He pulls out, taking 116th Street to Morningside. Twenty minutes later, we're over the Madison Avenue bridge.

The familiar streets of the South Bronx fold me back into their shadows, but my mind stays in that library, thinking about Edie and how that fuzzy sweater would feel against my face.

# Chapter Thirty-Six

EDIE

It's a miracle that Bender hasn't called by now. Am I off the hook? Is it possible?

Bad Bunny is blaring from Odetta's phone, and she's standing in front of our couch, wearing the mega-sexy, off-the-shoulder dress we refer to as Teal Tango. She got it for almost nothing at a resale shop due to a rip in the bodice, which she craftily sewed up.

"Thank goodness you're here!" she says breathlessly. "Are you good to zip it with that arm?"

"Of course!" I zip her up. "But don't you think it's a little dressy for movie night?"

"Noooo! I'm so sorry. Chad made a massive sale, and the client just threw in a weekend getaway in the Hamptons—at Gurney's! Five-course meals, couples massage with ocean views, hotel sex. The limo picks us up in like two seconds. Rain check?"

"Of course," I say, trying not to sound too devastated. "Oh my God, of course!"

"With or without the necklace?"

I focus on her outfit, glad for the distraction from stressing out over what happened with the big Milaga Hotel meeting, hoping that Luka got out of there in time.

"Are you wearing those earrings?"

"Yeah."

"Take them off. Less is more with Teal Tango."

She takes them off. "I'm so sorry I forgot about our night."

"I have to work on Iconic Regret anyway."

She winces in sympathy. "Worst weekend ever! Is your poor arm going to hold up to write with that thing?"

"I've been dictating." It's definitely weird that I haven't shown the injury to her yet, but you can still see the bruises from Bender's handprint on my skin.

"Don't forget to keep icing it," she says.

"Got it."

She fills her overnight bag with every toiletry possible, and then her phone pings for the limo. "Feel free to finish the carrot cake."

"Carrot cake activate! Have fun!"

She does ironic pistol hands at me, and then she's off.

I spend the afternoon and into the evening curled up in an overstuffed chair in the fourth-floor study lounge, legs hanging sideways over the arm, feet clad in the colorful socks Odetta knit for me, trying to first predict what questions might pop up on my Indo-European language exam and formulating answers to them and then search for sources in the Digital Library of the Medieval Manuscripts.

School isn't that hard if you stay ahead.

But I can't stop thinking about the big meeting. Sometimes I search for mentions of arrests in that part of the Bronx. There's been nothing, which is a relief.

It's not impossible.

I think about being back with Luka that night in his hotel room. He's standing, swaying slightly at the foot of the bed, beastly and desperate to fuck. I loved him like that.

I'm spreading salve over his back, caring for him with every stroke. Docile for once. I loved him like that, too.

And then he rejects me so totally the next morning. And it hurt so badly.

Could Bender be right? He took away the phone to take away the temptation?

Every time my phone makes a sound, I'm paranoid it's Bender calling or texting to let me know that Luka is at the restaurant and that I have to go there—or else.

Luka is bound to show up at the restaurant at some point. And then I'll need to go over like a needy stalker and get his hair and more information—or else.

In what world is that even possible for me to do?

It's like I'm trapped in a dark maze with no way out, and there are trapdoors hidden all over.

Yes, I'd love to see him again. Just not like that.

But then I realize if the worst-case scenario happens and Luka is at the restaurant and Bender makes me go... all I need is the name of a language and one human hair. Just one tiny human hair. Bender would have no way of knowing who I got the hair from.

Right?

One simple question. One strand of hair. And my sister could be coming home.

During a study break, I spin through outpatient drug rehab programs in the area.

Odetta already said it would be okay for Mary to stay with us for a couple of days, and she would stay with Chad. It seems like a dream to have Mary with me in the residence hall. I'd feed her and pamper her. Connect her with whatever support and resources she needs. I'm under no illusions about the rough road in front of her. I'd help her find a roommate while I finish my master's.

It could happen.

# Chapter Thirty-Seven

## EDIE

It takes me forever to get to sleep because the students on the floor above are blasting music, and the bass is thudding like a heartbeat in my skull. It doesn't help that at any moment, Bender could call, and I'd have to race across town to face Luka again.

A man whose face I still search for in crowds.

A man whose voice echoes in my dreams.

A man who might kill me if he knew what I was up to.

Or would he? I usually have good instincts about people, honed over years of watching my mother bring home iffy guys and moving us into neighborhoods where survival meant learning to read people fast.

I bury myself in a book. Eventually, the music stops, and I drift into a restless sleep.

The next thing I know, a rough hand slides down my cheek.

I gasp and try to pull off my sleep mask, but a hand is over it. "Keep it on."

*Luka.*

Adrenaline bolts through me.

"What are you doing here?"

His lips brush my ear. "Taking the princess in her castle."

He found me. Does that mean he knows about Bender? Am I in trouble?

"Is everything okay?" My voice is a whisper, breathless.

"Why wouldn't it be?"

"You shouldn't be here."

The bed groans as he climbs on. "Oh, I definitely shouldn't be here. You're right about that."

Something brushes my bare skin. His suit sleeve?

He seems to still. "What happened to your arm?"

"It's nothing."

His voice turns lethal. "Did somebody hurt you?"

"Walking and texting. One star. Do not recommend."

In the silence that follows, he touches it lightly, seeming to examine the loose wrap I wear to bed. I wish I could see his face. Did he hear the lie? Has he figured out about Bender and me?

Satisfied that I'm intact, he trails a finger down, down, down my belly.

His touch is electric. Wicked fingers slip down the front of my sleep pants, and heat floods my core, mixing with something sharper, something dangerous.

Luka is here. Luka the kingpin. Luka the killer.

A coil of unease wraps around my spine, but then his fingers find my clit, and I don't even care anymore. The forbidden pleasure of this bad man's touch overrides everything.

"Tell me to stop, princess. Tell me."

I lick his neck. He groans, stroking me nearly into oblivion.

And then it hits me. Luka is never alone.

He's always with Orton and that Arctic soldier. Sometimes, he even has more people around him.

"Are we alone?" I go for my mask.

He grabs my wrist. "What did I tell you? The mask stays on."

"But... your men." I wrench against his hold to dislodge the mask.

His lips brush my ear, teasing, taunting. "Ah. Would the

barbarian fuck the young princess in front of his men? Is that what you're asking?"

"W-what?"

His mouth claims my nipple through my thin nightshirt, and my body bows under the sensation.

"Just tell me if we're alone," I gasp.

He hums against my skin. "Your roommate seems to have won a trip. Pretty amazing."

My stomach drops. Luka arranged for Odetta's boyfriend to win the trip? Just to get me alone?

"And yes," he continues, pulling my pants and panties off. "My men are all around the bed, watching me defile you. They're dirty and brutish, dressed in furs. Some still carry their weapons from battle."

It takes me a second to get what he's doing—showing me he knows all about what I study.

Calloused palms slide over my hips, drinking in bare skin. "Their eyes all fixed on the princess who thought herself above them."

Images flood my mind of rough men watching from the shadows as I'm devoured by a brute of a man.

"Drinking in the sight of your utter submission."

"What the fuck," I whisper.

"Enough." Strong hands flip me onto my stomach, baring just my ass, and then—a wicked slap. The sound cracks through the air, sharp as my gasp. Pleasure slices through me.

This game feels wild. Dangerous.

He jerks up my hips so my ass is in the air. "They're watching me take the innocent princess, their hungry eyes tracing over all this soft skin."

I imagine their fists wrapped around crude weapons, knuckles white with tension, eyes burning. Heat pools between my thighs.

His fingers slide through my wetness, teasing, torturing. And then he's gone, and there's nothing. Just emptiness.

*Come back.*

"They know that only I get to have you." Another slap. "The sacred ritual of claiming royal bloodlines."

The scholar in me wants to correct his historical inaccuracy, but then he reaches around and twists one of my nipples, and all facts dissolve into the air. There's only his hot breath against my ear and his achingly male scent.

"They're barely civilized. None of us are civilized. We take what we want. When I see a princess pure as you, I need her hard and brutal."

I slide my palms over the cool sheets and then squeeze wads of it in my fists. Waiting. For him.

Is this really happening? It's so wrong... and so hot.

Cool air brushes my back as he pulls away. "Don't move."

I couldn't if I tried.

More like I *wouldn't.*

A belt buckle clanks. Fabric rustles.

My breath stutters as strong hands rip my sleep pants all the way off me.

He pushes apart my legs, and the thick head of his cock presses against my entrance, teasing, testing, but not pushing inside.

Desperation claws at me. I push back, needing him, needing to be filled.

He growls low in his throat. Another slap, sharper this time. "Be still."

I don't care anymore. I don't care how he found me or if I'm in danger. Right now, I only need one thing.

Again I bear back.

A cry tears from my throat as he thrusts deep, his claim absolute. He fucks me long and strong. He takes what he wants.

At some point, I am on my back, still with the sleep mask on, and we're fucking like animals, crying, losing track of ourselves in this strange dance that we do.

Pleasure detonates through me, an explosion of every forbidden color, every wrong need.

He comes with a guttural grunt, his massive hands holding me in place.

# Chapter Thirty-Eight

LUKA

Edie's dorm is bursting with personality: artsy prints, posters of singers I wouldn't be able to name with a gun to my head, pastel hats on hooks surrounding a mirror, and a bulletin board full of memorabilia and photos of her with different people. And a harmonica.

She comes over to where I stand, long legs under a red T-shirt, and hands me a small bottle of some sort of flavored water.

There's a logo on her shirt, some college thing, probably, but it's not enough to disguise her sexy nipples that I already want to suck again. I already want her again.

"You have... a harmonica."

"Yeah. Also, I have a bone to pick with you," she announces. "Taking my phone like that and sending me away? You cut me off like I was nothing after I showed basic human concern."

I move to the window, looking out at the campus below—this world so different from mine. It's late, the dark streets nearly vacant. "I don't do concern."

"Clearly."

When I turn back, her green eyes are fixed on me, unwavering.

This is what draws me to her—that fearlessness, even facing someone like me.

"It was fucked up," I say.

She waits, seeming to want more.

I wrack my brains and realize she deserves an apology. "I'm sorry."

Her eyebrows rise slightly. "Excuse me, what?"

"Don't make me repeat it." I step closer to her. "When you talked about my scars, about wanting justice for me... no one's ever —" I stop, searching for words that don't come easily. "People don't usually see that part of me."

"The part that was hurt?"

"More like vulnerable. Weak."

She shakes her head. "That's not weakness, Luka. It's humanity."

"In my world, they're the same thing." I reach for her hand, relieved when she doesn't pull away. "You cared, and I didn't know what the fuck to do with that. It's easier when people are trying to kill me."

"Oh my God, I can't believe you just said that. Don't I get to care about you? Do you actually hate it when somebody gives a shit about you? Is that the situation here?"

"The caring act usually means they want something from me."

"Well, maybe I just want you."

I study the wisp of hair on her cheekbone, going against the impulse to laugh her off. I want to give her some bits of truth, at the very least. "I'm not used to this caring thing. Loyalty, blood oaths. That's all I get. But the caring thing. It's... hard."

She watches me, her expression softening just slightly. "No shit. You took my phone and told me we were done."

"Dick move, I know. I'm gonna do better. At least I'm gonna try. I want to be better for you."

If she knows how big it is that I'm saying this, she doesn't show it. She doesn't need to know. It's for me to know that she's inspiring me to raise the bar for myself and what it means to be a man.

I tuck a strand of hair behind her ear. "You're nothing like anyone I've ever known."

She grins. "Yeah?"

"Yeah. I've never met anyone who could lecture me on historical accuracy one minute and threaten to firebomb a reformatory the next."

She laughs despite herself. "I did not threaten to firebomb—"

"You were thinking it." I brush my lips against her forehead. "Most dangerous bookworm ever."

"Most secretly soft-hearted villain ever," she counters.

"Only for you."

She snorts and kisses me.

I tunnel my fingers through her hair and deepen the kiss. I cannot get enough of this woman.

Standing on her bedside table is a framed photograph of a young Edie alongside a girl who looks to be a few years older. Matching freckled noses. Matching honey-colored hair. Christmas tree in the background.

"Your sister?" I ask. She has an older sister, according to her file, and that girl's been in a lot of trouble.

She searches my eyes, and I get this flash of something not right. "You found me. I guess you know the answer to that question."

"I do know. I know all about you now."

"What does that mean?"

I take the bottle from her fingers and set it aside. "It means I read your papers, for one thing."

"You read my papers?"

"Three of them are online, Edie. It doesn't take much to find them. Anastasia Laskarina: Scholarly Ambitions and Diplomatic Challenges of a Young Byzantine Royal was especially fascinating."

She blinks at me, stunned.

"I do read, shocking as that may seem."

"No, it's not that it's... shocking."

"But maybe it's a little bit shocking."

"It's just weird to think of you reading my papers."

"But it was so very interesting," I say. "The princess in her pastel gown strolling past marble columns. Writing down her observations."

"On parchment made of animal skins," Edie adds.

I slide a finger down the side of her face, tracing her cheekbone. "With a quill pen made from the feather of a swan."

"Right." She starts going on about how they made pens because she's nerdy like that. She wants to find a picture.

My phone buzzes. I glance down, seeing Orton's name, and check it while she roots around in her schoolgirl books.

*Spoke with counter person at bakery - woman matching Edie's description exactly. Paid cash. Three blocks from her residence hall. Circle cookies delivered precisely when we discussed the meet.*

The words blur. Blood rushes in my ears, drowning out Edie's voice.

Each detail hits like a hammer blow: the timing, the location, her fucking description. The pieces lock together with sickening clarity. And her studies. She clearly understands Latin. She heard us set that meeting.

She heard us.

She told the cops—it could only have been her.

Edie betrayed us—*betrayed me.*

The realization punches through my chest with the force of a bullet.

How could I have let my judgment get so clouded?

And yeah, maybe she thought better of it and sent cookies to warn us, but it doesn't matter. It's a betrayal all the same.

My chest tightens as she holds up a book, open to a page with an image of a quill pen. "Right?" she says.

Were we talking? I don't even remember, and it doesn't matter.

A lifetime of ruthless survival has taught me what to do with traitors. It should be simple. Clean.

"W-what's wrong?" she asks.

God, even now, knowing what she's done, I want to mark her as mine in ways that have nothing to do with death.

I barely recognize the abomination I've become—a kyre who hesitates to kill a spy because he's drunk on the taste of her scorn.

"Tell me, princess..." I bite out, voice like ground glass. "What did the barbarians do to those who betrayed them?"

"Excuse me?" She searches my eyes—warily. She's hiding something. How did I not see it?

I force my voice to stay steady. "What did the barbarians do to those who betrayed them?"

"I-I don't understand..."

"Betrayal. Surely you've heard of it. What punishment did they deal to those who violated their trust?"

She shuts the book and clutches it against her belly.

I move in like the predator I am, my blood a roaring inferno.

"Luka..."

"Did they make examples of them?" I settle my four fingertips onto her jawbone, ear to chin.

She's trembling now. *Good.*

I force myself to imagine choking her, squeezing the air right out of her. The way her skin would redden. The way she'd struggle.

"Tell me," I demand.

"M-maybe they would listen first. Let the accused explain the reasons—"

"Explain the reasons?" I wrap my hand loosely around her throat, skimming the side with my thumb, up and down, up and down. "Make up stories to save their ass? You think they'd allow that?"

"I wouldn't make up stories." She pulls at my hand. "Please, if you'd just—"

"Tell me," I demand. "Would they allow excuses? Would they care?"

"What happened to *secretly soft-hearted*—"

"Tell me! Would they care?"

"No."

"What did they do to traitors?"

She tries to turn away, but I catch her chin, forcing her to meet my gaze.

"Tell me."

"They... they killed them."

"How?" The word comes out like gravel.

"Luka, please—"

I slide my other hand into her hair, fisting it tight. "Tell me how they died. Paint me the picture."

"Exile..."

"Try again."

"What? Exile would be a death sentence."

"What else?"

Tears spill down her cheeks. I force myself to tighten my hold on her hair because traitors don't deserve mercy.

"Impalement, dismemberment... they would make it gruesome to serve as a warning to others." Her voice shakes. "Make sure everyone saw what happens to those who betrayed the clan."

I study her eyes, pale green shot with brown. For one insane second, it comes to me to make a joke about the standard-issue criminal punishment for betrayal.

But that part of us is gone now.

She gazes up at me like a rabbit that knows there's no escape from the predator—terrified but unable to look away. My chest fills with unnamable darkness.

It would be so easy to snap her neck. I'd send somebody to make the body disappear. They'd wipe down the room, not that I touched much—aside from her.

Storm had a guy spray-paint the cameras I couldn't avoid before I arrived. I'm a ghost. I always have been.

I let her hair go. "Pack your bag."

I watch her hesitate. She wants to say no.

"You could always refuse. Yell out. Sound the alarm. I promise you won't like the results."

I watch her think through what I could do to her. To her people. To her world.

I see the moment she realizes compliance is her only option.

With shaking hands, she gathers up her things.

# Chapter Thirty-Nine

## EDIE

Luka doesn't speak as he leads me to a black SUV parked in the shadows. Storm is at the wheel, waiting for orders.

We get in the back, Luka on one side of the backseat, me on the other, clutching my pink Pusheen overnight bag like it might save me or something.

The city blurs past the tinted windows, neon streaks of light reflecting off wet pavement.

The silence between us is thick and oppressive against my ribs. I keep waiting for the explosion, but he's too cool for that, I guess. Too controlled.

Somehow, that's more terrifying.

Would he really kill me? But he told me to pack my things. A dead girl doesn't need a toothbrush and a change of clothes.

Unless he wants it to look like I went on a trip.

My heart sinks. We had that conversation about caring, and I thought we were really together. But now it's like somebody else has taken over his body.

I have to get away. But how can I outwit a battle-hardened killer like Luka?

I steal a glance at his profile—the sharp set of his jaw, perfect lips, dusky brows like angry slashes. A bruise still kisses his cheekbone from that fight. He's like a Renaissance sculpture of dangerous beauty, all shadows and light.

Quickly, I look away. I have to figure this out. He took my phone, but maybe I can get it back when he's not looking.

A dark thought comes to me: what if he forces me to unlock it? I try to think if there's anything incriminating on there for him to find.

But then again, he already wants to kill me. How can it get worse than that?

Then I remember Mary. Things could get worse for Mary. If Bender tries to contact me and thinks I'm blowing him off, what would he do to her?

"Can't I just tell you why—"

"No. Ask again, and I'll make you sorry," he grates out.

Anger flashes through me. "This isn't the twelfth century. There are such things as exculpatory reasons."

"Not in my world," he growls. Some animal instinct in me knows not to say anymore. He probably wouldn't care anyway.

Eventually, the car pulls up in front of a penthouse, steel and glass against the night sky. "Where are we?"

He doesn't answer; he simply pulls me out and leads me through a sleek, glittering lobby. The doorman hands him a package without so much as a glance in my direction. I catch sight of his name on it.

So this is his place—a perfect fortress for a king. Or a prison.

When the elevator doors close, I huddle in the corner, as far from him as the small space allows, but it's no use. His presence brushes against my skin. We get off on the top floor, and I follow him into his place.

"Put your things on the couch." His voice is quiet. He moves to the bar, pouring himself a drink. The clink of ice against glass is impossibly loud in the silence.

"Are you gonna kill me?" I ask.

"You'll find out when you find out," he says, all quiet menace.

My mind spins. Except... if he was planning on killing me, why would he have brought me to his own home? The doorman saw us come in, and I'm sure there are cameras. It seems foolish, and Luka is far from foolish.

Maybe he'll toy with me first. Punish me or whatever a man like this does. Which means I have time... to get the hell away.

I put my bag on the couch and wait, wringing my hands and looking around.

I don't know what I expected from his place, something hard and cold, I suppose. Full-on Spartan. Everything gunmetal gray.

Instead, the place is posh and bright—chic, even—like we've walked into the pages of an interior design magazine. A mod statement chandelier made of swirly glass. Floor-to-ceiling windows. There's even a blue chair in that knobby sort of fabric.

It's not him.

But then I almost want to laugh because it's actually *so him* to live in a place that's not him.

This man who lives in the shadows and treats everything as a transaction. Nothing to pin him down. Nothing to define him. He *would* live in a magazine. Another way to stay hidden.

"You warned us about the meeting." He turns, swirling amber liquid. "With the cookies."

My breath catches. I hadn't expected him to lead with that.

"That was your mistake, of course."

"I couldn't let anything happen to you." The words spill out before I can stop them. "No matter what you think of me, I never wanted to cause trouble for you. I care—"

"Another mistake," he murmurs, stepping closer. "So naive."

Excitement churns in my stomach. Even now, just his nearness turns me on. "It's not naive to care."

He takes a slow sip, gaze locked on mine. "You and Anastasia Laskarina."

I blink. "What does she have to do with anything?"

"You're alike. The two of you living in your cloistered worlds of pastel gowns and leatherbound books, spinning elaborate theories about the world outside your castle windows. Fascinated by brutal men."

"Fascinated by brutal men? That's not true of her or me."

"It's why you study her. You're both fascinated by the barbarians—from a distance."

"You clearly don't know anything about her. If you did, you would know that she was interested in all the issues of her time. Diplomacy. Matters of state. Charitable causes. She was the first teen historian. As you would've read in my papers."

"According to your papers, she was obsessed with barbarians."

I fold my arms over my chest. "That is what's known as a flawed interpretation."

"You know what else I think?" he rumbles.

"No, but I bet you're going to tell me."

A predatory smile curves his lips. He sets down his drink. "I think you love it when your princess talks about how brutish and dirty they are. You love those parts. Hot for a little bit of danger."

"It's an academic concentration, not a sex fantasy!"

He comes close. Electricity crackles between us.

Gentle fingers skirt over my breasts.

I suck in a breath, trying to look indifferent.

"You sure about that?"

"Quite sure."

"Your stiff little nipples beg to differ."

"No, my entire academic career begs to differ. The nipples are responding to the thermostat settings."

His lips are a hair's breadth away from mine, spicy with scotch and so kissable, I can barely think. "Is that so?"

"I can read your body the same as I can read a dark street. Same as I can read a fighter's eyes. I know when you're aroused, princess. It's in the flush creeping up your neck." He kisses my neck. "It's the rhythm of your breath, the way your pupils dilate when I get close." Another kiss. "Your body's screaming for me."

"Ummm," I say, voice husky. "Screaming for ice cream," I say nonsensically because all the blood in my brain has drained down to my throbbing clit.

I should put a stop to this. He'd stop if I asked.

"Tell me I'm wrong. Tell me no."

"You so suck."

He fits his hands over the collar of my thin T-shirt, his touch electric, grasps the collar... and rips the shirt down the middle.

Cool air rushes over my bare belly. "You're such an asshole! I liked that shirt!"

"The scornful princess, imposed upon by the uncivilized barbarian."

"For your information, they're called Pechenegs, and they *weren't* uncivilized."

Rough lips brush my throat. The harsh scrape of stubble makes my knees buckle. "Unlock the bra, princess. Now."

"And if I don't?"

He traces patterns on my skin, branding me with heat. "I so suck, remember?"

My hands tremble as I undo the front clasp. My breasts pop free, and he claims them without mercy, thumbing, sucking, devouring them. I can't think. I grab his shoulder for stability.

"You hate the way I take you over." He mumbles against my nipple, voice like dark velvet. "You hate that you love it."

"No, I just hate it," I lie.

My back talk seems to spur him on. "Liar."

He sucks harder.

*Fuck, it feels good.*

Suddenly, he's on his knees in front of me, pushing down my yoga pants.

"Craving my dominance. Giving you what those pampered boys can't."

I snort like it's so ridiculous.

His lips hover over my mound as he skims my thighs with his rough palms, pushing the fabric to my ankles. He rids me of my shoes and every stitch of clothing below my waist, and I'm bared to him, way too turned on for life, pussy wet and throbbing.

His lips are still in the vicinity of my clit, and I'm desperate for him to touch me there, to lick me like in the restaurant.

Anything.

*Everything.*

Miracle of miracles, he shoves his tongue between my legs, rough and warm and invading.

My hand tunnels into his hair. "More."

He fucks me with his tongue. My legs are like noodles, and I'm holding on for dear life as he switches to a finger, fucking me ruthlessly with it. He nips my belly. My eyes flutter shut.

"The prim princess, corrupted by a savage man," he says, breath hot on my skin, finger owning my clit.

*Yessss.*

I'm sinking so deep into this strange reality we create together that I don't know which way is up. It's everything.

He stands, letting the angle of his finger grow sharper, hitting just the right spot.

I whimper.

He slows, dragging his fingertip around my sex like a god trailing energy with his touch.

"Don't stop."

"Shamelessly begging for more."

My eyes fly open. I *am* begging.

When I vowed I wouldn't.

But I want more. More of this. More of him. "Fuck off, you dirty beast."

Something dangerous flashes in his eyes, and the last thread of his control snaps. His jaw clenches, his nostrils flare, and his pupils dilate until his eyes are almost black. A wild, dark energy radiates from him—primal and untamed.

I've awakened something in him that should probably terrify me, but I love it way too much, and my world's upside-down now anyway.

"That's right," I say. "You're not fit to lick the leather bottoms of my gold embroidered shoes."

He growls, long and low. With one violent swipe, he clears the bar surface. Glasses and bottles fly off, bouncing and shattering across his floor.

He hoists me up.

"You're mine," he rasps, claiming my thighs with rough hands. "Your body is mine. Your breath is mine. When you come is mine, and your begging is mine."

My chest heaves as he presses my thighs apart. Our mutual heat cranks to eleven.

"Do you feel me owning you? You're in my castle now, princess. I own this world. I'm setting the law."

"You can lick... the... bottoms... of my... embroidered..."

His gaze is merciless as he drags his fingers through the slick proof of my undoing. My breath stutters, my fingers twitch with the urge to shove him away, pull him closer—maybe both.

"I should destroy you," he murmurs, voice like gravel.

A shiver rips through me. Fear and need tangle together so tightly I can't tell them apart.

"Do it," I plead, reckless now. "Just do it."

His thumb strokes my clit, slow, torturous. "Oh, I will," he promises, lips brushing mine in a whisper of a kiss.

# Chapter Forty

## LUKA

I'm inside her in a flash, this woman I can't get enough of. This woman who, by all rights, should be in the Bronx River.

Her heat clenches around me, gripping like a vise, and I curse, dragging my hands over her hips and locking her against me. She closes her teeth around the skin of my neck. She could do some damage if she wanted. She could kill me with a bite there.

But she won't.

She's too gone, too ruined.

So am I.

There's no control left. Just instinct. Heat. Hunger.

She grabs onto me, nails raking down my back.

I want her to mark me. Want to feel her teeth, her rage, her surrender all in one. We move together—rough, frantic, chasing something violent, something that isn't soft or safe. We move like animals, desperate and raw, tearing each other apart, losing ourselves in the wreckage.

It should be meaningless.

But fuck, it isn't.

The orgasm rips through me, a lightning bolt of pleasure, leaving me wrecked and breathless.

A hazy bliss I never let myself have.

My grip loosens, and my body sags against hers, not fighting for once. Just being. Feeling. Holding her.

She moves in my arms. Whatever she's doing, I'm too out of it to care.

Until a sharp crack of pain explodes across my skull.

The world tilts. My vision goes black at the edges as I stumble back, my knees nearly giving out.

What the—

*She hit me.*

I shake my head, trying to clear the daze, and through the haze of pleasure and pain, I see her.

She's moving fast, yanking on her clothes with frantic hands, breathing hard. She takes my suit coat from where I'd thrown it over a chair and puts it on over her ripped shirt. Her gaze flicks to me, wary. She grabs her shoes and heads for the foyer. The elevator.

Rage and something else—something raw—burns through me.

I touch my head. Bleeding. I take an unsteady step forward.

"Ow!" She stops. "Fuck!" She looks down, mouth twisted in pain.

She stepped on glass, but she isn't letting it stop her—she's hopping on one foot now.

I blink, instincts flipping so fast it makes me dizzy. Before I can stop myself, I'm moving toward her.

She limps toward the door, but I'm there first. I sweep her up and carry her to the kitchen island, her body stiff in my arms.

She pounds on my chest. "Why can't you just let me go?"

I don't answer. Because I don't fucking know.

Blood drips from her heel.

"Stay right there." I grab the first aid kit stocked with everything from butterfly bandages to surgical sutures from under the sink. In my world, you learn to patch yourself up.

I set it on the expanse of granite beside her and pull out antiseptic, tweezers, and gauze. My movements are practiced, mechanical. I've stitched up bullet wounds in pitch-black basements with less than this.

"Is it bad? It feels deep," she says.

"Not so bad," I assure her.

"Okay."

She's not pulling away. That's a start.

Blood wells from the cut as I examine it. A shard of glass is embedded in her heel, not deep enough to need stitches but enough to make walking painful. I grip the tweezers and extract it.

She doesn't make a sound. She's done being vulnerable.

"Almost done." My words come out gentle, which sounds strange to my ears.

I clean the wound thoroughly, my hands steady despite the pounding in my head. The back of my skull throbs where she hit me. Smart move, going for the base of the skull. Another inch lower and I might be unconscious.

"You have good aim," I say, pressing gauze to her foot.

"Not good enough, apparently."

"Hold still," I murmur, wrapping a bandage around her foot and securing it snugly. Not too tight. Just right.

When I finish, I look up to find her staring at me, confusion clouding her eyes.

"You're still bleeding," she says suddenly.

I touch the back of my head. My fingers come away sticky.

Before I can react, she reaches for the first aid kit, pulling out an alcohol wipe. "Turn around."

I hesitate, every instinct screaming not to show my back to someone who just tried to crack my skull open. But I turn anyway.

Her touch is surprisingly gentle as she parts my hair to find the wound. I wince when the alcohol makes contact.

"Not so tough after all," she says, but there's no venom in it.

"Everyone bleeds."

She works in silence for a moment, cleaning the cut. "You'll live."

"Disappointed?"

"I haven't decided yet."

I turn to face her, our bodies close, the air between us charged.

"I didn't have a choice," she gusts out. "I didn't. This cop, he's got some sort of control over my sister. He can get to her. Horrible things'll happen to her if I don't do what he wants. I was so scared."

I listen, emotion coiling in my gut. I had told myself I didn't need to hear what she had to say, but it was a lie.

She tells me about Mary sliding into the underworld and her attempts to find this sister of hers she loves so much. Searching everywhere without considering her own safety.

"Mary cared for me. She's the only reason I'm not dead or in a gutter. And then she went missing, and I had to find her." She searches my eyes. "So I went out to where she worked, dressing to blend in..."

My blood boils as she tells me how this cop picked her up and exploited the fuck out of her. Then sent her to sit with Dardan, for fuck's sake.

She must have been so frightened. I can barely grate out the next word, but I slide a gentle hand over her shoulder to show it's not her I'm angry with. "Name."

"Bender." She wrings her hands. "I think it's fake, though. I looked it up, and I couldn't find any cop named Bender that matched him. At first he said all I had to do was sit at the table for a few hours and leave. It was all it was supposed to be, and then he would bring her home to me. I didn't know what to do. But then you showed up..."

"And took you for my own."

I scrub my face as I see how fucked up I've acted. Not letting her explain. This woman is mine. Mine to protect.

"I just need you to know—I was determined not to tell him

anything, but then he got all scary and made these threats. So I told him a few things that seemed like common knowledge with you, like the Lazarus rumors. But he kept demanding more from me, and if I reminded him it wasn't our deal, he'd get so scary. Unhinged. And I'd panic. I swear—I never wanted to tell him anything. And when I heard you planning the meeting, I wasn't going to tell, but it's like he knew I was holding something back. Like he could read my mind. And he got angry, and I was so scared and..."

Her gaze points down to her wrist.

Ice spears through my veins.

Gently, I take her bandaged arm, cradling it in my hands, and I'm vibrating with rage. "*He* did this to you."

Her lips tremble. "He wouldn't let go. He kept squeezing and twisting." Her eyes glisten with unshed tears.

The room temperature seems to drop as ice floods my veins. "Show me. Now."

"It's nothing, just—"

"*Show. Me.*"

She unwraps the beige bandages. The moment I see the hand-shaped bruise marking her delicate skin, something dark unfurls in my chest. I trace the outline with trembling fingers, memorizing every detail of what this bastard dared to do to what's mine.

Her eyes widen in alarm. "You can't go after him—"

"Go after him?" I laugh, and it's a terrible sound. "I'll do more than go after him. I'll hunt him down like the scum he is. I'll break every bone in his hands, starting with the ones he used to touch you. Then I'll start on the rest of him, piece by piece, until he begs for a death I will not give him."

"Please, you don't understand—"

"No, *he* didn't understand. You're *mine*." I'm shaking with barely contained violence.

"But he'll kill my sister!"

I close my eyes. Right. The sister. "Do you think he kidnapped her?"

"I don't know. All I know is that she's somewhere against her will. I'm sure of it because why wouldn't she call me? It's been five weeks now, and she always reaches out. And he seems to know the people holding her..."

I cup her face in my hands, forcing her to meet my gaze. "Then he's a dead man who just doesn't know it yet. We'll get your sister back. And then..." My thumb brushes away a tear. "I'll make him pay."

She swallows hard.

I trace the bruise one last time. "I'm going to tear this whole world apart to find her. I'll make sure she's safe. And then I'll rain bloody hell on this Bender. I will make him so sorry, and then I'll make sure nothing like this ever happens to you again."

"Thank you." She throws her arms around me.

"No thanks needed."

She holds me more tightly. "I've been so scared. And just so tired."

"I know."

# Chapter Forty-One

## LUKA

I carry her to my spa bathroom, set her down in a chair, and start a bath. She tells me not to fuss over her, but that's not an option.

I had every wrist-healing device and hot-cold wrap known to humankind sent over. Every salve and balm—even the hippie shit. I set them out methodically, arranging everything with military precision.

The pressure she's been under blows my mind—it really does. But she's made of tough stuff. This is a woman who's used to fighting for things others take for granted, and she's been carrying this huge burden alone.

She gazes up at me. Relief has softened her face.

I was an asshole, but she sees now that I have her back.

It hits me suddenly how much deeper I've gotten with her than I've ever gotten with anybody in my life. Sara and I were kids —sneaking around, defying authority—but Edie? I know her heart. Her sense of humor. I know the contours of her desire like I know the warmth of a fire on a cold night. I know she loves pastels and is a hat person. Thanks to that visit to her dorm, I know she plays the harmonica, of all things. And she's an organizational wiz with several planners and an elaborate color-coding system.

"Tell me about your sister," I command gently.

She smiles up at me. "Mary is the bravest person you could ever meet. A total free spirit who loves music, especially all that nineties stuff, and an amazing artist. She used to draw tiny animals on everything—little mice and rabbits and possums. Unicorns if I begged her. And she's so resourceful. We had a hard time growing up, but she was there for me when Mom was checked out, which was kind of always toward the end."

She describes little games Mary would invent, candies and sparkly jewelry she would procure, and the dinners she'd make out of three sad ingredients.

"She ended up being my mother and making our life livable. She sacrificed her childhood for me, and I didn't even realize it. I should've paid attention."

"You can't take that kind of thing on yourself," I say firmly, leaving no room for argument. "You were doing the best you could."

She makes a little sound. She's not so sure. Or maybe she doesn't trust me now. I wouldn't blame her.

I test the water with my hand, gauging it with expert precision. "Too hot?"

She swishes her hand around in it. "It seems good."

"Come on, then," I say softly but decisively. I slide my suit coat over her arms, my fingers deft and sure.

"Are you coming in with me?"

"This is just for you." I help her with the rest of her clothes, taking care to avoid touching her arm but watching her with protective eyes all the while.

"It's not like it's broken," she says at one point. "It's really fine."

I fix her with a look that silences further protest.

I kiss her shoulder. Her skin is soft, and of course, I would love nothing more than to consume her on every level. But I stay with the caring shit, outrageous as it is coming from a man like me.

The lion caring for the mouse, which, again, would never happen in nature, but it's happening now because we're different. We're more than that. It's wrong, but there it is.

The lion can't get enough of the mouse, though she's hardly a mouse.

She sinks more deeply into the water, surrendering to my care, looking more relaxed than I've seen her look... possibly ever.

"I have this dream for me and Mary. Or I shouldn't call it a dream. It's more like a plan where I find her and pull her out of whatever hell she's got herself into. I get her into rehab, and once I have my teaching license, we live in a little seaside house and help each other. And we'll grow flowers in the window boxes and things like that."

Rescuing her sister. I'd expect nothing less of her.

She's calm enough now to give me some halfway-decent details. "So what does this guy look like?"

She regards me warily.

"Don't worry," I promise. "I'll get your sister home first. Then I'll deal with him."

She seems to relax at this. "He has short, dark wavy hair. He's about your height but wide. His shoulders are really wide, and his eyes are dark brown and also really wide. His neck and arms are super thick. Like he might be a wrestler or something."

"That's good." I test the water again, my movements controlled and deliberate. "Distinguishing marks?"

"Umm... he has a small white scar on his chin." She narrows her eyes. "He's a bad shaver; seems like he always has a shaving nick. That's not a very good description."

"Anything else stand out? Birthmark? Tattoo? Limp?" I press, mentally cataloging each detail like the predator I am.

There's not much to go on with this guy, but she tries her best.

"What sorts of things did he want to know about me?" I ask, my jaw tightening.

"At first he just wanted me to report anything I heard—names, dates. He's desperate to know where you've been all this time, like all the years after you disappeared."

"You didn't tell him... any of it?"

"No way. That's your story," she says. "And when I told him that you didn't want to see me anymore, he was pretty upset. He wanted me to do one last thing where I show up at your restaurant and start quizzing you on what languages you speak and why you came back. He really wants to know why you killed your brother the way you did. Oh, and I'm supposed to get a strand of your hair —complete with the root."

I straighten. "Hair?"

She shrugs. "I doubt he wants to clone you."

"That's not what he wants," I say darkly.

"The hair and more details on where you've been—those were supposed to be my final assignments. He said he's watching your restaurant, or at least he has somebody watching it. He plans to text me the next time you're there, and I'm supposed to show up like I need to see you again. Did you know people were watching your restaurant?"

"I've always assumed."

She swishes her hand through the water. I'm glad to see her using her injured arm—it'll heal up fine. But it should never have happened.

"Okay, so don't laugh, but I have a plan."

"A plan, huh?"

She tells me this plan she's concocted where she goes to the restaurant, I invite her to sit with me, and we pretend to dine together. Then I pretend to get mad at her, and I make Orton throw her out with a warning to never come back again. Then she feeds Bender a fake story involving a military school in Montenegro to explain where I've been all these years.

"Montenegro? Why Montenegro?"

She shrugs. "It seemed believable?"

"Standard-issue criminal place to send a kid to military school?"

She splashes me. "Do you want to hear the rest of my plan or not?"

"Go on."

"I don't think he ever really expected me to ask about your brother, so we're clear on that. And I'll bring a hair, but not yours. We find a different one with the same hair color. What do you think?"

"Bad plan."

"What? I think it's great. He won't know if the hair is yours. He won't know if the story is real. He has no way to verify any of it."

"And then what incentive does he have to help you reunite with your sister? Once you've given him everything he supposedly wants? Assuming he doesn't see through it."

"I would've fulfilled my end of the bargain and..." She trails off here as she realizes the man has zero reason to help her. "Oh."

"We don't know if he has her. We don't know if he knows where she is or even if she's alive. That's job number one."

"But he had a recent picture of her!"

"I could show you a recent picture of Scarlett Johansson. It doesn't mean I have her stashed away somewhere or that I could get to her. A recent picture doesn't even prove she's alive. And how do you know how recent the picture actually is? Even if he really did have her or has some control over her, what use is she?"

"Y-you think he's probably killed her by now?" The horror in her eyes is a blade in my gut.

"No, I don't specifically think anything," I say, but the damage is done.

"She could be dead either way, that's what you think!"

"No, princess," I grate out, regret surging through my veins.

"Don't pretend you didn't say it. You think it could be true." She lies there in the tub, blinking back the tears.

"I'll do everything I can to find her." This is all I have for her. I wish I had more, but I won't lie.

She gazes miserably at the skylight. "You think she's probably dead."

"Neither of us knows. You don't know anything, and I don't know anything." All this, I say with too much vitriol.

She's full-on crying now.

It kills me.

Kills me.

I reach down and hoist her clear up from the tub, holding her tight to my chest, dripping wet, but I don't care.

I just hold her, my throat tight with emotions I've never allowed myself to feel.

"I got you, princess," I finally manage, voice rough. "You're not alone. We're in it together."

She loops her arms around my neck, forehead pressed to my shoulder, but I can feel the stiffness in her body.

"If she is out there, I will find her," I promise. "If somebody hurt her, I will kill them. If somebody's holding her, I will hunt them down."

She wriggles out of my arms and grabs a towel, wrapping it around herself. The distance between us suddenly feels like a chasm.

"What's wrong?"

"I appreciate your help with my sister. So much..."

I can hear the 'but' loud and clear. I force myself to say it. "But..."

"You couldn't trust me just a little bit? Hear me out? You had to jump to the worst possible conclusion?"

I run a hand over my face, struggling with unfamiliar vulnerability. "I know."

"Do you? I thought you knew me at least a little bit."

"I do know you."

"You thought I betrayed you, and you wouldn't hear different.

And you fucking kidnapped me and made me think you were gonna kill me!"

"I fucked up, Edie. Not just a little. Kidnapping you, scaring you, refusing to let you explain—it wasn't just wrong. It was unforgivable."

"Then why did you do it?"

I suck in a breath, unaccustomed to having to explain myself. "Because I've spent my entire life knowing only one way to handle betrayal. Because it was easier to treat you like an enemy than admit... how much power you have over me."

"I never betrayed you," she says, her voice cracking. "I was trying to protect my sister while still protecting you."

"I know that now."

Her eyes meet mine, guarded but listening.

"In my world, explanations and intentions don't mean shit. It's survival—black and white. But with you..." I struggle to find the words. "Nothing's simple. Things are messy and complicated and sometimes saying stupid things like 'I'm sorry' feels harder than robbing Fort Knox. And I *am* sorry. And I love this thing we have. I want this thing. I want it. I want you."

She studies my face. "Is this going to happen every time? Because I can't live waiting for the next time you decide I've crossed some line without letting me explain. I can't live by your mafia rules."

"You shouldn't have to."

She blinks. "So... that's that?"

It's not enough, I can see that. "The rules I've lived by, the ones that kept me alive—they don't apply to you. Not anymore. I've never apologized to anyone in my life, Edie. I've never needed to. But I'm asking for your forgiveness now. Not because I deserve it, but because I can't lose you."

"Pretty words," she challenges, though her eyes soften.

"I mean every one of them. I need you to know you'll be heard. Always." I press my lips to her hand. "I can't promise I'll never make mistakes. But I can promise to remember this moment," I say, my voice rough with emotion. "Almost losing you because I couldn't see past my own code killed me."

Tears glisten in her eyes. "I appreciate that."

"I don't deserve you," I admit.

She places her palm against my chest, over my heart. "You don't get to decide that."

# Chapter Forty-Two

LUKA

I sip coffee and watch from the pillar that divides the kitchen area from the sunken living room area as Edie explores my place, running her fingertips over the marble surfaces, the couch, a chair. She touches the elaborate moldings around the windows and then gazes down at the Hudson and the Palisades.

I follow her gaze to where the rugged cliffs are tinged with the faint green of newly budding trees. The blue sky soars above, and fluffy white clouds cast fast-moving shadows on the water.

"This view in the daytime. Just wow." She's already said "wow" twice.

I iced her arm, followed by a heat wrap and a lot of balm, and now it's bandaged to the best of my abilities, which is pretty fucking good if I do say so myself. We slept in, then ordered donuts that arrived just as the coffee was ready. She takes hers black, and her favorite donut is a French twist with white icing. I file it all away with the hats and the harmonica, which she's going to have to play for me at some point. Harmonica. So old-timey.

She wanders to the oil painting above the fireplace. Three black blobs over a field of blue with one white dot in a random fucking place. The thing's as big as a bicycle, loaded up with so much paint it's practically sculptural. I never really thought of it, not since the day the real estate agent suggested I get my own art, and I told her to fuck off.

I see now that it's a ridiculous painting, but Edie looks at it for a long time, giving it a chance, maybe.

It's not her style, that much I know; I saw the way she decorated her dorm. She'd hate statement art designed to go with couches, and that's what this is.

I never cared before today.

Only Orton and Storm have crossed into this space, and they would never look at the artwork. They would never touch the furnishings just to touch them. None of us ever thought to even care about what we surround ourselves with. We're so used to moving through other people's spaces, usually with bad intent.

Edie turns around, done with her perusal of the piece, and looks at me.

"What?"

"Nothing."

A lie. She has thoughts. She always does. It's the art.

She heads to the bookcase, pausing at the shelf of framed pictures. One is some bridge. One is a painted door, probably in Europe. One is a boy flying a kite.

She picks it up. "Is that you?"

"No."

"Is it a relative?"

"It's a boy flying a kite."

"You don't know who it is?"

"Nope."

"You have a picture of a random boy flying a kite?"

"Yeah."

She smiles uncertainly and puts it down.

"Are we almost done with the inspection?"

She gives me an indignant look. "Are you kidding?" She moves on to the books themselves. "You have some really interesting books."

"There's nothing interesting about those books, I promise you."

"Are you kidding? *The Dawn of Western Civilization?* That is nothing if not—" Her words die as she attempts to extract the book from the shelf and instead gets the boxy cardboard shell disguised to look like a row of books.

"Oh my God! What the hell?" She holds the thing like it's a dead rat.

"I told you they weren't interesting."

She regards me with horror. "It's just a cardboard facade! Are all of these...?"

"All of them." I take it from her hand and put it back.

"Why would you have fake books on your shelves?"

"Well, they *are* bookshelves."

She squints at me. "But those aren't books!"

"Who cares? Do I look like a librarian to you?"

"You do read books, don't you?"

"Of course."

"Well, where are the books that you've loved? Are there books out there that you imagine you might like to read? Or that you're currently reading? I mean... shells made to look like books? Who does that?"

*Shells made to look like books.*

The phrase is jam-packed with scorn. Leave it to Edie to get this upset about fake books.

"This stuff out here is just for show. It was here when I moved in. It's just staging stuff."

"This is a staged home? And you kept it like this? Why would you live in a home that's just for show?"

"What's wrong with it?"

"Well, for starters, what if you want to read an actual book?"

"If I wanted to read a book, I'd go out and buy it, or I'd order it as an ebook. I'm not somebody who collects a lot of stuff."

"But you own this place, right?"

"Yes, and I like it the way it is."

"So you like fake books?"

I go to her. "Maybe."

"Shut up! Don't you want to have things you love around you?"

It's the sort of thing the real estate agent said to me. I gave her a flip answer, but I won't do that with Edie.

"I don't have things I love. Objects. Art I've gathered or whatever. I'm used to being on the move. I'm used to spending my time in hotels, barracks, and bombed-out buildings. A home has always been more of a transaction. Something temporary that serves a specific need."

"As opposed to something personal."

"Yes."

"But this place, it's beautiful. Out of all the homes you could have chosen, you picked this one. The fact that you picked it out makes it personal."

"I picked it out for the location, exits, access to major roads, and resale value."

She takes a deep breath, just a hint of a smile playing across her sexy lips. "Nothing personal, then. Just a transaction."

I go to her, wrap her up in my arms, and kiss the top of her head.

"She can't be dead. I still feel her." Because, of course, that's what's on her mind.

"Good," I say. "That's a good sign."

"You really think Bender never planned to help me?"

"That guy only wants to help himself, but it ends now. Our number one task right now is to figure out if he knows where your sister is. I'm gonna have you ask some questions."

"He hates it when I ask him questions."

"Too bad. You're gonna text him and say things are moving along, but you want proof of life."

"I can't do that! He'll be mad. And he holds all the cards."

"He's holding some cards, but you're his golden goose. You have something he can't get from anybody else—access to me and my secrets. And secrets are power."

"I wish I'd never told him anything."

"You told him nothing of importance. You were amazing. And brave."

She rolls her eyes.

"You were. Most people would give up everything in your position. Here's what's going to happen. You need to figure out a question that only your sister would know the answer to. Something obscure. That will be your proof of life. He has to get her to answer that question."

"He'll freak out!" she says. "You don't know him."

"Oh, I know him well enough. I know he hurt you," I say, trying to hide the murder in my voice. "I know he intimidates and bullies you. I know he constantly breaks his word. That right there is a weak man. We can work him—"

"But if he takes it out on my sister—"

"Proof of life is a normal ask, and he knows it. I guarantee you, he expects you to ask for it. He's probably surprised you haven't already."

She looks thoughtful. "Have I been a patsy?"

"You've been amazing." I pour more coffee. "After that, you'll text him and let him know you've got the story and the hair."

She takes a seat at the kitchen island. "But... the plan was that he'd text me when you showed up at the restaurant, and I'd burst in. Obviously, that never happened. So how did I find you?"

"Tell him I hunted you down, but you don't know how."

"I *don't* know how."

"Always best to stay closest to the truth."

She narrows her eyes. "But between us, how *did* you find me?"

"Fingerprints. You were fingerprinted for your university job."

Her eyes widen. "So you *fingerprinted* me?"

"Well, I *am* a brutal criminal."

She stares at the window.

"Go ahead. Ask."

"What happened with your brother? Why did you... gouge out his eyes?"

"Not an easy rumor to come by," I observe.

"It took a bit." She gazes at me, strong and steady. She wants to know. She's different, this girl.

I line my mug handle up with the edge of the counter. "Growing up, it was just the two of us—Alteo and me. Alteo was seven years older and very much my father's son. Violent, angry, and excited to be in the Ghost Hound Clan. For me, the last thing I wanted to do was to follow in his footsteps. But I was expected to. In my world, the sons follow the father."

"Even if they're not into it?"

"It's like the royal family in a way. There's a whole bloodline thing with the clan leaders, the kyre, descending from an ancient king on a mountaintop like our fucking Jesus. It's hard to explain. Our lore and the superstitions that have been handed down are a sort of gospel to us. You don't opt-out. The oldest usually takes over control of the clan, but the younger brother is in the clan, too. Anyway, the fights between my father and me got worse every year. He was a lot harder on me than he was on Alteo. Nothing I did was right. And then, one hot July night, men came to take me to a school. They wouldn't say anything about it, just that it was a school. I absolutely didn't want to go; they had to drug me. I woke up in a cell in St. Neri Reformatory deep in the jungles of Tucumayo."

"Oh my God. Just... no warning?"

"No. The place... it was extreme. It's not exactly the kind of place where you get to go home for Christmas break, either. A lot of troubled kids were sent there. The sort of kids whose parents" didn't want them to go to military school and acquire any sort of skills that could be used against them. I didn't know that then, but it seems obvious now. And maybe that's how they got my mother on board, telling her that it would be rigorous instruction, which there was a lot of. History, math, languages. Classics right alongside rigorous discipline methods. In the end even she didn't lift a finger to get me out of there. And they knew what was going on. If not at first, they surely knew from the letters I smuggled out to them."

"They were whipping you, and your parents don't see fit to get you out?"

"Nah."

"And nobody ever noticed that suddenly this clan family's son had disappeared into thin air?"

"It would have been a problem if not for this prophecy that was circulating at the time. That the youngest son would blind the king and then kill him."

"I heard about it. It's like a really mixed-up version of Oedipus."

"You have done your homework."

"I'm a diligent student." She shrugs. "You said they went too far. Which is hard to imagine considering the whipping."

"People are adaptable. You'd be amazed at what a human being can get used to. Them going far wasn't about draconian punishments or deprivations. It was what they did to the girl I loved then. Her name was Sara."

"Oh no."

"She was a student—an inmate like us, really—at the girls' reformatory connected to the place where we boys were. The girls had it worse than we did." I pause and force myself to look her in the eye for this confession. She needs to know. "Sara died because of me. Because of my carelessness, my selfishness."

She reaches out for my hand. I let her take it.

She says, "Tell me."

"I didn't think. I wanted what I wanted."

"Doesn't sound like you're the one who killed her."

Of course, she'd say that. "Sara was from a town south of Tucumayo. She was a year younger than me but eons more innocent. I mean, a little ruffian, but she'd never even kissed a guy. Things never got much further than that."

"And you loved her."

"To us, it was love, or whatever love is when you're sixteen and seventeen. There was a huge wall between the girls' wing and the boys' wing, but there was a hole in that wall we'd use. Kids sneaking out wasn't unheard of. You put a lot of teenagers in a cage, they'll find ways to do things. She was always really nervous about it, but I promised her she'd be fine. I had no right to make that kind of promise."

"You were just a kid."

"Still," I say.

"So what happened?"

My phone pings right then. It's the doorman asking if he should let this charcuterie delivery team up. Within minutes, there's a dizzying spread of cheeses, dips, crackers, and chocolates, and Edie's eyes are wide as saucers.

"Eat," I say, loading up a cracker with cheese and some sort of jam and handing it to her.

"For me?"

*It's all for you.* But I don't say that. I shove a chocolate into my mouth and continue.

"We were discovered one day, kissing in a nook in the chapel. I was punished, but Sara? She disappeared. I searched all over. Even snuck into the girls' wing to ask the girls what they knew. I wondered if she'd been sent home, but they said that she hadn't, that she was simply taken away. A few weeks later, one of her friends smuggled a note to me telling me that I had to come. That it was about Sara. I followed the directions the girl gave me to a small stone room at the far end of the basement, adjacent to the cemetery. It was full of caskets."

"Oh, Luka," she says.

I can't believe I'm telling her this. I haven't spoken of it to anybody, not even Orton, though he knows what I saw.

"I started throwing open the lids, wrenching them apart with my bare hands. That's when I found her body. She'd been beaten. Killed."

"No."

"Savaged, really. I couldn't see straight, and I went wild. By then, the alarm was up. Three of the schoolmasters rushed down to subdue me and bring me back. They had stun guns they'd use on the boys, and I don't know if they missed or if they jammed some electricity into my veins and I just had too much fury for it to even matter. I ripped those things out of their hands, and I bashed in their heads with a small boulder. I just bashed and bashed. I was so angry, so grief-stricken, and killing them? It was beyond cathartic."

"Is that when you made the bag of rocks that you swung around by a rope?"

"Yup. I was an unstoppable killing machine making my way down through the main hall in the chapel. I grabbed keys at one point and started letting boys out of their cells in the basement, and that's when it became a full-on bloody uprising. The schoolmasters and priests employed guards from the local area, but once these guards saw what was happening, they simply left."

"Wow."

"Someone thought to let the girls out, too, and they went for their teachers and nuns. They'd been amassing weapons, as it turned out, making knives out of pencils and combs. We all had a lot of pent-up rage, which was very unfortunate for the people running the place when the shit finally hit the fan. Calls were put out for help, but the local officials were slow to react. Nobody liked the church down there—not this church, anyway. I killed so many people that day. Once I started, it was hard to stop. I suppose it was in my blood."

"They were your tormenters. It would be in anybody's blood."

I kiss the top of her head, just fucking loving her style.

"Orton was in there, too. He was my friend. Once we got out, we fell into the mercenary life. Twenty years we were in the field."

"Fighting for whoever hired you?"

"We had our standards, but that didn't mean we were good guys. We met Storm a few years in. He's been with me since."

"You inspired two loyal followers before you even took over the Ghost Hound Clan," she observes.

"I wouldn't put it that way, exactly. Orton has a dream, and Storm has a debt, at least in his mind."

"Oh, yeah, okay. Nothing about you."

"Everything's a transaction," I say. "That's what you learn out there."

She takes a chocolate-covered strawberry, inspecting it from all sides before deciding to take a bite off the end.

"Anyway, we weren't planning on coming back. Orton wanted to because he always felt like our place was in the clan. But I wanted nothing to do with the Zogajes. We were in Tunisia one winter and ran into someone from one of the rival clans. That's when I found out what really happened to Sara. It wasn't the schoolmasters and priests who did that to her. It was two men sent by my own brother."

She straightens up, eyes wide.

"Not that the schoolmasters and priests were blameless, but it turned out that my brother was getting reports about me. When Sara and I were discovered meeting in secret, he sent people after her."

"He went after Sara just to... be cruel to you?"

"That was very on-brand for Alteo. Not that I'm trying to excuse myself. Ultimately, it's my fault she died—"

"No, nobody could fault you for having a girlfriend."

"I asked her to meet me. I engineered all of our meetings, and I got her killed. And I didn't even avenge her death well—if I hadn't been so rash, so quick to unleash maximum bloody chaos, I might have taken the time to ask a few questions and get to the truth. My brother and those who helped him kill her wouldn't have been walking free for so many years after." I grab a cheese square. "Not that I'm sorry I killed the St. Neri people. I just would have liked to kill Alteo and his guys sooner."

"Do you think Alteo knew it was you who destroyed that place?"

"It's hard to say. The official story was a rebel militia attacked the place. That story was more convenient to the authorities from a propaganda standpoint, and it certainly worked for us. Most of us were presumed dead."

"So you killed your brother to avenge Sara."

I give her a level look. "Is that really what you want to ask?"

She slides a finger down the foggy side of her glass and back up again before meeting my gaze. "Why did you poke out his eyes?"

I gaze out the window. What I did to my brother is not something I like to talk about or even remember, but I find that I want to tell her. I want to know her. I want to be known by her.

I say, "This part is just for you."

"Okay."

I pick up a toothpick with a bright little bit of cellophane on one end and twirl it back and forth. "If Orton were to tell it, he'd say that an unseen force moved my hand, that it was predetermined rather than a decision."

"But it was a decision?"

"I got him out on a boat. I had to trick him to get him out there."

"Do you think he knew you wanted to kill him?"

"Once we were out there, he did, but by then, it was too late. I was battle-hardened on every possible level, and he'd spent the past two decades smoking cigars and ordering people around."

She picks out another strawberry. It comes to me that she's hungry. "You need some real food."

"I need the rest of your story. I need to know."

"You like to know the bloody things."

"I like to know the real things. The true things. A lot of them just happen to be bloody."

"Like medieval invasions."

"Yeah, we know why you think I study that."

I settle in on the stool next to her. "I wasn't going to kill Alteo like that. I don't have any interest in making people think prophecies come true. People believe enough bullshit as it is. My only goal was to make him suffer. But then he told me something when we were out there. He said that I'm not a real Zogaj, that my mother had had an affair, and that's why I was sent away. He said my father had paid one of the crones in the old country to invent the prophecy about me putting out his eyes so that he'd have an excuse for sending me away."

"So he isn't your real father?"

"Who knows? The idea that I'm not a real Zogaj is the kind of thing my brother would invent. But it also makes sense in explaining why my father hated me. Ultimately, I don't care. I wanted my brother to suffer and die for ordering her killing, I wanted the names of who else did the killing, and I wanted to make them sorry, too."

She nods, rapt.

"Of course, my brother knew he was a dead man out on that boat, and he refused to tell who he'd hired to do the job on Sara. He meant to go to his death in silence, thereby ensuring I'd never learn the truth. Some people, you can inflict maximum pain on them, and they'll pass out before they tell you anything. My brother, that's how he would have been. Not out of bravery so much as spite. He'd always had so much spite toward me."

I can see the wheels in her mind turning. Still not understanding. Of course, she's an outsider.

"Here's the thing you need to know about the Ghost Hound Clan or really any Albanian clan," I say. "It's a very secretive organization. When you're outside of it, you're nothing. But when you're inside, you're in the club. His talking about the prophecy gave me an idea. What if I were to kill him in a way that would align with the prophecy?"

"You blind him and become the promised king."

"Exactly. They'll obey their promised king because they believed in the lore."

"So you forced yourself to put out his eyes," she says. "To fulfill that prophecy and mark yourself as king."

"*The son will blind the kyre and ascend the throne.* I pressed my hands to the sides of his face and gouged out his eyes with my thumbs—slowly—so that he knew what was happening. And then I broke his neck and threw his body near the shore so that everyone could see what had happened."

"Was it..."

"Difficult?" I supply, searching her green eyes. "He was my brother, cruel as he was, so yes, it was difficult." I never told anybody that, but I need Edie to know. I'm done playing monster to her. I need her to know my heart.

"And the people of the clan seem like they've accepted you as their new leader. They really have."

"You saw the situation with the cookies. Most of these people take the lore very seriously. They accepted me instantly."

"You seem good at it."

"It's the lore shit. Even Orton—he's the kind of guy who needs his king to have royal blood. I could be the worst king, and he'd follow me."

"Oh my God, that's why they want your hair," she says.

"Exactly. Truth or fiction, it's gotten around that I might not be a Zogaj. Why a cop would be interested in that angle... let's just say it's odd."

"What would happen to you if it turned out you weren't a real Zogaj?"

"Putting myself up as a false king? Perpetrating that kind of fraud on a dangerous clan? Somebody would have to kill me. Orton might kill me first, just for the sake of his own honor."

"No!"

"Don't worry. Nobody's killing me."

She twists up her lips, eyes squinted. "Orton loves you. I don't see him killing you."

"He can love me and still be able to kill me."

"Luka," she gasps, and I kiss her. She grabs my hair and kisses me back.

"Well, we can't give Bender your hair," she declares. "He'd use it to hurt you if it turned out that what your brother said is true."

"Even if he got my hair, I'd deal with it."

"But obviously, he'd try and test it and find out if you're in the bloodline."

"Don't worry," I say as she plops back into her seat. "A DNA test is just some asshole in a lab. A lab is not Fort Knox. I'm the fucking kyre until I say I'm not."

She smiles and dips a cracker in a spicy berry dip. She likes that. I like that she likes it.

This woman is different. She's different from everyone I've ever known. And suddenly I need to clear the air on something.

"Remember that morning in the hotel after I got in that brawl? With the concussion and all of that, and I told you about the school in Tucumayo?"

"Yes."

"You were so upset. I promised you that the kids were long gone, but it was about more than the other kids for you. You were up in arms because it happened to me. It seemed like you wanted to personally go and firebomb that place."

"I did."

"You had a personal stake in it because it was a shitty thing that happened to me, and you wanted to go after those people."

"Yeah," she says. "And then you acted like an asshole and took my phone away."

"Yeah, I was a total asshole. I couldn't think of what the fuck to do with this fierce, sexy woman who got it in her head to fight for me. What the hell is that, right? It was a good feeling that I didn't trust. I didn't have a category for it. So I ejected you."

She studies my face. Pale green eyes serious. "You hurt my feelings."

"I know. And I'm sorry for that."

She blinks. "Thanks for saying that."

"It meant a lot to me that you wanted to do that. I'm used to being the one to avenge somebody else."

She reaches out and takes my hand.

"So... you hungry?"

She grins. "Is that your limit of caring and sharing?"

"Maybe."

"Well... I'd eat." She looks around. "Don't tell me you cook, too."

"Not at all, but one of the best sushi restaurants in the city is a few blocks up."

She gets a sly grin. "Is your oven an empty cardboard box, too?"

"Are you gonna stop giving me shit about my books anytime soon?"

"No. But yes to the sushi. I love sushi."

"I know."

"How do you know?"

"Takeout menus on your bulletin board. Come on."

# Chapter Forty-Three



The sushi place he likes turns out to be an extremely popular spot with a line out the door.

"Ohhh, no," I say.

"It's fine. There's a table for us."

I follow him up to the host desk. "So nice to see you, Mr. Zogaj." The host heads off. When I look up at Luka, he's giving someone a ferocious stare.

"What?"

I follow his gaze to three men on the other side of the host's desk. He points at his eyes. They straighten up, raising their gazes to the space above my head. "Learn a little respect."

I set a hand on his arm. "It's okay."

"Disrespect is never okay," he says, gaze still fixed hard on them. They seem to have shrunken in size, somehow, huddled together, eager to demonstrate that they're innocent guys talking.

I tug on his shirt, trying to wake him up from whatever fever state he's in and go up on tiptoes to kiss his cheek.

He grabs my hair and kisses me roughly, like all of his dark, protective energy is pouring into that wild and dangerous kiss, and I could live in it forever.

When he pulls away, he seems calmer. And I feel alive. I have the strangest thought that we really do fit together. Like forbidden puzzle pieces nestling right into each other.

I lean my head on his shoulder. Everything smells delicious, and I'm thinking about Mary. Does she have decent food? Tampons? And what will I use as my proof-of-life question? I'm stressing out about it a lot.

Another guy appears—the owner. He shakes Luka's hand. "It's so nice to see you. Please. This way." He leads us to a romantic window table.

Luka pulls my chair out for me as he chats with the owner about some kitchen things.

I grin up at Luka when we're finally alone. "I feel like we got the best table!"

He sits. "My brother was bringing hell down on this place, and let's just say this guy's glad I took over." He hands me a menu. "Everything here is amazing."

"So you like sushi?"

His lips quirk. "It's my favorite."

"What's so funny?"

"Us. Having normal things in common."

We figure out our order and hand back our menus.

"I bet we have a lot of normal things in common," I say.

"Like what?"

"We both speak Latin," I point out.

"Yeah, we haven't discussed that yet, have we? Orton's and my secret fucking language. Nobody's supposed to know that."

I shrug. "Language of medieval manuscripts. Whadya gonna do?"

He grumbles in the joking way he sometimes does. Eventually, our drinks arrive—a scotch for him and a cosmopolitan for me.

I say, "My classics teacher's head would *explode* if he knew people were using Latin to discuss nefarious criminal enterprises."

He picks up his glass and swirls the amber liquid around and around. "The more nefarious, the better."

We talk about his travels and random city things and my textbook idea with my fave girl historian.

It's fun, though sometimes I catch him looking grimly at my wrist, which he so carefully bandaged up before we left.

I'm keenly aware in these moments of what he is, a dangerous—and yes, nefarious—criminal who'd hunt and kill for me. He wants to hunt and kill Bender for what he did to me. He'd rip him apart with his bare hands if he could.

It means everything.

But he'll hold off in order to find and protect Mary. That means everything, too.

Our gazes meet. His dark angel eyes sparkle.

Shivers slide over my skin. I just want to live in this moment.

Our first course comes, and we dig in. The salmon rolls are incredible. He encourages me to taste the surf clam, a.k.a. the hokkigai. "It's mind-blowing when it's fresh."

I sell him on the natto roll, which he seems to have categorized in his mind as hippie sushi. He's shocked that he likes it, which is highly enjoyable due to how expressive I'm learning he can be.

We order another round of just our favorites, and then his phone dings. The way his eyes narrow slightly when he reads the message—not quite his full intimidation squint, but close—is something I've come to recognize. I love how I can read these tiny shifts in his expressions now, like a secret language only I understand.

"Here we go," he says. "Pictures for you to look at."

"To see if any of them are Bender?"

"You good to check them out?"

"Let me at them!"

None of them are Bender, as it turns out. I try not to feel hopeless.

Luka is undeterred. "It means we ruled these guys out, that's all. We'll find him. And we'll find Mary. He'll get what's coming to him."

I nestle a ginger slice onto a bit of sushi, creating a perfect bite. "So you became king—kyre—just to get the killers' names?"

"Yup."

"And then what? When you find and take care of the final guy, will you pass the crown to somebody?"

"I like being king—for now. I'll leave when I decide to leave, and it won't be in a casket, I promise you that. And it won't be because of some DNA test."

It seems so sad. "Your home is temporary. Your job is temporary…"

"Everything's temporary, Edie."

"That's such a cop-out. Even a rental apartment deserves curtains."

He raises an eyebrow. "You suggesting I need curtains?"

"I'm suggesting you stop acting like you're just passing through your own life."

He grunts his neutral grunt. Not a yes, not a no.

We walk down Johnson Avenue after dinner. I haven't spent a lot of time in the Bronx, and it's kind of delightful. Luka can't believe I haven't been to the Bronx Zoo.

"I get that life's temporary," I say, "but it doesn't mean you can't put down your flag and say, 'This is what I want now.'"

"Act as if things aren't temporary?"

"Exactly!"

"That's what's known as a delusion."

"No, it's called hope. It's called defiance." I stop walking. "It's called not being a commitment-phobic fatalist."

He pulls me close. "You're hot when you're worked up."

"Don't deflect. I've seen you running the Ghost Hound family. You went through all this trouble to—you know…"

"Brutally kill my brother?"

"To take the throne," I correct. "And now you run it like you were born for it. That restaurant owner practically genuflected when you walked in."

He gives me his Luka squint. "What'll it take to get you doing that?"

"Shut it!" I give him a playful punch and set back off walking. "You've been king for what—a month? And already, your guys would follow you anywhere."

"You sound like Orton."

"Smart man, that Orton."

"Practical man. He wants to serve a king. The men just want to survive. The restaurant owner just hated my brother. It's not about me."

"And Storm follows you because... what? He likes your cologne?"

"It's all transactions, Edie."

"Oh, please."

He takes my hand. He kisses my fingers.

"You won their loyalty, and you're not gonna convince me otherwise. Not even with sex. The 'nefarious criminal' thing suits you, and you'd throw it all away?"

"The schoolgirl approves? I thought the schoolgirl hated criminals."

I find that I do approve. This is who he is... and I'm rolling with it. "The schoolgirl likes this criminal. And his barbarian might-makes-right thing."

"You are so hot when you're a little bit bad."

I snort and gaze across the street. That's when I spot a bookstore. "Look!"

"Uh-oh," he grumbles.

"Murderous rampages are one thing," I say, "but fake books? That is not a character flaw that I can overlook in a boyfriend."

There's this sudden silence where we both realize I just called him boyfriend.

It's awkward on about ten different levels—at least for me.

Luka not so much. He smiles at me. He likes it. He pulls me to him and kisses me. "Let's get some fucking books, princess."

The bookstore is a labyrinth of worn wooden shelves housed in an old three-story building tucked between a bodega and a laundromat. Inside, the mustiness of aged paper mingles with sandalwood incense and the faint scent of coffee from a tiny counter in the back.

"I could live in this smell," I say.

Luka takes my hand. He's not a man who puts down his flag, but he just agreed he's my boyfriend. It feels strange and dangerous and a little bit wonderful, and I'm not thinking of the future. I suppose you could say I'm ripping a page out of his book for now.

We wander around the main floor, all shiny new books on every subject imaginable.

The upper floors hold the used books. Dusty old scholarly affairs from other centuries, colorful cookbooks and art books, and endless sections of tattered, well-loved paperbacks—mysteries, romances, fantasy, and more.

I find an old edition of a favorite werewolf book of mine. "This is the cover it had when I first read it." I show it to him. We compare it to one of the later editions and discuss which covers are best.

We ramble through the travel section, and I make him show me pictures of Tucumayo. They didn't get out of the prison-like school much, but there was a jungle-y courtyard complete with monkeys.

We head on through the genres. Luka, as it turns out, gravitates toward military science fiction. He shows me a few favorites, but he refuses to buy those because he "already read them."

It's so him not to be sentimental about the past or to buy something he might read again in the future. He thinks of today and possibly tomorrow.

But he does pick out a few new books by authors that he's liked. That's something.

Eventually, we drift over to nonfiction.

"Maybe we should get you a book on meditation, like something on ratcheting down your nervous system," I joke.

"Why would I need that?"

"You almost gutted three men for looking at me."

"I like my nervous system just fine the way it is."

I give him a mischievous smile and threaten him with meditation lessons.

We move as a unit down the rows of books, making comments and showing each other our finds. It feels easy. Even silent browsing feels easy. At one point, he stands behind me with his arms wrapped around my waist and his chin on my head. I feel like we're bandits, spending stolen time together.

I examine some old children's books, and that's when it comes to me. I turn to Luka. "I thought of the proof-of-life question. My sister had this doll named Brittany, and the only food Brittany would eat was chocolate chip pancakes."

"You think she'd remember that?"

"A hundred percent. It was a constant theme. Mom would be angry about it, which was so weird since it was completely imaginary. Mom would randomly add her two cents about eating healthy when she decided to give a shit about us. Which made us embrace Brittany's love of chocolate chip pancakes."

"Perfect. Text him that you have what he wants."

"Right now?"

"You want to move fast on these things—it gives you the advantage. Want me to?" He puts his hand out for my phone.

"No, I'll write it. I just need to think how to put it."

"I'll draft it."

"Shouldn't it be in my voice?"

"The man's not a forensic linguist."

"Fine." I hand over my phone.

He types a while and shows it to me.

> Luka found me somehow. I have his story—it's a shocker—and I have the hair. Ready to meet. But I need proof of life. Ask my sister what Brittany's favorite food was and text me the answer.

"I can't order him around like that! He'll freak out!"

"This is how you do it."

"Maybe how *you* do it, but nobody my age would call something a shocker."

"What would you say?"

"Probably just WTF."

"As an adjective?"

I grin, surprised. "Yeah."

"What?" he says, typing. "Is it such a WTF thing for me to know what an adjective is?"

"Kind of."

"I attended a harshly regimented school run by priests and sadists, princess," he says as he types. "Check it out."

> He found me somehow. I have his WTF story and the hair. Ready to meet. But I need proof of life. Ask my sister what Brittany's favorite food is and text me the answer.

"You don't want him to know your story, though, right?"

"If we have to tell him, we have to tell him. Not much he can do with it."

"Here. Let me." I take the phone back and fix it:

> I have his story WTF!!!! And the hair I'm ready to meet but need proof of life please understand I need to know! ask my sister what Brittanys favorite food is and text me the answer

"Did you just fuck up the punctuation on purpose?"

"Nobody punctuates texts except exclamation points, and periods come off too stern. It's perfect."

"Periods are stern now? Jesus Christ," he says. "Also, you don't say please to a man like that."

"I do."

"Fine. Go ahead and send it."

"Right now?"

"What's there to think about?"

"I don't know. Maybe I want to sit with it."

"You have to get in front of him. Acting first lets you set the terms."

"Maybe I want to think about it, though."

"Don't you want to set the terms?"

"I don't know," I say.

"There's no other way." He takes the phone and hits send.

My jaw drops nearly to the floor. "What did you just do?"

"I sent the text."

"I wasn't ready!"

"Won't improve this situation. You have to start managing this guy before he starts managing you."

"Sending the text was my call to make—mine. This is my sister we're talking about!"

"All the more reason to be fast and firm. That's how we keep her safe."

"I'm not one of your mafia underlings you can order around. I need to trust you to respect my wishes, and you knew I wasn't ready. Did we not just talk about that?"

"I was sure."

"Do you hear yourself? And now he's gonna be mad as a hornet when we meet. Mary is my sister. You can't just take over and decide things."

"There are only two ways this can go. Either Bender will text you with proof of life, in which case I'll scoop him up and make him tell me where she is. Or, if he doesn't have proof of life..."

He doesn't bother to finish the sentence. He doesn't need to. They find him and kill him.

I sit there hating everything.

"This is my world, Edie," he says softly.

"I get it, but let me tell you about *my* world. I grew up with my mom getting jerked around by a string of guys. I watched my sister get jerked around by all kinds of guys, too. I vowed not to let that happen, but I ended up in this Bender situation with another man jerking me around and making me feel like I didn't control things. And I hated it. And I thought you were gonna be different. Like, on my team."

"I *am* on your team. We created a plan that needed to be executed. I've dealt with a million Benders; I know how those motherfuckers think."

"Maybe so, but you needed to get me there. I get a say. Didn't you promise that I didn't have to live by your mafia rules? It means that this thing we have can't be a dictatorship with you as the all-powerful king. It needs to be a democracy."

He stares out the ancient-looking window. You can see bricks and the corner of a pizza place sign, lit in red and green neon.

I wait, holding my breath. I need him to get my point of view. I need it more than most things I needed lately.

He finally speaks. "You're right. What the fuck. I just said I wouldn't do that kind of thing, and then I went and did it."

"I mean, I get that you're invested," I say. "So am I."

"It was a fuckup, Edie. Other people having a say... it's not natural for me."

I slide my finger over his. "We both count. Our opinions both count."

He narrows his eyes at me. "You are not going to make this easy."

"I'm not."

"Nothing good is easy, though." He comes to me. "We both count. Maybe I'll tattoo it on my hand or something."

"I think that would be weird? And open to a lot of weird interpretations?" I say.

"We both count," he says in a really serious tone. "Except when it comes to coming. You come first, and you count more."

"I'll allow that exception."

I check my phone constantly on the way back to his place with our haul of books.

"He's not going to get back to you for a while," Luka says, setting the box on the kitchen island. "He wants you to sweat now. He wants you to feel nervous, but I promise you, if he has her or has any kind of line on her, he's finding the answer to that question."

"How long do you think he'll try and make me sweat? Because I'm already sweating."

"And he knows it."

"I'm not made for this."

He comes to me. "It's alright. I am. I got you."

"While also soliciting my buy-in on important decisions."

He snorts softly into my hair. "Yes."

I pull away. "It's almost dinnertime now, and I have a major paper due that I'm wildly behind on."

"You'll do it here."

"No, I'll do it at my place. I'll hole up in the study commons."

I can see him really, really wanting to order me to be at his place.

"I have to write this paper, or I'm so screwed. The worst thing that could possibly happen to me is the vending machines running out of corn nuts."

"Bender's dangerous."

"I'll promise to contact you the instant I hear anything from him if you promise to think things through like what we talked about."

He comes to me. "In my all-powerful kyre brain, you mean?"

I kiss him on his whiskery cheek. "Yes, please."

# Chapter Forty-Four

### EDIE

I've made decent progress on my paper by the end of the weekend, organizing the shape of my argument, marshaling supporting research, and then roughing out my opening and closing. I grab a snack from the room and find Odetta there. I get the highlights of her glamorous weekend and then head back down to polish up my masterpiece. I'll give it one more good pass tonight and wake up bright and early to do a final pass before turning it in.

Just as I'm settling into my spot, I get a Snapchat alert.

I fumble through my bag and pull out my phone. It's Janey.

*D has some important new deets on that research project and he wants to give you your book back he'll be in his residence hall cafeteria tomorrow morning at ten if you want to stop by it took him an hour just FYI*

I sit up. I forgot about Darren. Does he have intel on my sister? Is it possible we could bypass Bender altogether?

Me: *Can you say which research project this pertains to?*
Janey: *Of course not bc enigmatic!*

I deposit the bitcoin money immediately into Darren's account to show him I'm interested. Ten o'clock is totally doable. I'll have turned in my paper, and my Classics seminar ends at nine.

I text Luka before I turn in to let him know there's been no text from Bender.

---

There's still nothing from Bender the next morning. I let Luka know, finish my paper like a boss, turn it in, and head off to class. I have the rest of the day to study for Indo-European after I meet with Darren.

The first thing I notice when I get to Darren's residence hall is the line of police cars with cherries blazing. I head straight for the cafeteria, wondering if Darren will know what happened, but he's nowhere to be seen. It's just a few minutes before ten, so I wait. And wait. Did he give up on me? I walk around the place as the time ticks by. He's five minutes late. Then ten. Did the police spook him?

I find his room number from the directory and head up. Students are clustered in the hall, some talking to cops. I ask a girl if she's seen Darren.

"They just took him out of here. He's in a coma. Somebody tried to kill him."

My blood freezes in my veins. "Is he... gonna survive?"

"No clue," she whispers.

"Do they know who..."

She shakes her head.

I'm mortified. Did Darren get hurt because of the research he was doing for me? I have this horrible feeling that he did.

Cops are interviewing students up and down the hall. I push my way up to where bright yellow tape blocks one of the doors. Darren's room.

A uniformed officer stands just inside the door while other

police officers mill around inside; most are clustered in and around the far room, probably one of the bedrooms. You can see special lights and techs with foot coverings in there.

"Stay back," says the officer at the entrance.

"What happened?"

He doesn't answer.

My heart pounds. Did Darren find out where my sister is and get attacked for it? Did he do more research on Luka and get attacked for that?

My gaze drifts to the little table next to the door. There's a copy of *The Elements of Style* with a pink Post-it stuck to it and ED scrawled on top. He probably set it there to take down when we were going to meet. Did Darren stick notes inside the book like he did last time? Is the key to finding my sister in there?

I've seen enough police procedurals to know they probably wouldn't let me take it.

"I was supposed to meet Darren just this morning," I say to nobody in particular.

This gets the attention of a woman with a notepad—a detective, I think. She comes over. "When did you last see Darren?"

"Last week. He was helping me with some research, and I lent him a book. We had plans to meet for coffee this morning, but he wasn't there."

"You're a student here?"

I nod, getting up my nerve to ask for the book. "Yes. History. Medieval studies."

She asks if he seemed agitated in any way or if he mentioned any enemies or upcoming appointments he was worried about. People having it in for him. The nature of my research. I tell her it had to do with European families that stretch back centuries, which isn't entirely a lie.

A guy in a red sports jersey pushes past me, bursting right in. "What the fuck! Where is he?"

It's unclear if he's talking about Darren or whoever did this to

Darren, but it's enough to grab everybody's attention. This is my chance to nick the book.

I hesitate. It's a big move, but then I think about Luka and force myself to channel him. Luka doesn't fret about the future. He would make a bold plan and execute it.

I reach out, swipe the book, and shove it into my pocket.

Did I just do that?

Yes. Yes, I did.

It seems like nobody saw me take it. I think.

My pulse whooshes in my ears.

I'm no master criminal, but I think I'm in the clear... unless I try running out of here. I need to wait because the detective obviously wasn't done with me.

I go for a bored face, but the inside of my head feels like a blaring siren.

The detective comes back and gives me a card. "If you think of anything more that might help us—even if it seems insignificant—gimme a call."

I assure her that I will, and I get out of there as fast as I can.

I force myself to walk a full two blocks before I duck into a bagel shop around a corner and get in line. I check around for cameras—more of channeling Luka—and, satisfied there aren't any, pull out the book like I'm just a bored college student grabbing study time in line.

There is, in fact, a scribbled note stuck inside on light blue paper. I pull it out and open it up.

There's a name at the top—*Zamir Prifti*—underlined twice. *Born: St. Louis Fernbrook Health Center. Data leak: boon!* There's a date of birth that makes this person a little older than Luka.

*Mother: Felicia Warner. Father: Besa Zogaj. BA, Psychology; University of Missouri–St. Louis. Scholarship: track, 3x state champ - hammer + shotput.* Then: *Half Zogaj brother.*

*Discuss:*

*•Dropped off face of earth 7 yrs ago*

*•Track team photos: ALL missing ???*
*•Name change / NYC?*
*•THE CHATTER!!!*

I stand there staring at the paper.

Luka has a half-brother? This is important information for him.

This is how Darren did the notes last time, with the discussion topics arranged in bullet points, and he filled me in on each one. But none of them were in all caps. What is the chatter? What did he find, exactly?

He told me nobody would be more thorough. He seemed proud of that. And he had said that he had more leads. This must have been what he was talking about.

And it very well might have gotten him killed.

What's up with the track team photos? I pull out my phone and do some googling around collegiate Missouri championship track teams from the years that would put this half-brother in his late teens and early twenties. Sure enough, the Hammer team is missing all three years where Zamir's name is mentioned. The shotput squad is missing two years when Zamir's name is there. But the team pictures are there in the years before and after in their matching red shirts.

There's some sort of hammer team insignia on the shirts that looks oddly familiar. I zero in on them and realize they look like Thor's hammer.

The exact same insignia that was on Bender's red shirt that day at the fountain.

Is Bender Luka's brother? Is that why he wanted the DNA?

# Chapter Forty-Five

## LUKA

The call comes in the next morning just as Orton and I are getting out of a meeting. My guys located Declan, the last of the guys who attacked and killed Sara.

My vengeance is wrapping up.

"Bundle him up and bring him to the tech dock." I pocket my phone.

"They got Declan?" he asks.

"Yep."

The tech dock is a gloomy stretch of waterfront. There's a direct shot out to open water where sharks are sure to find a corpse before the authorities ever will.

I get Orton up to speed on the situation with Bender. He's shocked and angry and has lots of feelings about Edie, but I give him a hard look, and that's that.

"Fine." Orton looks thoughtful. "In other news, I heard rumblings of some guy offering serious money for a hair off your head. The guys were talking about it. Now that I hear all this, I'm thinking it must've been this fucking cop. Bender."

"Bender needs to die," I say.

"He wants to show you up as a fraud and make us turn on

you," Orton says. "If he gets that hair to test, he'll be sadly disappointed."

*Or not,* I think, marveling at how convinced Orton is that I'm a true Zogaj after all that my brother said.

"I knew that girl wasn't right," he grumbles as we reach the door.

I give him another hard look. "She kept important secrets in the face of enormous pressure, and she warned us off."

"She lied," he says.

I slam him against the wall, forearm across his throat. "She's mine."

His gaze sharpens. "Is that how it is?"

My voice drops to a deadly whisper. "That's exactly how it is."

Shouts from inside.

I let him go and barge in. There's a man tied to a chair, and that chair is currently on its side.

"Good job," I say to the guys. "Go get a sandwich. We'll call you when we need some cleaning."

The guys clear out.

The man makes pleading sounds from behind the bandana that's tied around his mouth.

Orton rights the chair and yanks down the bandana.

"Please. Whatever you want. I've got money. I'll do a freebie kill. I'll do ten."

"Are you looking for mercy?" I lean in close, my voice a razor. "You didn't have any mercy for that girl you killed down in Tucumayo, did you?"

"It was a job."

"She was a kid."

"Just business," he says.

"She was a kid," I repeat.

He straightens. "She was a whore."

I grab his throat, meaning to rip it out.

A calming hand holds my arm. Orton. "He wants you to kill him fast." *Don't take the bait,* he means.

"Right." I leave him there, bleeding and broken, and grab a Dr. Pepper from the machine.

"What's up?" Orton asks, strolling over.

"I'm not feeling it."

"We could keep him on ice for you."

"It's not that." I take a sip and stroll over to the guy. "A young girl suffered because of you. She was just a kid."

The man eyes me, panting. Bleeding.

Orton comes up beside me. "Still not feeling it?"

"I don't know."

"What does your intuition say?"

Orton's a big believer in intuition, especially with me. He buys into the idea that the *kyre* has divine prescience.

The guy squirms and whines.

"Shut up," I say to him.

"You know what I think? I think you're not ready to be done with this whole thing." Orton makes a hand motion meaning *the whole Ghost Hound Clan thing.* "Once you complete your vengeance, the mission is complete. We've always waited for the next mission to come up. What if we say we're done with missions? We could choose this. Permanently."

"Yeah, I know your feelings on the matter."

"But do you know your feelings? You like it. It suits you."

"You sound like Edie."

"You've discussed this with Edie?" he asks, shocked.

I nod. If you had told me that night in the hotel bar that I'd be discussing this sort of thing with her, I would have been shocked, too.

Orton and Storm have always been my inner circle. Women were always just transactions.

"So you're just... all the way in with her," Orton says.

"I'm all the way in. And that's not up for debate."

"You need to think long and hard before you let a girl influence you," Orton warns. "You have power. You have wealth. People are fucking scared of us. We're at the top of our game. Once you walk away, you can't come back. This is your destiny."

"You're not listening," I say. "She's good with all this."

Orton straightens. "That little girl?"

"Don't let the pastels fool you. She's one of us."

I tell him about Bender threatening her family and fucking her up. How she gave him nothing he could use, and what she did give, it was to protect us. A fucking civilian and she ran that cookie op. I tell him about her impulse to go down to Tucumayo and make them answer for what they did to me. Bloodthirsty. Loyal.

"In the world of fight or flight, she fights," I say. "Right in there with me."

"You have seemed more focused since she's been around," he observes. "And she's really down with this life?"

"She's down with this. Down with me."

Orton grunts.

I gaze out the dusty high window. It's so dirty, you can barely see the sky. "And she's mine," I say with finality. No need to use the L-word with Orton.

Edie with her unicorns and cherry lip balm and sexy lips and fake squints that are supposed to look like my squint. *Mine.*

"And I love her."

Orton stands there, just staring at me. "Wow."

The guy whimpers. We still ignore him.

"Not like she doesn't make me crazy, though," I confess. "She thinks relationships have to be like democracies. Even when one person knows a shit ton more than the other person about how something should be played, it doesn't matter because, apparently, it's a fucking democracy."

Orton laughs. "Trouble in paradise."

"Fuck off."

"What happened?"

I tell him about the text fight. I don't know why I'm telling him. He's never had a real relationship, either.

The guy is moaning.

"You came for the vengeance, but you're staying for the power—and the girl," he adds.

"You're right." I pull out my piece, level it at the hitter's head, and pull the trigger

"It's done," Orton says. "With every prick, the spider's web tightens, thorn for thorn, blood for blood. And now the vengeance is done." Orton lights a match, lets it burn down to the end, and then throws it into the small puddle near the drain.

I grab my phone to turn on the sound and see the texts, the first string from Storm:

> They have your DNA at Stackhardt Labs out near La Guardia. Fuck that. Bust some heads?

Then another:

> Now or never. Shut this thing down?

Then another:

> DNA thing is up and down the grapevine. People already saying you're not blood. We can get to the lab if we leave now.

And then there's a string from Edie, ending with:

> Need to talk ASAP.

# Chapter Forty-Six

## EDIE

"Did you have an order?"

I look up into the exasperated expression of the man behind the bagel shop counter.

I've texted Luka twice and there's been no reply.

"If you need more time, can you please step aside?" he asks.

I mumble something about having to leave and bolt out of the place. My knees are shaking. Bender is Luka's half-brother. Is he even a cop?

Did he erase those pictures from the web? And if it's that important for him not to be recognized, did he kill to keep his secret? God, did I get poor Darren hurt—or worse?

And what does it mean for Mary?

I tell myself that Darren probably had his fingers in a lot of secret information. Isn't the dark web full of killers and criminals?

But the timing seems suspicious.

Did he follow me to Darren's? I feel like I shouldn't go back to the residence hall.

With shaking hands, I text Luka yet again.

Heading to your place.

I can't think of what to do next. My blood is racing, and I can't think straight.

I should take an Uber, but what if Bender is tracking my credit card activity or something? If he sees that I called an Uber, he might be able to find out where I went.

I decide on the subway. I'm about to look up the best route on my phone, but then I set it to airplane mode, turn it off, and shove it back in my pocket because I'm in full-blown paranoia now.

I'll do the old-fashioned thing and check an actual map. I make a beeline to the 116th Street station, stop at the map and figure out how to get myself near Luka's condo. It's just one transfer. I could be there in under an hour. But then I'd use tap-and-go and that could be tracked.

"Hey, fancy meeting you here."

I know that voice.

*Bender.*

I fix my gaze on the map, pretending not to hear him. What if I darted down the steps into the subway? Would he chase me? But it's not like I can run forever down there. Could I bolt up the sidewalk?

Running for it will probably tip him off that something's up.

My stomach folds in on itself once and then again and then a third time. My stomach is a diamond of fear at this point. It's a wonder I'm standing upright.

"Hey." He comes up and stands next to me. He looks like his normal self, except he has a uniform on. He's Luka's half-brother. *And* he's a cop.

"I got your text."

I slap on my most neutral and bored face. My first thought is that he got the text I sent to Luka, but then I realize he's talking about the proof of life ask.

"You didn't respond," I say.

He grins. "Well, I was busy asking your sister your completely random question."

"You were?"

"What is her doll's favorite food," he says. "That would be chocolate chip pancakes, I believe?"

Something in my chest unclenches. "She's alive?"

"Of course she is," he says. "And I believe you have something for me now?"

"I—I don't have the hair with me."

"That's okay. I got the hair from another source."

"You did?" My mind spins. I have to warn Luka.

Bender smiles like a Cheshire cat. "But I will take the story. Tell me where he was."

My pulse races. This isn't how it's supposed to go. "And you'll tell me where my sister is?"

"Yes. In fact, she's been asking for you."

"So... you talked to her? Is she okay?"

"As okay as she can be in rehab. I know she's been complaining about the food."

"She's in rehab? Where?"

"Here in the city." He puts out his hands. "But don't you have something for me first?"

"The story," I say.

"All ears."

I did tell him I had the story, but something about all of this feels too easy. But he's watching my face, waiting. Luka did say he didn't care if we had to tell him.

"He was in South America. Some reformatory in the jungle. When the place was attacked, he and Orton got out and went into the mercenary life."

"Hold on. He was in a correctional school?"

"Yes, and they were kept under lock and key and taught by harsh priests. The whole thing."

"Did you happen to get the name?"

"Saint something?"

"You don't remember?" He pulls in a breath like he's struggling to keep his voice pleasant. "You were supposed to remember. Fine, never mind. And now I suppose you want your sister," he says mockingly.

The whole thing feels weird, but I can't tell if it's because I'm still so freaked out about Darren or the fact that Bender is being so pleasant. "Yes, I want to know about my sister."

He sighs dramatically. "I suppose you've earned it. She's in the south wing of St. Benhilda. It's a locked rehab facility."

"And she's been in that rehab this whole time?"

"It was the only way to keep her on ice for you, and no offense, but she wasn't gonna clean up on her own. It's a little bit beyond the pale, I know, but I think you'll agree we've both gone beyond the pale."

"So if I go there... I mean, can I just show up?"

"No, I'd have to sign her into your custody. She's on what is known as a ten-week lockup. We could take care of that right now." He checks his phone. "Otherwise, you're going to have to wait for the weekend. I'll sign her into your custody, and we'll call it even. Your record'll be clean, and we never met. Got it?"

He nods his head at a police car double-parked near the crosswalk.

I feel so confused. What if he didn't kill Darren? What if this is exactly what it looks like: that Luka has a half-brother who's obsessed with knowing about him? One thing I know for sure is he has my sister. She's alive and well. There's no other way he could have gotten that information.

"Where is this place?"

"Queens. Just over the bridge."

"Why didn't she contact me?"

"Rules. Like I said, it's a locked facility. Come on. I have to be back across town at three. We're doing this now or next week. Up to you." He walks to his car.

I catch up. "All this time and they didn't let her contact family?"

"What part of locked rehab rules do you not understand?"

"But isn't it illegal to hold someone against their will for more than seventy-two hours?"

He opens his door.

I step back. This is all wrong. "You know what? I'll arrange to contact her myself. I don't need a ride." I will not be getting in a car with him. No chance. Plus, I have to warn Luka.

"You can't visit without an official in."

I stand firm. "I'm good."

He comes to me. I back up. "I'll go on my own." He grabs my arm and takes my phone before I feel a prick like a needle jab into my neck.

"Hey!"

He turns me around, and I feel cuffs being slipped over my wrists. My injured one screams out in pain. I try to call out, but my voice is suddenly as feeble as the rest of me. I feel like I'm in one of those dreams where you try to fight back but your limbs won't cooperate.

The sidewalk goes tilted. People are avoiding us and walking around us. I can hear him reciting my Miranda rights before he shoves me into the back of his car.

# Chapter Forty-Seven

## EDIE

A familiar voice calls my name. "Edie! Oh my God, Edie! Wake up!"

I don't know if it's an hour later or a day later that I become conscious. I'm lying sideways on a cold, hard floor with something soft under my head, like a sweater, and all I know is that I just want to sleep through whatever nightmare this is.

Gentle hands shake my shoulder frantically. "Edie! Please! Wake up!"

I feel like I'm in a dream, like we're back in school, and Mary's bugging me to get up. "Sto-op," I complain, my head pounding.

Gentle fingers pat my cheek, then more urgently. "Edie, Edie, Edie! Oh God, what did he do to you?"

I force my eyes open through the fog. A face swims into view, one I've been searching for desperately. For a moment, I think I'm hallucinating.

"Mary?" My voice breaks. My heart nearly stops. "*Mary*?!"

"Oh, thank goodness!" Mary's voice cracks with emotion. She's crying, her eyes red-rimmed and wild. "I thought you were— I didn't know if you'd—"

"Is it really you?" I struggle against the handcuffs digging painfully into my wrists, desperate to touch her, to make sure she's real. "How are you here? Where is here?"

"That psycho cop brought you in unconscious. I've been going out of my mind!" She's trembling, her hands fluttering over me like she's afraid I might shatter. "What the hell is happening? Why are *you* here? You're the one who's supposed to be safe!"

Blinking, I pull myself up to sit against the wall, my head spinning. Dim light filters through a filthy window at the far end of the place, beyond the bars that surround us. The reality of our situation crashes down on me.

"We're in a cage," I whisper, the horror of it sinking in. "Both of us."

"That jackass's basement," she says, her voice cracking as she pulls me into an awkward hug with my hands still cuffed. "I've been here for weeks, but you—oh, Edie. *Why* are you here?"

"I've been looking for you everywhere," I manage, tears streaming down my face. "I was so scared you were dead."

"I'm so sorry, I'm so sorry—" Her voice breaks into a sob.

"Stop with the sorrys. Are you okay?" I ask, scanning her for injuries. She looks thinner and her skin is sallow, but she's whole.

She laughs bitterly, wiping tears from her cheeks. "Aside from being trapped in this hellhole for five weeks? Aside from watching that creep walk in dragging my practically lifeless little sister? I thought he killed you!"

"Mary." I wish I could hug her back properly. "I was so scared I'd never see you again."

"How did you get mixed up in this?" Her eyes are wide with terror. "He showed me pictures of you with those men—"

"Looking for you. It's a long story, but I've been searching everywhere."

"He said—" she choked on the words. "He said you were working for him now. That you were with those men because of me. That you went out to talk to the girls on Garrison to find me because I didn't take your call on my birthday, and he caught you in a sweep and made you his bitch. He says he's making you prostitute yourself to disgusting, cruel mafia guys because of me and you go home crying and you're flunking out—"

"Mary, he's messing with you."

"But I saw the picture of you looking miserable in a butt-ugly skin-tight dress you'd never ever wear with a hairdo done like a sad clown 1980s news anchor at some bar. He says that's how you dress now—"

"And you believed him? That I dress like a sad clown 1980s news anchor now? You have insulted my fashion choices in the past, but seriously?"

She sniffles and laughs through her tears. "But the picture—I know what I saw."

I shift my shoulders around, trying to ease the pressure. One of the things they don't tell you about wearing handcuffs behind your back long-term is that it's really painful for your shoulders. And my injured wrist is throbbing like crazy.

"Those handcuffs look tight," she says.

"Never mind about that," I say. "What happened with you?"

She tips her head against the wall. "I'm sorry I didn't take your call."

"What happened? It was your birthday."

"I know. I was so drunk and so baked, and I couldn't deal with talking to you like that. But then I felt like an asshole the day after. I couldn't call because I knew I was making bad decisions. I promised myself I'd straighten up and call you with good news for once, and then one day turned into the next. I was such a shit!"

"You have nothing to apologize for."

"I have everything to apologize for. I really wanted to have cleaned up my act the next time I talked to you. And I was starting to—ten days I was sober—and then I was at this shelter in New

Haven, and this guy showed up. He was in uniform, telling me that you're in trouble, and then he tricks me and brings me here. I'm so sorry, Edie. And you ended up having to do all this stuff for me..."

"There's no amount of stuff that I could do that would repay you for the way you saved my life growing up. You gave up your childhood to care for me. You gave up everything—"

"That is so not true," Mary says.

"It is true. I survived because of you," I say. "You saved me. You took every kind of bullet for me."

"Edie, no—"

"You made everything better, and not one day goes by that I'm not aware of the sacrifices you made. I'll never repay that debt. Not ever."

"You don't know what you're talking about," she says. "Saving you saved me."

"You're just saying that."

"Fuck off if you don't believe me," Mary says. "Taking care of you kept me from going off the deep end. If there's any debt to pay, it's the one I owe you."

"Disagree," I say.

"Disagree with your disagree."

"Disagree with your disagree with my disagree." We go on like this for a while. It's an old game.

She holds up a dingy plastic water bottle. "You thirsty? I could pour this in your mouth. It's drinkable. He gets it out of the sink over there."

"As long as you don't dribble it on me," I say. "Sad clown doesn't like water on her."

She snorts and carefully pours it into my mouth. "That guy's a real prick."

I wipe my mouth on my shoulder the best I can.

"There are some bits of truth to what he told you. I did go

looking for you, and he did scoop me up and make me sit with some mafia men wearing that horrible dress. But I didn't have sex with somebody gross, so you don't have to worry about that."

"You promise?"

"Promise. But... I did have sex with somebody I met there, and if I could do a chef's kiss right now, I would. And that's all I'll say on the matter."

"Wait, what?" She blinks. "You had sex with somebody from the mafia?"

"Yeah," I say.

"You? And a mafia guy?"

I shrug.

Her eyes go wide.

"What? Don't be so shocked."

"Edie, you hate criminals."

"Not all criminals. Apparently."

"Ohmigod. He told me you had to blow ten men at once—"

"Excuse me? Absolutely not true. And gross!"

Mary gusts out a breath of relief. "I wanted to kill myself!"

"Well, now I want to kill him."

"Get in line," she says.

I hoist myself up to standing and kick at the bars, finding the spot where the bar meets a crumbly-looking wall.

"Don't bother. I've tried. Every which way."

"Fuck." I awkwardly slide back down to the floor. "Seriously, these cute cowboy boots? But you believed my new fashion is sad clown 1980s? This is what you believed?"

"No, the boots are good." She lowers her voice. "Do you have any paperclips in your pockets or an underwire bra on?"

"No, why?"

She looks around. "Check out what I've been making." She pushes away some crumpled papers and pulls out a long, skinny, gnarled stick with a bend at the end like a shepherd's crook.

It's maybe four feet long and rigid but sort of fragile.

"I made it out of dried celery and chicken bone and gum. It's wrapped with threads from my socks and some of my hair."

"Ummm... I guess it's nice? Maybe just not my style."

"Fuck off." She hides it again. "Sometimes he leaves his keys on the bench over there, and if I get it long enough, I feel like I could hook them and let myself out."

"Wow. That's actually kind of amazing."

I can't feel my fingers on my right hand. The wrist he injured is probably swollen up like a balloon, cutting off the blood supply to my hand. It hurts, and I'm getting worried. Could that do permanent damage? Could I literally lose my right hand?

"Seriously want to kill him," I say.

"I'm so glad you're okay. You have no idea," Mary says.

"Well, I don't have a gross pole made of dried celery and my own hair, but other than that..."

"That gross pole is gonna get us out of here."

I give her a solemn look. "We've seen his face, Mary."

"I know," she says softly. "He's completely unhinged. You have no idea."

"I have some idea." I stand up again and go to the bars, staring hopelessly out at the dank basement. Bender is an outright sociopath who probably killed Darren, but it doesn't seem like a helpful detail to add.

"Hey." She comes up to me and pokes me in the shoulder. "We'll figure this out. We're the Flying Frittatas."

I manage a smile at the stupid name we used to call ourselves. Blast from the past. "Where did we even think of that?"

She shakes her head.

"Frittata," I say.

"Forget frittatas—a mafia guy? You?"

"I know."

My right-hand fingers are all pins and needles now. It hurts.

"Miss Straight-A Proper Girl? *You* are into a *literal* mafia guy?"

"Yeah. Luka. He's hot and wild and brilliant, and we have fun together, and he's a caveman and a gentleman—"

"Ohhhh, hold on. Luka Zogaj? Bender's brother Luka?"

I nod. So it's official. Darren was right, and Bender knows.

"Bender is obsessed with him! He talks about him constantly. Luka fucked up his life or something."

"Nothing like how Luka's gonna fuck up his life once he finds us," I say bravely, even though I have no reason to think Luka would be able to find us. "He's gonna fuck him up so hard…"

Footsteps sound out, coming down the stairs.

Bender appears.

I back up—I can't help it.

Mary puts a protective arm around me. She always knows when I'm scared.

"Who's gonna fuck up who?" Bender asks, coming right up to the bars. "My brother? Is that who?"

"Fuck you," she says.

"I'm talking to your sister."

"I have nothing to say to you," I say.

"Hey, those handcuffs are really tight," Mary says. "How about you gimme the keys so I can take them off her?"

"They're really tight?" Bender says with a mock face of concern.

"I can't feel the fingers on my right hand," I say. "I don't think there's any blood going to my fingers."

"Come on," Mary says, ever my protector. "You already have her in a cage. There's no need to handcuff her."

"It pleases me. Isn't that enough?"

I glare.

"Fine, come here," Bender says. "I'll adjust them."

"You will?"

Bender taps the bars with his keychain. "Put 'em here." He points at Mary. "You—back to the wall."

Mary backs up to the wall.

I go to the bars and turn so that he has access to the cuffs.

Can I grab his phone? His gun?

He circles my wrists with his hands, and there's a sickening click before he makes them tighter.

"Ow! Hey!"

Mary rushes up, but he backs up just in time, laughing. "Any other requests?"

"Gimme the keys!" Mary demands.

"She's not gonna need those hands anyway."

"Come on," Mary pleads.

"Psycho," I say.

"My goodness, such attitude! I said I'd help you find Mary, didn't I? And look. I brought you right to her. And now you're giving me attitude? Is that any way to treat the newest kyre of the Ghost Hound Clan? The last remaining brother?"

My blood goes cold. Luka is dead? No, there's no way. "You're lying."

"Your boyfriend is currently ensnared in what I like to call a triple trap. Do you wanna know what that is?"

"No," I whisper miserably.

"A triple trap is a trap inside a trap inside a trap," Bender says. "By now, he'll have learned that one of his own loyal men gave up his hair for testing. Sad."

*So he's not dead yet. Okay.*

"Doesn't say much about his leadership, does it? His own guy heard I wanted one of his hairs for testing and sought me out. He was that desperate to bring Luka down. The Albanians are extremely serious about their bloodlines," Bender continues. "Sadly for Luka."

I grit my teeth. Luka was good to his men and a good leader, and one of them turned on him? He'd hate it.

Worrying about Luka helps take my mind off my hand, at least.

"He'll have the address of the lab by now, as well as the schedule, which is slated to be on the testing docket..." He glances at his phone. "In about one hour. The place is out in New Jersey, and my guess is that he's already there. I've got sharpshooters in place, and he'll be killed before he even gets in."

I feel like throwing up.

"I've also got an assassin inside just in case he makes it that far. And you know what else is so perfect? If I'd killed Luka myself, I'd have the whole clan gunning for me, but if somebody takes him out trying to stop a DNA test?" He gives me a smug shrug. "Nobody avenges the death of a fraud."

I shift my shoulders, trying desperately to ease the pain. "He'll smell your trap."

"He'll still go in."

Bender's right, of course. Luka doesn't back down from things. Nobody takes what's his.

"Not only that, but he'll go in alone. It's not the kind of thing he would ask his men to help him with."

"If Luka wants to stop the test, he'll stop the test."

Bender just laughs and shakes his head as he checks his phone.

I exchange glances with Mary. In another life, we might think it was funny that he was explaining his whole plan like a Bond villain or something. But maybe that's an actual problem for criminals—the only people you would tell about your plan are the ones you're planning on killing.

Bender's right that Luka wouldn't bring his men to raid a testing facility.

*A lab is not Fort Knox.*

Miserably, I think of my fight with Luka. He was being bossy, but he was just trying to help.

If only I could figure out a way to warn him. My gaze falls on Bender's phone. If we could get it away from him...

"If he *does* manage to get in and stop the test—pretty big if—it won't matter because I split the hair sample so it's being run concurrently at another lab. Once the test results are out there, he's a dead man. His own people will kill him. The men of the clans hate a fraud."

"How are you so sure that he's not a real Zogaj?"

"My mother told me, and she heard it from my father."

"Oh, so it must be true," I snip.

"I doubted it myself at first. Mom was off her rocker, especially at the end there, so I didn't think she meant it literally. Nobody cared because Luka was out of the picture. Quite possibly dead. But when he came back and I heard the rumor and looked at the photos, I realized my mom was telling the truth. You only have to look at the pictures. Alteo and I look like the old man, whereas Luka doesn't."

"Sounds like a lot of wishful thinking to me."

"More like a wish come true." Bender scrolls on his phone. "I had a good thing going. I kept our clan safe from law enforcement, and Alteo set me up with more money than I'd ever be able to spend. But then Luka had to come in and ruin all of that." He glances up at Mary. "You know he gouged out his own brother's eyeballs? I'd call that a red flag."

"Depends on the brother," Mary says.

Bender doesn't think that's funny. "I decided it was time to take over. My first idea was to get Luka arrested, connecting him to clan crimes that I knew about, but this is much better, don't you think? The mysterious Luka Zogaj killed while trying to conceal evidence that he's a false king."

I stand there wishing desperately that I knew Luka's number. That we could get Bender's phone and send him a 'here's my location' text. But then I remember the restaurant. He owns it, right? Mary could look up that number and leave a short message there.

"Luka totally looks like his father," I say.

"Are you kidding?" Bender scrolls furiously.

Mary leans against the bars nearby, playing it cool. We've always been really intuitive with each other, and she's decided to follow my lead.

"Also, what father banishes his kid to some jungle correctional school?" Bender continues. "The father of a bastard, that's who."

"Yeah, yeah, yeah," I say.

"Here." He holds up his phone with an image of Bender and Alteo. I recognize Alteo from one of the newspaper articles. The phone is too far away to grab, unfortunately.

"I can't see," I say.

"Do I look stupid to you?" He waves his phone around. "This what you want?"

Sigh.

"My fake brother has finally met his match," Bender crows.

"So that's your triple trap?" I ask. "You kill him when he goes to the lab, or else his men kill him?"

"Keep up, that's only two parts of it. If my shooters don't get him and if he somehow survives his own people killing him, I'm guessing he takes his millions and heads overseas. Or will he? That's where you come in. A few fingers in the mail might encourage him to change his plans. Albanians can't resist the siren call of a severed finger."

I feel sick.

"A good cop covers his bases," he adds.

"Too bad you're not a good cop."

He laughs. "True enough, but I'll be an amazing kyre. But I know what you're thinking. That that part of the plan is pretty weak. Are you really that good of a piece of ass? Will he come for you? Or will he look at the fingers I send and toss them on his way to hashtag beach life? We'll see about that."

"Yeah, we'll see," I say.

I have this strange sense right then that's hard to describe. It's something good, like the feeling of peace and hope coming over me.

Like Luka might be near.

Wishful thinking, no doubt. After all, Luka has the DNA hair test to deal with, which is a matter of life and death. My last text was just that we needed to talk.

Still, I have the uncanny feeling that he's near.

Bender rakes his gaze over my body. "Maybe I'll even take a taste for myself before I kill you. Or we can have some hot sister action in exchange for a merciful end." He draws near. "Maybe we do a twist on Scheherazade where you two can cook up increasingly exciting thrills for me in exchange for extra days."

"Gross." Mary goes back and sits against the wall.

"Personally, I'll go with death," I say.

He snorts and checks his phone once more.

Just then, I catch movement on the basement stairway—one black shoe silently alighting on the edge of a step and then the next.

*He came.*

My pulse races in my ears.

I hop up and go right up to the bars, determined to distract Bender. "Can I tell you again that you absolutely don't look like your supposed father? I've seen pictures of the patriarch, and it's like night and day with you two."

"Are you on crack?" Bender says. "I look exactly like him."

"I know what I see."

"Have you even seen a picture of my father when he was young? There's no question we're related. And if you really think about it, it's obvious that the prophecy was about me, being that Luka was never truly a son. I'm the true son who will kill the king and ascend to the throne."

Bender's back on his phone, sauntering toward me. He's really invested in showing the world he's a Zogaj.

Luka creeps down. I can see enough of him now to see his gun.

"Thinking about side-by-side images of you and Luka's father reminds me of those memes where people supposedly look like their dogs, except one is human and the other is an actual dog, and nobody in their right mind would think they were related."

Bender glares at me and looks back down. He's near enough now that I can see an alert flash up on his phone.

He furrows his brow.

"That's how much you don't look like that old geezer—not even the same—"

He moves like lightning, grabbing my hair through the bars. A gun barrel presses into my cheek.

"Drop it or she dies," Bender says.

# Chapter Forty-Eight

## LUKA

Edie is in a fucking cage with a gun in her face. My worst nightmare.

Her eyes rivet to mine. I love this woman. I fucking love her. And this guy's dead.

Her sister stands back, arms crossed. There's no question it's Mary. Has she been down here all this time?

My rage burns so high it's a miracle the entire place hasn't burst into flames. Somehow, I keep my focus. Chalk it up to long years of experience.

"This is between you and me," I say.

Bender smirks. "Drop the piece and slide it to the middle of the floor with your foot. Slow."

I set down my gun and slide it across the floor. "This doesn't end well for you, Bender."

"The name's Zamir. Zamir Zogaj." He nods at me. "Now, the one in the back. I know you carry there."

I pull my Glock from my belt and slide that one across, too. "You'll let them go, now."

He chuckles.

I knew he wouldn't let them go, but it's best that he thinks he's in control.

I wait for him to ponder his options. I can practically see the gears moving. He's realizing that he's got one shot—at me—and he'll have to take his gun off Edie to make that shot.

It'll be just enough of a pause to allow me to dive for his legs, a move I've trained many times and done only once—a lightning-fast takedown that has the added benefit of dropping me out of the range he's likely to shoot in.

The odds of not getting hit are fifty-fifty, but that's the risk. I risk taking a bullet going in, but then I've got him. A man can't shoot you when you're on top of him, destroying his face.

I just have to get him to take the gun off Edie.

More than that, I have to touch her. I feel like I could tear apart the metal bars with my bare strength—that's how intensely I need to get to her.

She's being unbelievably brave, standing there calmly, hating on Bender.

"I'll admit, this was unexpected," Bender says.

"You two okay?"

"Fine," Edie says. A lie. She's in pain—it's all over her face. "This is my sister, Mary. Mary, this is Luka."

The woman sitting on the floor on the far side of the cage raises a hand in greeting.

"You do know the DNA test is happening right now, right?" Bender says to me. "There's no stopping it. That train has left the station."

"Yeah, yeah, yeah." As if I'd choose anything over Edie.

He smirks. "One of your own men supplied me a hair sample. All your guys know it's happening now. They know there's a question about your blood, and they're all waiting for the result. And what do we think it'll show?"

*One of my own guys gave up my hair?*

If I weren't so focused on that gun barrel shoved into Edie's cheek, I might give a shit.

"How 'bout you ease off on her," I say.

"That's how much you suck as a leader," Bender continues. "That's how eager your men are to be rid of you. Once they got wind that you might not be a true Zogaj, they couldn't wait to provide a hair sample. And it's at two independent labs, so there will be no question. I have it from good authority that the result will be a resounding F. F for fraud."

It's right about here that I notice Mary slowly moving to the side of the cage behind Bender. Inch by inch.

I nearly have a heart attack thinking she's going to try and attack Bender from the inside of the cage—a sure recipe for getting Edie shot. But then I notice that she's got some lumpy-looking Vaudeville hook in her hand. She slides it out the bottom of the bars—across the floor—and toward my gun, just beyond Bender's periphery.

Fuck. She's going for the gun.

"So, one of my guys brought you my hair? I have a hard time believing that." I move casually to the side, drawing his attention away from Mary.

"Believe it," Bender says. "I hear even my brother, Alteo, knew you were a fraud. I'm not surprised. I knew Alteo. We were working together. Did you know that? We made an excellent team, the two Zogajes."

"Did my guy give you a name? The one who gave you the hair sample?"

"Wouldn't you like to know. But I promised I wouldn't reveal his name, and I keep my promises."

Edie snorts.

"Shut up!" He yanks her hair.

I've never wanted to kill a man so badly.

Meanwhile, Mary's hooked the gun and is dragging it slowly toward the cage. Does she know how to use it?

I distract him with more bullshit about Alteo. Mary has the gun in her hand now.

If Edie notices what's going on, she's not showing it. She's tough as nails.

I fucking love her, and I can't believe I bulldozed her with that text bullshit. I should have trusted her to handle this guy. Maybe she would've wanted to stay at my place and do her homework. She'd be safe right now.

I can tell by the way Mary's holding the gun that she's used one before; she seems to be checking for the safety, which she'll find off.

She gives me a look.

Will she take a shot if Bender takes the gun off Edie? It's the obvious move.

I have to get the gun off Edie.

"Do you have the Zogaj birthmark?" I ask Bender suddenly.

"What Zogaj birthmark?" he asks.

"It's usually on the belly."

"Is this where you try to trick me into looking for a birthmark and jump me?"

"I'll show you mine." In one quick motion, I pull up my shirt. It's enough to trigger his cop training, and he takes his gun off Edie.

Mary takes her shot, getting him in the knee. He collapses from the impact, his gun arm pointing skyward. Another shot sounds out. His gun.

I launch into his legs.

He falls.

I whip him around and get on top of him. My fist crashes down into his face with the fury of a thousand hells. "Here's your prophecy." Blood spatters everywhere. Over and over I hit him. There's the sick crunch of cartilage—his nose. I drive my knuckles straight into his windpipe, crushing it.

I let him choke on his own blood while I take the keys from his pocket and open the door.

"Edie!" I go to her, grab her shoulders, pull her to me. "Fuck, what did he do?"

"I'm okay."

"Get the cuffs off," Mary says.

I turn Edie around and kneel behind her, unlocking the handcuffs. Her right hand is swollen.

She gasps the moment she's free, rubbing her wrist.

I put the cuffs and the keys in my jacket pocket and cradle her face in my palms. "Edie." I brush my thumbs over her cheekbones, gliding my fingers over her neck and over her shoulders.

She gazes up at me as Bender gurgles out his last breath. "You came."

"Of course." I kiss her lips. I kiss her nose. I kiss her cheekbone. "Let me see."

She holds out her hand.

I trail my fingers over the back of her hand, her fingers. "Make a fist, baby."

She slowly makes a fist.

"Good. Now straighten."

She straightens her fingers. "Ow."

"No, that's good. Keep it moving," I say.

She repeats the motion. She rotates her wrist and moves it every which way while I run my hands over every inch of her—head, shoulders, hips, legs and back up, ferally fixated on consuming her with all my senses—touching her, breathing her in, knowing she's there.

"You came," she whispers again, tears glistening in her eyes.

Mary comes up and sets her hand on Edie's shoulder. "Frittata. Hey."

Mary has the same sparkle in her eyes—that Edie sparkle.

"Nice job," I say to her.

"I was aiming for his head," she says. "But I'm good with how it worked out."

Edie pulls away from me and looks me in the eye. "How did you find us?"

"What kind of badass criminal can't find his girl?"

She blinks. "But... what about the DNA test? Did you somehow get into the lab and switch it already?"

"What the fuck do I care about a DNA test?"

"You'll care when the results might make your own guys kill you!"

"Let 'em try."

"You let the tests go through?"

"First things first. We're in a basement with a dead cop. Come on."

"What should we do?"

"You nurse that hand," I growl. "We got this, Mary, right?"

"On it," she says.

Mary and I get shit from the kitchen and wipe the place down. I find his home surveillance setup, because of course he has that, and destroy it.

We fill a trash bag with everything that might tie us here, scolding Edie to leave it all to us, but of course, she tries to do random little things.

I flip on the gas in the basement, and once the sisters are safely in the car down the block, I throw a hastily improvised Molotov cocktail through the window and get the fuck away. A blaze lights up the sky.

---

We drop Mary off at Edie's place. Edie's roommate, Odetta, is going to take Mary out to eat and buy her clothes.

I leave behind a stack of bills with strict orders to spend it all or else.

Edie's wrist is looking and feeling a lot better, but I need to be sure, so I get her into a clinic to be seen right away. The doc gives us a heat therapy wrap and a positive prognosis.

Back at my condo, I reheat the wrap in the microwave and wrap it again—soft and loose.

"You can stop fussing now," she says.

"Not likely," I growl.

"I was so worried. He said he had sharpshooters around the lab, just waiting for you to show up!"

"I would've done the same." I tuck in the edge of the thing just so.

"And there were more shooters inside, in case the outside guys weren't successful. The whole thing was a trap!"

I fasten the clip. "How is this? Too tight? Impinged?"

"Not in any way impinged," she says.

"Your sister is awesome."

"Right? She's probably got Odetta running around outside and visiting every ice cream shop in a ten-mile radius. But seriously —how did you find me?"

"You're not going to like it."

She narrows her eyes scornfully with that scorn that gets me so hard. I'm gonna miss that.

"I've got a few tracking devices on you."

"What?"

"You got complaints?"

"Now that Bender's dead? Yes, I've got complaints. I want them off."

I kiss her.

"Seriously, you can't do that. Tell me where."

After some playful arguing and a dead-serious make-out session, I give it up. "Your shoe, your belt, and your bra strap."

"Three? So, I'm like a walking transmitter here."

A text pings. It's Orton.

> We need to meet ASAP Trevor St

So this is it, then. The results are back. I know what they'll be. Like I told Orton, deep down, I know I'm not my father's true son.

And somebody's gonna kill me.

But I made my choice, and I'd do it again.

I text him back.

> One hour.

"What's up?" Edie asks.

I pocket my phone and head to my living room safe. I open it up and pull out the money. "We need to find something for you to carry this in."

"What are you doing?"

"I'm giving you money." I throw the stacks of bills on the couch.

"What the hell? Why?"

"In case something goes wrong."

"What do you mean, 'In case something goes wrong'?"

"Exactly what I said." I pull a backpack from the closet and stuff it full. "Unmarked and un-sequenced. Even so, don't spend it all in one place, if you get my meaning. There's also an offshore account in your name at the First Royal Seashield Holdings in Monaco. I'll text it to you."

She looks at me in alarm. "They're going to come after you for impersonating royal blood, aren't they?"

"I got this."

"What does 'I got this' mean?"

"It means I got this." I go to her and kiss her. I can't get enough of her.

"Fuck off," she whispers into the kiss. "Tell me what it means."

I carry her to the bedroom and set her on the bed. "Let me help you off with these." I start unbuckling her belt.

"Are you trying to distract me?"

I kiss her belly. I kiss her mound under the denim. She hisses out a breath, shoving her fingers into my hair. "What was the text?"

I've got her belt undone, and I'm undoing her zipper. She helps me, wriggling out of her pants.

I take down her panties. "God, you're so wet for me."

"Talk, Luka. You need to tell me things."

"It was Orton. He wants to meet later on."

"Did the results come through?"

I kiss the inside of her thigh. Up, up, and up toward her core. Goosebumps flare across her skin. "Presumably. It's probably why he wants to meet."

I kiss higher. Higher.

"So... the results. Did he say what they were?"

I press apart her legs. "I think we know what the results are."

"What the fuck?" She snaps her legs back together and sits up. "You can't go meet him! You said yourself he'd kill you if you weren't of true blood, and everybody who knows anything thinks you're not. Including you."

"This is my world, Edie. Trust me."

"You just gave me all your money! Not a good sign!"

"My world, my code," I growl, pushing her back down on the bed.

She rolls away. "To walk into a meeting where a guy probably wants to kill you? That's what I call a shitty code!"

She's wrong. A guy doesn't want to kill me. It'll be *guys*—plural.

This is the choice I made. I protect what's mine.

"Let's run away!" she begs. "We can go live in Rio or something like that."

"Run away from my own clan? A man has to be able to look himself in the mirror."

Her eyes widen. "Not if he's dead! A man can't look in the mirror when he's dead! A man can't look at anything when he's dead except the worms eating his brain."

"Come here."

"No, not if you're just going to walk to a meeting where they want to kill you!"

"You need to trust me."

She mumbles something about having to pee and stomps off.

I lie back on the bed, staring at the ceiling. It's only here, lying here, that I appreciate how much I really have loved being king.

But not as much as I've loved Edie. I love her. Every last thing about her.

Things have been very good for such a short time.

But a man protects what's his. He protects those he loves. And a king doesn't run from his men. He sure as hell doesn't drag the woman he loves along with him. Or worse—run and leave her behind. Exposed.

A low rumble sounds from the kitchen, followed by the *pock pock pock* of the refrigerator ice maker.

What is she up to? Getting ice? Does she have some sexy plan with ice?

Edie comes back, naked as the day she was born; her hands are behind her back, and her eyes have the look of pure devil.

# Chapter Forty-Nine

## EDIE

"Whatcha got?" he asks.

I smile. "You're going to have to guess. Lie back and grasp the headboard."

He gives me a suspicious look and scoots back, grabbing the metal bars at the top of the thing.

"Now close your eyes," I say. "You're going to have to tell me what you feel."

He closes his eyes.

I crawl up over him, trying to keep everything quiet so he doesn't hear the telltale clinking. I straddle his chest and lean up to kiss his Arianiti's eagle tattoo. "I love this tattoo," I say.

"Me too. And I love that you knew it."

"Me too." Quick as lightning, I handcuff him to the bed.

His eyes fly open. "Edie, no."

"Sorry, but…"

"What have you done?"

"You know what."

He yanks, trying to free himself. "Where are the keys?"

"Nowhere you're going to get to," I say. "And don't think you can get out of them. They're Bender's cop cuffs."

He swears softly under his breath.

I've been thinking about the cuffs ever since he said he was going to that meeting. He wouldn't be in danger from his own men if it weren't for me. It's my turn to protect him.

"I need to be across town in under an hour," he says. "Take these off."

I climb back on him and kiss his chest. "You saved me; isn't turnabout fair play?" I move down, kissing his abs.

"The kind of man who wouldn't go to that meeting? The kind of man who runs from his own men with his tail between his legs? Putting you in danger along the way? That's not a man you want, Edie."

"Spare me the patriarchal bullshit because that's exactly the man I want." I kiss his belly button. I kiss the lightly furred stretch of hair below his belly button, the soft place that rises and falls with his every breath.

"I wanna wake up in bed every morning with the man who doesn't go to that meeting."

I plant another kiss.

Another.

I look up to find him watching with those angel-devil eyes, watching my every movement.

I slide my hands over his abs, trailing kisses back up his hot skin, over each and every muscular contour, all the way up to his strong chest.

"I have to go, princess."

"Not happening."

"You don't get to decide that."

I unbutton his pants.

He whooshes out a breath. "Edie... God... what are you doing?"

"You know what I'm doing."

I lower the zipper. My wrist is killing me, but I don't even give a shit.

"Edie," he gusts out.

His cock is a rock-hard ridge. I kiss it. "I could make out with your cock for days. Days and days and days."

His breath sounds ragged. Everything feels wild and real and a little bit dangerous. Because it is.

"You can't... you...."

I yank down his pants and boxer briefs. His cock springs up.

Luka isn't a man who likes to be managed. Or stopped from doing things, but there's no going back now.

I lick the bead of precum off the tip, and he hisses out a ragged breath.

"Need you..." he groans.

That's more like it. I pull his pants all the way off, down his legs, off his ankles. I want him so bad I can't think.

"Yes," he rumbles. "Show me that scorn, princess."

"Forget it. That's so far from how I feel right now. So far away." I kiss the side of his cock. "You came for me, Luka. You knew it would cost you, but you came anyway."

"Don't make this more than it is," he whispers. "Nothing but a transaction—"

"You could've stopped that test. You could've stayed king, but you rescued me instead."

I kiss the other side.

"I was only here for the vengeance," he grits out, "and you were only here for your sister. We both got what we wanted. End of story." He mumbles something about *a transaction*.

"This is more than that. Look in your heart—you know."

"You don't want to know what's in my heart."

I crawl up more and kiss his chest. "I already know what's in your heart, so you can fuck the fuck off because I love you."

"You don't know what you're talking about."

"I love you, and I think you love me too."

His eyes blaze. I can't read his expression for once. Is he happy? Angry? It doesn't matter.

"You loved being king, and you came for me because you know this is more than a transaction. We make each other better, and it's my turn to rescue you now."

"You can't."

"Watch me." I whip out a condom and unwrap it. "I love you like crazy, and you can't stop me."

"You're gonna see that I'm right."

I caress the sides of his cock, silky and hard. I wrap my hand over it loosely, exploring the shape of him, tracing the vein on the side with my thumb. I'm torn between taking him in my mouth and having him that way or getting right to the fucking. "I want you on every level possible."

"God, put it on already."

"There's the spirit." I roll on the condom.

I hover over him when I'm done and look down at him, right into his eyes. The whole world seems to have fallen silent except for our tandem ragged breathing.

"Luka."

His expression gentles.

Maybe he knows I won't let him go. I fit us together, enjoying the tip of him in me, lingering in this place.

His breath is ragged.

I lower down on him, watching. I've never felt so connected to anybody ever.

Warmth floods my body.

With a groan, he thrusts his hips, filling me deeper.

"Yes," I say.

He thrusts up again, hard. It's delicious, the feeling of him hard in me, quelling the ache between my legs.

He speeds up, but it comes to me, then, what he's doing. He's going for our usual feverish pace, all desperate and clawing.

"No, wait." I press down on him and stay. "This isn't that kind of fuck." Slowly, I grind on him, making small circles of pure magic.

"This can't be something it isn't," he says.

"It already is." I bend down to kiss him. "And it's already another kind of fuck because I love you so much."

He squeezes his eyes shut, trying to cut me off, to cut us off. But what we have is undeniable.

We've imprinted on each other, primal as thunder.

I skim my palms down his body, consuming him, being consumed. I want to stay in this delicious feeling of being lost with him. It's all I want.

I lean down and nestle against him, pressing into him as we roll against each other.

Time slows. Everything falls away. My mind is mush, and I don't even care.

"Princess." He kisses my forehead.

Shivers lick over my skin.

His lips are magic. My clit is a bundle of nerves and sparkles.

His hands skim down my arms, a detail I'm too gone with pleasure to process.

He turns us so that he's on top. He moves into me sweet and slow.

I gaze up into his eyes, mesmerized by his expression, so serious, so intent. He tries to act like he's not with me, but there's no denying it.

Pleasure blooms inside of me.

He leans down to kiss me. He thrusts into me again.

I shatter apart into a billion shards of light.

He gasps my name and presses his forehead to mine. Over and over, he whispers my name. *Edie, Edie, Edie, Edie.* I hold him tightly as he comes, shuddering into me.

*Edie, Edie, Edie, Edie.* He kisses my cheek, down my throat.

He takes my lips with his.

I mumble into the kiss.

Strong hands skim up my hips, my ribs, my arms, up to my hands, pressing my hands over my head.

There's a clinking sound coming from somewhere. Cold metal on my wrists.

What?!?!

I come to my senses too late and realize he's gotten free, and he's cuffing me to the metal headboard now.

"Hey!" I jerk at the bonds.

"I'm sorry," he says, standing up.

"What have you done?"

"Is that okay on your wrist? I tried to make it loose, but I can't let you get away."

"What the hell?"

"I have to go. You know I have to go."

"You *don't* have to go!"

"I can't run and hide, I told you. Running from danger is not what a dirty barbarian does. And it's not safe for you."

"Who cares?"

"I do." He leans down to kiss me. "I don't run from my men, and I don't put you in danger."

"Fuck off, don't kiss me if you're gonna let yourself die!"

"Nobody knows the future."

"I have a pretty good guess!" I yank desperately on the cuffs.

"Shhhh." He pulls my panties back on and then my pants. He pulls the sheets up over me. "I'll message your sister to come free you."

"You can't leave me here!"

He removes his archangel Michael medallion and puts it over my head.

"Omigod," I whisper, my vision blurring as unshed tears burn behind my eyes. My chest tightens with a pain so raw it's almost physical.

"A man protects those he loves." His voice is steady, but there's something in his eyes I've never seen before—a vulnerability that cuts deep.

"Did you just tell me you love me?" The words catch in my throat.

"Yes." Just one word, but it changes everything—the air between us, the rhythm of my heart, the entire universe.

Rage surges through me, hot and unstoppable. I yank at the cuffs until metal bites into my skin, but I don't even feel the pain. "You can't tell me that and then voluntarily go out in a hail of gunfire!" My voice breaks on the last word, a sob threatening to tear me apart.

"Edie." He stands at the foot of the bed, gazing at me. "Do you mean go out in a standard-issue-criminal hail of gunfire?"

"Stop it! That's not love, Luka—that's goodbye."

"A hail of gunfire straight from criminal Costco?"

"It's not funny!"

He kisses me on the cheek.

"Fuck off!"

He takes one last look at me. "There's that scorn."

With that, he's gone.

# Chapter Fifty

## LUKA

I stroll past trees with branches like fingers, the bright green buds appearing here and there. The steely sky above me stretches to infinity over the brick and concrete city. My city.

For now.

A text will go out to Edie's sister later today. She'll get free, and she'll use the money to make a life. Live her dreams. Help her sister. She'll use that money out of spite, if nothing else.

I never gave a shit about the future. I never planned for it. Until now. A woman got under my skin and made me weak. Made me strong in different ways.

It was good for a while. It was very, very good.

I turn the corner at Trevor Street, enjoying the crisp air and the din of traffic and birds and planes and the sense of the earth under my feet. This is my domain, whether I live or die. I feel it all with this strange ripple in my chest that might be gratitude. And love. Both foreign concepts until her.

My heart is still full. It feels rare and strange and wild as a hurricane. Is it possible that there are people who walk around like this all the time? Full of love and gratitude? How do they function?

I knew what I was signing up for, killing my brother and taking over the clan like I did. I set myself up as a king, and I accepted the risks. I took what I wanted. But it was worth it to me. A true alpha doesn't hide behind facades.

The vengeance wasn't really worth it in the end, but the path I followed to get there led me to Edie, and she's worth it.

Orton'll be the one to kill me, but it'll be good to see him one last time all the same. A king couldn't ask for a better knight. A truer man.

Even a false king couldn't ask for better.

The bright beer sign flashes up ahead.

She's still on my skin. Her taste on my lips. Her claim stamped into my very cells.

I take a breath and pull open the door, ready for death. I knew the deadly price if I was found to be anything less than a true blood, and deep down, I knew I probably wasn't. But I claimed the throne anyway.

It takes a while for my eyes to adjust to the darkness. The place is packed—more men than I expected. Figures hunched over tables, profiles edged in red neon from the beer signs. All Ghost Hound Clan. My clan, until they decide otherwise.

The conversation dies as I enter. A glass shatters somewhere in the back, and the sound of a shotgun being pumped punctuates the silence.

Men turn slowly. Eyes narrow. Jaws tighten.

Several hands drift toward waistbands or inside jackets. The air crackles with tension, like the moment before lightning strikes. I count at least twelve weapons already half-drawn.

I step further in. Somebody kicks the door closed behind me with more force than necessary, making sure I understand there's no retreat.

"We wait," somebody hisses from the darkness.

"Bastard," comes another voice.

"We'll have proof of *that* soon enough." Gianni spits on the floor in front of me.

I turn toward him, keeping my expression neutral. "Gianni."

His eyes are hard, glittering. "What kind of man pretends to be what he isn't? What kind of rat thinks he can rule over us?"

So, the story has spread and taken root. Probably Bender's doing. *Zamir.*

Someone else calls out, "Dead man."

A blade catches the neon light. "Even your brother proclaimed it."

I think of Edie handcuffed to my bed. Her face. The way the light caught in her hair. If I die here, at least she's safe. That thought steadies me. I've protected what's mine to the end.

"Orton is on his way with the proof. Any last words?" Gianni asks, weapon drawn.

I look around at the faces of the men I've led, meeting their eyes one by one.

"A false king who served true," I say, voice hard as steel, "is better than a true king who serves false."

The words hang heavy in the air.

West is at the bar, staring into his drink. Kress the Shadow, who'd follow me anywhere last week, now sits with arms crossed, face blank.

Orton's shout cuts through the din. "The kyre is here!"

He pushes through the crowd, a folded paper clutched in his hand. Storm towers behind him, face like granite, hands gripping what I know are dual Glocks beneath his coat.

Orton stops a few feet from me. His eyes are unreadable. "The results." He holds up a paper.

He'll execute me himself. Fulfilling his oath to the bloodline. I can see it all unfold, clear as day.

"It's true then?" I ask quietly, just for him.

Orton's eyes flash. With what? Anger? Regret?

He turns to address the room, voice carrying to every corner. "I hold in my hand the DNA test results."

A man near the bar stands. "Read it!"

Another voice, "Show us the proof!"

"Let's end this tonight," Iron Jaw Dardan snarls.

Orton unfolds the paper with deliberate slowness. The room is so quiet you could hear a pin drop. Someone cocks a gun, not bothering to be subtle.

"The DNA analysis shows"—Orton pauses, his gaze sweeping the room—"that Luka Zogaj carries blood more ancient and more pure than any living Zogaj."

Confusion ripples through the crowd. Men exchange glances.

He looks up, face dead serious.

I blink. Stunned.

It makes no sense to them.

It sure the hell doesn't make sense to me.

"Bullshit!" someone calls.

Orton shakes his head. "A test was run in two different labs. The results are beyond conclusive. His blood carries markers consistent with a direct lineage to The First."

A beat of stunned silence.

Orton continues, voice rising. "Not just a Zogaj—a direct descendant of the original *kryetar* himself. The First."

Chaos erupts.

"Impossible!" Gianni pushes forward. "Let me see that paper!"

"How could his mother have—" another begins.

The room teeters on the edge of violence. I stand rooted, as surprised as any of them. This wasn't the end I expected.

"It's a trick!"

Orton's voice thunders above the din. "*You question the blood?*"

The room falls silent.

Orton is a true believer—everybody knows it. He's like a fire-and-brimstone preacher, a Crusader clutching his cross on the battlefield.

Orton holds up a fist. "I swear by this ring, a relic preserved for generations in my family. Science confirms what the prophecy foretold!"

Men cross themselves instinctively. Some make the old gesture against evil.

Orton's face is flushed with fervor. "The true king has been revealed! A bloodline purer than we imagined!"

"It's not possible," Florian argues, but his voice wavers. "How could the *kryetar's* blood—"

"Do any of you claim to understand the workings of fate?" Orton's voice drops and takes on an almost mystical quality. "Do you presume to know how the unseen powers move through generations?"

The atmosphere in the room shifts, almost imperceptibly at first.

Orton would sooner cut off his hand than question what's written in the ancient texts.

To lie about something like this?

Unthinkable.

My pulse races. What. The. Fuck.

"Our ancestors foretold this day," Orton continues. "A king whose blood reaches back to The First, who would restore the Clan to glory."

I feel the change in the air. The hostility gives way to something else. Uncertainty. Then awe.

Storm steps forward. Without speaking, he sinks to one knee before me.

One by one, others follow. First the older men—those most steeped in the old ways. Then, the younger ones, pulled by tradition.

West, still hesitating, finally slides off his stool and drops to a knee.

"The promised king," Orton says, voice thick with emotion.

A man approaches, takes my hand in both of his and bows his head over it. Then another. And another.

"Luka!" someone calls out. The name ripples through the crowd, building into a chant. "Luka! Luka! Luka!"

I catch Orton's eye over the heads of the kneeling men. There's something in his gaze—a glint of fierce protectiveness. Of loyalty deeper than blood.

He knows something about the test that I don't.

What?

But right now, surrounded by men who minutes ago were ready to riddle my body with bullets, all I can do is play my part.

"The promised king," Orton repeats, dropping to one knee himself. "Gëzuar!"

"Gëzuar!" the room echoes.

Bottles appear. Raki flows. The Chant of the Brotherhood rises.

And somehow, impossibly, I'm still alive.

Later, when the men come back to earth and stop treating me like Zeus descended from the mountain, or at least once the men tone it down a little, I turn to Orton.

"I'm directly descended from somebody four centuries old?" I lower my voice to a harsh whisper. "I'm telling you, my mom wasn't running around fucking mummies."

Orton leans closer, his eyes intense. "You don't understand how much these men want to believe—in you. In the specialness of the clan. They're making sense of it already. Some are saying perhaps your mother crossed paths with another true bloodline— one hidden from our records. Others..." He gestures toward the celebrating men. "They see this as confirmation of the old prophecies. A king with blood more ancient than we knew."

"That's crazy," I mutter.

"Is it?" Orton's voice drops further. "These men follow power, but they crave meaning. A bloodline connecting you directly to The First? It gives them something holy to serve." He taps his glass against mine. "The impossible blood of a true king is a far better story than a leader who earned his place through blood and willpower alone. Men die for stories, Luka. They always have."

I give him a hard look.

"The unseen powers work in mysterious ways." He throws back his raki.

It's then I see it—the dull shine of the stone in his ring. The smoothness. "Your ring looks different."

"What?"

"Your ring. It was beat up, but the stone was always shiny. But now it looks so dull. And wait… it had a chip on the side of it—"

Orton grabs his glass, effectively moving his ring out of my sight. "The men need you to speak. Some of them need reassurance you won't be angry. They moved to kill you when they thought you were not true blood."

"Is that even your ring?"

He stiffens. "I think I'd know my own ring."

I grab his arm. "That's not your ring. It's a fake."

"Stop."

I look into his eyes. "What have you done, old friend?"

"Nothing."

I squeeze. "What. Have. You. Done?"

Orton puts his hand over mine. "I serve the kyre. You are the kyre."

My heart pounds in my chest as the pieces of the puzzle fall together.

"You faked the test?" I hiss.

Orton frowns. "How could I? I had no access to the test. The results were certified and sent all over the place."

"No, the samples. You broke your ring to get at the ancient hair. You offered that ancient hair to Bender."

"Madness," Orton hisses.

"You told him that the ancient hair from your ring was my

hair." Orton rolls his eyes, but I know I'm right. Bender said that one of my own men offered up my hair for use in DNA testing.

That man was Orton.

Orton pried open his treasured heirloom relic ring and took it from there. His relic ring that was passed down through generations.

He probably ended up destroying his beloved ring to get the hair out.

"Orton," I say.

Orton fixes me with a hard gaze. "I serve my king. I am loyal to my king. You are the true king."

# Chapter Fifty-One

## EDIE

I've loosened one of the bars that the handcuffs are attached to. How did Luka even get free?

And he did it without my noticing. I've been wailing away on the cuffs, fueled by angst and worry and terror and rage, and it makes a lot of noise.

I'm ragey that he chained me here.

Ragey that he said he loved me and then left to go be all alpha and honorable and shit, marching to his death. I hate him for it—I really do. I love him and hate him.

And he loves me.

And I could lose him just when we found each other. He could be dead right now, but I'm trying not to think of it. I'm channeling my anger into getting free.

I'll figure out where he's meeting Orton. I'll somehow get in there and then... I don't know what.

I feel like I might be loosening one of the bars when I hear the main door open.

I go still. It could be anybody coming in here. Is it my sister? If she frees me, maybe there's still time to go after him...

"Princess."

I gasp. "Luka?"

He strolls in looking sexy and relaxed, pocket square gleaming, hair roguishly mussed. Face still faintly bruised.

"Ohmigod, what happened? Did you change your mind?"

"Not exactly." He climbs onto the bed next to me and unlocks the handcuffs.

"What happened?"

"Remind me to teach you how to get out of these one of these days."

He's talking about the future—*us in the future.*

"Luka!" I get up on my knees and grab his shoulders. "You changed your mind! You decided to blow off the whole he-man-stroll-into-a-hail-of-bullets thing!"

"No, I went."

"What?"

"You know I had to go." He checks the bandage on my wrist. "This okay?"

"You went?"

"Your hand—"

"It's fine." I yank it from him. "Tell me what happened."

"The DNA test worked out in my favor."

"Wait, what? So that means you're your father's son, after all? You seemed sure you weren't."

He hauls me into his lap. "The DNA test suggests that I'm descended from The First—a purebred kyre, I suppose you could say."

"So you're not... related to your father?"

"I'm related to my father in that my father is descended from The First, but my blood is purer. I'm more closely related to The First. At least that's what the test said."

I blink. "So... your mom had an affair with some super pure-bred guy or something?"

"Well, no." He gazes out the window, thinking. Processing. "It's actually bullshit. You know that ring Orton wears?"

"The one with the big red stone?"

I explain to her about the relic ring. How our people took relics from The First's body—usually hair or bits of his burial shroud—and shut them up into those rings. And now Orton wore a fake ring.

"The hair is old, probably degraded, but there was enough DNA in it to make me look like the second coming of the original kyre."

I look at him in disbelief. "The man who one hundred percent would want to kill you if you turned out to be a regular guy posing as a true blood? That's the guy who fixed the test."

"It's... a lot to process."

"Is it, though? It's called loyalty, Luka. You earned his loyalty."

"I suppose."

"You suppose?!"

"It's a lot to get used to."

I trace his cheekbone. He's so beautiful and damaged, and he can work out complex operations in his head and do ultra-dangerous things that would put the fear of God in any normal mortal, but somebody doing something for him because they give a shit about him personally is beyond his comprehension. "He would do anything for you."

"Maybe."

I poke him in the chest. "No maybe about it."

He clasps my hands in his. "I would do anything for *you.* Because I love you."

This bloom of happiness fills my heart. "I would do anything for you, too." I kiss him, then I pull away. "After you apologize for handcuffing me to the bed."

"What?"

I wrestle him to his back—or, more like, he lets me do it—and climb on top of him, looming over him. "You heard me."

"Excuse me? I should apologize for cuffing you to the bed after you cuffed *me* to the bed? Trying to make me miss my meeting?" He flips me over. "Not thankable."

"Oh, it was thankable," I say, looking up into his deep chocolatey eyes.

His mouth is all frowny and serious, but his eyes are smiling. "Everything with us is thankable, even the unthankable stuff."

"Mind blown," I whisper.

He kisses me. I lose myself deliciously in the kiss, deliciously in him, so growly and feral and full of life, and my last thought before my mind pretty much explodes with pleasure is that I'll never get enough of him and his brutish, uncivilized ways.

# Epilogue

LUKA

**One month later**

I set the third and final box of books in front of my bookcase.

Edie wanders over. She's in her favorite light green dress and beige hat, hair curling softly around her heart-shaped face. "What are those?"

"I've been shopping," I say to her. "Take a look."

She opens up the box and gasps. "Books!"

"A man can't have fake books on his bookshelf."

She beams at me, delighted. "You know what this means."

"What?

"We have to figure out categorization!"

We spend the afternoon putting the books in piles in what she calls preliminary categorization, and then we start filling the shelves.

It seems like a lifetime ago that I pulled her out of that fucking cage that psycho put her in.

We spent a few weeks searching for a seaside home for Edie to share with Mary. We ended up getting two side-by-side cottages, one for Mary and one for Edie and me for when we drive out from the city. As much as I've enjoyed getting to know Mary, I want privacy, especially since I plan to spend a good deal of time there doing things that require privacy.

I head around the kitchen island and start putting together a charcuterie board.

Edie turns and grins at me. "You ready?"

"Ready for what?"

She goes to where I put the hated fake cardboard book facades and rips one of them the best she can, which turns out to be half ripping and half folding, and then she stuffs it into the recycling bin, repeating the process with the others.

"You know those were perfectly good fake book shells."

"There's no such thing as a perfectly good fake book shell, thank you very much."

I go to her and kiss her. "So, how long have you been waiting to do that?"

She laughs into the kiss. "Since the moment I laid eyes on them."

"Hate at first sight."

"You got that right."

I could not love this woman more.

I dump a tin of candied nuts into a small bowl and set it next to a hunk of brie. "We need a gouda on here."

She holds up a yellow trade paperback. "What is this one? *Million Dollar Teams*? What is that?"

"It's about creating high-functioning teams," I say.

"I didn't know you got this. It looks good. I'm making a contemporary nonfiction section, which I might split into business because you have a few of these." She grins. "Your *businessman* books!"

Edie is endlessly amused that I might apply business principles to running my clan, but it's gotten to be a fad among the Albanian clan leaders.

In any case, a crime organization is a multimillion-dollar enterprise, and a good business book can be valuable for somebody in my area of work. Thanks to the last book I read, I'm focusing on the strongest lines of business and learning how to streamline resources and functions to support them.

I never wanted to follow in my father's footsteps to be a *kyre*, but I'm loving it, truth be told. And I have my own vision for it that's different from whatever fuckery my father and brother were up to with their shitty management, which I'm still unwinding.

I've created a stronger alliance with the Dragushas; we helped him and his brother get that meeting with Razvan, no circle cookies, no cops. If Lazarus is out there, Razvan Bektashi will find him. And he'll kill him.

It's almost sad. Lazarus is such a fucking psycho, such a force of nature. The seventh criminal wonder of the world.

"Next thing you know, you're going to be hiring an HR manager," she teases, slotting in another one of my business books.

I set a bowl of crackers next to the finished charcuterie board. "I don't know if there are a lot of HR managers who'd be willing to deal with an untrustworthy employee by putting a bullet in their head."

"Mr. Big Bad," she teases.

"That's right, princess."

I fix us each a lemonade raki smash, a drink we invented together that involves fresh-squeezed lemonade, simple syrup, and mint, while she arranges the books on the shelves.

I catch sight of the book on forgiveness, which she puts next to the management books. It's one she brought over here.

She bought the book thinking about her mother.

Mary had completely fallen out of touch with their mother, and Edie always did the bare minimum, showing up for quick, sad little holidays. The three of them are trying now, and it seems like their mother has mellowed a bit.

I haven't met her yet. Edie says she's not ready. She confessed one night over dinner that she's protective of our happiness, and her mom has a track record of wrecking things. "I've always kept the precious parts of my life away from Mom. My favorite people, my passion for history. I want to change that, but she has to show me she's ready."

I assured her that I was not going anywhere.

Mary has been doing great. She's been keeping up with her sobriety and attending Narcotics Anonymous meetings religiously at a community center out by the seashore home. She even has plans to start a little dessert bakery in the nearby town. She's identified a storefront that will be perfect and is rumored to be going on the market soon, and she's been developing recipes and sourcing ingredients. Orton, of all people, has expressed interest in being an investor.

"What's the problem?" Orton protested when I roasted him about it. "I can try out a legit business sideline. It's called diversification. You should look into it."

Edie and I sometimes suspect it's about more than simple diversification. We've had dinner parties where Orton and Mary seem to get lost in their own little world of conversation. They excitedly agree on the most random subjects, too. Who knows what will happen, but with Orton as an investor, they definitely won't be selling any ring-shaped cookies.

Edie is finishing up work on her degree, and she's writing a proposal for her young adult nonfiction book on Anastasia Laskarina. She wakes up some mornings bursting with new ideas for it. Sometimes, we'll be in the middle of a meal or sitting in the jacuzzi or walking somewhere, and she'll get an idea and start scribbling furiously in the little notebook she carries around.

She stands back. "So far so good."

I hand her a drink. "So good."

We continue on, debating how the arrangement would work best. In the end, we decide to make distinctions between classic and contemporary works, genre fiction and literary fiction, business nonfiction and general nonfiction, and historical books.

It's nice. It's not about just looking better, though it does, but this place is mine. This life is mine. Edie is mine. I pull her into my arms for a kiss.

"What?" She's laughing.

"You."

She wriggles away, still laughing. "I was thinking about adding an 'up next' section where we identify books we might want to read next. For convenience. For grab and go."

"When I'm in the mood to grab and go, I'm not thinking about books."

"You are the worst," she says. "They're your shelves. You want a grab-and-go section right here?"

"Nearest to the door. I like that."

There is a twinkle in her eye. She goes over and picks up the fake book shells. "And these? Where should we put these? I know they're your favorite."

I go to her and take them from her hand, tossing them aside. "You're not going to let me ever forget about these, are you?"

"How could I? Of all your many horrible crimes—" She picks up her glass and takes a sip. "Mmm."

"All my many horrible crimes." I go to her. "Tell me again what you think about criminals."

She gives me her mischievous smile.

"Tell me."

She slams back her raki drink and hands me the glass. "I love one of them very much."

Some months later....

The setting sun paints the horizon in stripes of amber and rose, casting a golden glow across our weathered porch. I curl my legs beneath me in the Adirondack chair, listening to the rhythm of waves against the shore. The breeze carries the scent of salt and late summer flowers from my garden. Perfect evening doesn't begin to describe it.

Luka hands me a glass of wine, his fingers lingering against mine. He settles into the chair beside me, propping his feet on the railing. The champagne bottle chills in a bucket between us.

"To my favorite historian," he says, clinking his glass against mine. "Columbia University Press. Not bad."

"I can't help the grin that spreads across my face. "I still can't believe they accepted my proposal. A whole series about Anastasia Laskarina."

"I can," Luka says with that quiet confidence that still makes my heart skip. "They'd be idiots not to."

The letter arrived this morning – my book proposal accepted, with a contract for two more volumes if the first performs well. I've been floating all day, caught between disbelief and elation.

"They loved the angle about female historians being erased

from history," I tell him, still processing it myself. "And the teen audience focus."

Luka stretches, that predatory grace never leaving him even in repose. "I may have been wrong about your princess," he admits grudgingly.

I gasp in mock shock. "The great Luka Zogaj, admitting he was wrong? Should I call the papers?"

He narrows his eyes, but there's no heat in it. "Maybe she wasn't completely obsessed with barbarian invaders."

"Thank you," I say primly. "Her interests were varied and scholarly."

"Unlike someone I know," he says, voice dropping low as he leans closer, "who definitely has a barbarian obsession." His hand slides up my thigh.

I swat him away, laughing. "Behave. We have a beautiful sunset to enjoy."

His dark eyes never leave my face. "You still play hard to get, even when we're alone in paradise."

I give him a witchy glance and take another sip.

The porch swing creaks as the breeze pushes it. Our little cottage isn't large or fancy, but it's ours – our weekend escape from the city. The main house is just down the beach, but we've made this little guest cottage our own.

"Did Storm call today?" I ask, trying to sound casual.

Luka smirks. "Business talk? During our celebration?"

"I'm just making conversation."

"Things are going smoothly," he says after a moment. "Storm says the Bratva is respecting our new boundaries. The Pruszków will fall into line."

*Or else,* I think.

What would my professors think if they knew I could now identify most Eastern European criminal syndicates by name? Or that I've developed opinions on territorial expansion strategies?

"That's good," I say. "Less headaches for you."

"Mmm," he agrees.

The business is thriving under Luka's leadership, and he's forged stronger alliances with the other families. The Ghost Hound Clan has never been more powerful or stable.

Not that I approve of criminal activities. But Luka is who he is, and I've made my peace with it. We have boundaries – things I don't ask about, things he doesn't bring home. It works for us.

I get up and cross to the weathered trunk we use as a coffee table, lifting the lid.

"What are you doing?" Luka asks.

I pull out my harmonica, holding it up with a flourish. His eyes light up like I've produced a golden orb or something.

"Really?" he asks, sitting forward.

I grin. His fascination with my harmonica skill has been endlessly amusing. I'm always telling him that harmonica playing is something I do for myself and nobody else—completely true— but things have shifted so much in the last year. Luka isn't somebody else anymore. It's us against the world, and I wanna share everything with him.

"Consider it part of the celebration."

I take a deep breath. I haven't played for ages, what with nailing my master's degree and finding this place and finishing up the book. And of course, Luka.

But I bring the harmonica to my lips and start to play.

He watches with intensity.

It's nothing fancy – just an Irish folk melody I've always loved, and it has the bonus of being easy to play. Even so, I screw up a few notes, but then I get over it and the notes sound out against the crashing waves.

When I finish, Luka is watching me with that awestruck expression that I love.

"More," he says simply.

I play another tune, this one livelier. Halfway through, I notice movement on the beach – two figures walking toward our cottage, silhouetted against the dimming sky.

I stop playing. "We have company."

Luka follows my gaze, relaxing when he recognizes them. "Mary and Orton."

My sister and Luka's right-hand man. The unlikely couple that somehow makes perfect sense.

They climb the steps to our porch. Mary's curls wild from the ocean breeze, Orton's perpetual intensity softened by her presence.

"Don't stop on our account," Mary says, gesturing to the harmonica. "We heard you all the way from the beach."

"You're early," Luka growls.

I give Luka a look. "You're perfectly on time."

Mary takes a glass from Luka with a smile. "We sold out pretty early, so we hopped on cleanup right away. Here's to officially being on vacation for the next week while they install the new ovens."

"And if they go over schedule, we will have words," Orton growls.

Mary's brunch bistro, The Flying Frittata, has become a local sensation, and now she's expanding into the space next door.

"Congratulations on the book deal," Orton says to me. "Mary told me the news."

"Thank you! I'm still processing it."

We settle into our chairs, the conversation flowing easily as twilight deepens. Stars begin to appear, scattered diamonds against dark velvet. The champagne makes an appearance, glasses clinked all around.

Mary and I take our glasses down the steps to the beach and wade into the water, the waves licking at our ankles as we plan our bistro-vacay craft night: embroidery thread, a big couch, cheesy popcorn, red licorice, and Hallmark movies.

"I downloaded a really cute squirrel pattern off Etsy," Mary says. "He has this little flower crown? So sweet. And I found this fox curled up in a ball of grass. Oh—and there were some great bluebird ones, too. I'll send you the link."

"No, I've been designing my own pattern," I say. "It's a coat of arms. For me and Luka."

Mary stops mid-step. "A coat of arms."

"Yeah. Medieval style. I'm doing a shield divided into quadrants—Arianiti's eagle in one, a feather quill over parchment in another, a dagger in the third, and maybe the harmonica or a crown in the last. Symbols of us. I want to embroider it on linen and make a fabric tapestry for our reading nook. Maybe even do a couple of matching dish towels."

Mary snorts. "A coat of arms for you and Luka. Yeah, you're definitely not a nerd."

"It's gonna be the best," I say, already picturing the whole thing in gold, crimson, and midnight thread.

"You forgot to add circle cookies," Mary says. "Don't you want that on your coat of arms?"

I grin. "I'll put circle cookies on our coat of arms when you start baking them in your bistro."

"Not likely," Mary says.

The guys are talking intently up on the porch. I can't hear them, but I know Luka so well now that I can read his posture—shoulders just slightly tense. If we were closer, I'd see the tight line in his jaw. He doesn't like whatever Orton is telling him. If I had to guess, I'd say it's something about Lazarus, the psychotic killer they've been chasing halfway across the world. The coffee farm. The monastery. So many dead ends it's starting to feel like folklore.

"Hey, losers!" Mary calls out, holding up her empty glass. "Come on, the water's perfect—and I need a refill!"

That's when I see it. The ring.

I grab her hand. "What? Mary, what is this? Oh my God, Mary!"

"I was wondering when you'd notice. Some scholar you are."

"Mary!" I pull her into a hug. "I'm so happy for you. You guys are perfect. When?"

She holds it out to glitter in the moonlight. "Tonight."

"About three hours ago," Orton adds, strolling toward us, looking more pleased than I've ever seen him. "On the beach."

More champagne is poured. More toasts are made right there at the water's edge. I'm so happy for her. Of course, I tease her a little for always having to do everything first. First sister to do a cartwheel. First to graduate high school. Now first to get married.

"Maybe it's time to step up, mister!" Mary says to Luka, waggling her brows.

"Buzz off," I laugh.

Luka drapes an arm over my shoulder. "We've got our own timeline."

"Own timeline, huh?" Mary says.

"That's right," I say. "Some of us don't follow fireflies into the woods without a flashlight."

"Okay, okay," Mary says.

"Some of us don't get matching tattoos with people we just met at sunrise yoga and declare ourselves best friends for life."

Mary laughs. "In my defense, I *am* still friends with her."

"And some of us don't jump off the garage roof with a pillowcase for a parachute."

"Whoa, whoa, whoa." Orton raises his hands in mock surrender. "Am I the pillowcase in this scenario?"

Mary plants a kiss on his cheek. "You're no pillowcase, baby."

In truth, Luka and I have talked about the future together. A lot. But we both want to focus on the big things we're building—things most people can't see yet.

And yeah, we're a little less impulsive than Mary and Orton. Not that it's a bad thing. It's just us.

Eventually, we wander back up toward the porch as the conversation shifts to wedding plans and potential dates, and Lazarus and all his fuckery gets pushed aside—for now.

Later, as Mary and Orton head back down the beach toward their own cottage, Luka wraps his arms around me from behind, resting his chin on my shoulder as we watch them go.

"She's happy," I say softly. "Really happy."

"So am I," he says.

I lean back against him, solid and warm. I don't even need to answer. We get each other.

We watch the waves shimmer under starlight, the future stretching out before us unbounded. My barbaric king and me, writing our own improbable story one day at a time.

"Play me one more song," Luka whispers.

"Another?"

"Do it," he growls, lips brushing my skin, "or I'll make you scream a different kind of tune."

I smirk. "With an offer like that, I might never play again."

He leans closer, his voice dark and dangerous. "Careful, little historian. You're tempting fate."

I lift the harmonica and begin to play.

---

Thanks for reading!! I hope you enjoyed your time with Luka and Edie as much as I did!

But wait! Where in the world is Lazarus?
What devious things is that madman up to now?
Lazarus's book comes out in 2026!
Don't miss it!

# *Acknowledgments*

To my brilliant beta readers—Amy, Carla, Carol, Jessica, Jessica Fahey, Kat Pattemore, N.K., and Rebecca—thank you for showing up with sharp eyes, open minds, and exactly the kind of feedback that made this better.

And so much gratitude and love to everybody who stepped forward to be an ARC and ALC reader for this wild and crazy book! I'm just so appreciative of the time you took to read my book and the energy and creativity that you responded with. Heart eyes!

Deep thanks to my dear friends who helped me along the way: Jessica Lourey, who batted this idea around with me during the pandemic and helped to make it sing, and Molly O'Keefe and Adriana Anders, who read early drafts of this book and added incredible richness and insight with their freaking brilliant feedback.

Special thanks to Judy at Judy's Proofing and Pamela Clare for the meticulous eagle-eye work. I'm massively grateful to Molly at Novel Mechanic, who edited and proofed with brilliance and grace after I tore everything apart and rebuilt it. And to Shelley Charlton, who swooped in like a goddess with last-minute catches.

I'm also indebted to Maria at Artscandare for designing such a striking cover, and to Denise and Marnye at Audio Sorceress for their exceptional audio production. Heartfelt thanks to my talented narrators, Andie Eloise and Benjamin Sands, for bringing these characters to life.

All the love to my ARC gang – your support inspires me more

than you will ever know. My heart does a happy dance when I see what you do out there!

Tackle hugs also to the Fabulous Gang on Facebook for being so supportive and funny and loyal. You are forever my happy place on the internet.

Finally, I heart my readers so much! Thank you for cheering me on and leaving reviews and reaching out and most of all just for READING! You make me smile and you give my characters a reason to be evil and loving and everything in between!

# Also by Annika Martin

**Mafia Princes**

Dark Mafia Prince

Wicked Mafia Prince

Savage Mafia Prince

**Other mafia set in the same world:**

The Kingpin's Call Girl

Lazarus

*Romantic Comedy*

Most Eligible Billionaire

The Billionaire's Wake-up-call Girl

Breaking the Billionaire's Rules

The Billionaire's Fake Fiancée

Return Billionaire to Sender

Just Not That Into Billionaires

Butt-dialing the Billionaire

The Grumpy Billionaire

*Fun, super-smutalicious romcom*
*(read in order)*
The Hostage Bargain
The Wrong Idea
The Deeper Game
The Most Wanted
The Hard Way
The Best Trick

**Romantic Suspense** *(as Carolyn Crane)*
Against the Dark
Off the Edge
Into the Shadows
Behind the Mask

**Criminals & Captives** *(Dark and dangerous romance with Skye Warren)*
Prisoner
Hostage

**MM Spies** *(with Joanna Chambers)*
Enemies like You

*See a complete list of Annika's books at www.annikamartinbooks.com*

# About the Author

Annika Martin is a New York Times bestselling author who lives in Minneapolis with her husband; in her spare time she enjoys taking pictures of her cats, consuming boatloads of chocolate suckers, and tending her wild, bee-friendly garden.

Newsletter:
http://annikamartinbooks.com/newletter

Facebook:
www.facebook.com/AnnikaMartinBooks

Instagram:
instagram.com/annikamartinauthor

Website:
www.annikamartinbooks.com

Email:
annika@annikamartinbooks.com